Trilogy Order:

Decipis

Exodus

Eternus

The Rebel Christian Publishing

ISBN: 978-1-957290-62-1 (eBook)
Print: 978-1-957290-63-8

This is a work of fiction. Any references to historical events, real people, or real places are used fictitiously. Names, characters, and places are products of the author's imagination. Inclusion of or reference to any Christian elements or themes are used in a fictitious manner and are not meant to be perceived or interpreted as an act of disrespect against such a wonderful and beautiful belief system.

Cover designed by Valicity Elaine

The Rebel Christian Publishing
350 Northern Blvd STE 324 - 1390
Albany, NY 12204-1000

Visit us: http://www.therebelchristian.com/
Email us: rebel@therebelchristian.com

Contents

Eternus

Book III in the Treachery Trilogy
By Valicity Elaine

A Rebel Christian Publishing Book

1

Caesar

The sky is yellow gold, like someone cracked an egg and let the yolk spill across the clouds. I'm not one for sunrises but my eyes are glued to the horizon today. We've got a big delivery, so the timing must be perfect. If anything goes wrong—delays, poor directions, etc.—we could be sitting ducks and that's dangerous. Bandits and scavengers have been a real problem lately, the world is still reeling from this sudden war, people are hungry and desperate which makes them just as lethal as the enemy soldiers. I'm positive there are eyes watching (there's always eyes watching) which makes the hairs on the back of my neck rise. I've been a Runner long enough to know when we're in over our heads.

My eyes scan the horizon again; bronze and burnt orange have bled into the milky yolk. Just a few more minutes and the truck should get here. Eternus Campsite has set up connections to other safehouses and settlements so there's a healthy trade route set up now, but we fill the gaps with scavenging whenever we can. This load comes from a settlement over a hundred miles away. Everyone's been talking about the delivery, our biggest one yet. Packages of food, clothing, weapons, even medicine—which we desperately need.

Obviously, Raven and I couldn't handle this one alone so two other pairs of running partners joined us this morning. That's six people total, more than I've ever teamed up with on a single mission. Six may not sound like much, but Major Banks and her team have also joined us to provide backup. They're hidden in the nearby abandoned buildings, watching over us through the scopes of their automatic rifles. It's a scary realization. In just a few moments, we could be under fire. The Runners don't have guns to shoot back, but I've seen Keoni in action. I know she'll keep us safe.

I can't even imagine how frightened the delivery drivers have been all this time. Last month, we lost a driver to a group of looters. He was ambushed on the highway and forced off the road. Major Banks and her team were deployed to recover whatever they could. They found the truck abandoned in the desert, the supplies stolen, the gas tank emptied, and the driver's body tied up in the back. His throat had been slit, but he'd also suffered broken bones, lacerations to his face, and he was missing three fingers.

They'd tortured him. Probably to get him to unlock the back of the truck so they could steal the supplies, but also for information. Delivery trucks have a destination. A campsite. Eternus enjoys taking in survivors, but most looters aren't looking for the camp to join us. They're trying to find the location so they can take over.

We're at war; the entire world. No one is safe.

We'll have to separate into our pairs and take different routes home. If anyone runs into trouble, only part of the supplies will be lost. We also haven't shared our directions with each other, so we won't be able to rat out the locations of any other pair.

As the rattle of a delivery truck fills our ears, Raven tries to lighten the mood, "First pair to make it to Eternus gets first pick of the supplies."

Despite my nerves, I'm excited by the idea of a race. You already know I used to be captain of the track team, running is in my blood, but this race will be different. We won't be physically running, Keoni has already assigned a van to each pair. Once we get our supplies loaded, we'll travel with Keoni's soldiers to the coordinates she's given us and then hitch a ride with whatever driver is there waiting. Most of the race will be in the hands of our driver, but I'm sure Raven and I can shave off some time by hustling to the coordinates.

She must see the eagerness on my face because Raven touches my arm and smiles. "We've got this," she whispers. She squeezes my bicep and I'm not too ashamed to admit it makes me smile back.

I've spent the last few months in a hospital bed because of my own stupidity. Every face I saw had lowered brows and a wrinkled forehead. Major Banks was disappointed. Raven was pissed off. Even Dr. Brown shook his heavy head; he was kind enough to never voice his anger toward me, but I felt it all the same. That's why this mission means so much to me.

I made a huge mistake by trying to steal supplies and run off to find my friends. I knew it was wrong. I've learned my lesson. Now, I'm trying to prove to everyone that I can handle this. They can trust me. So, I can't mess this up. Especially since Raven's sister is here. I replaced her as Raven's new running mate when I first arrived in Eternus. She was recovering from a near-death experience at the time, but now she's well enough to join us here. Her name is Katia; she's tough as nails and will likely beat our team back to Eternus. Other than the occasional *hello* at church on Sundays, she barely acknowledges my existence, but still... I want to impress everyone I can, even her, and especially Major Banks.

Keoni is in charge of the Search-and-Rescue Team for Eternus, that means it's her job to go out and find survivors to bring back to the camp. If I have any chance of ever seeing Mya again, it'll be with Major Banks. I've got to do my best here.

The rumble of a car engine grows louder, accompanied by puffs of smoke that rise above the broken buildings surrounding us. We're hiding in an open parking lot that three other buildings share; a small restaurant, a hair salon, and a tiny smoothie shop. There are abandoned cars in the lot, covered in thick layers of red Arizona dust, there's also an empty shopping cart that's burnt black like it'd once been on fire, and

4

in the corner of the lot is the body of a dead dog rotting behind a dumpster.

The truck pulls in beside the dumpster; it's a semi that coughs out smoke as the driver puts it in park. A few agonizing moments of silence yawns through the lot before the driver opens the door and hops out. It's a hefty woman wearing goggles and a vest which I instantly recognize as bullet proof. Hopefully, she won't need it.

I watch through unblinking eyes as the driver unlocks the bed of the truck and lifts the gate. The sound of the metal cage echoes through the abandoned lot far longer than it needs to. I feel like I can hear my own heartbeat, and each one pumps fear through my body, straight to my brain. My hands clench into fists, my breath hitches, I swallow and realize my throat is dry.

Raven nudges me but she doesn't speak, when I glance over, she holds up three fingers. *Three minutes until we can move in.* Raven takes the lead on all of our missions; she's taught me her signals and even a bit of sign language so we can communicate without words. Right now, we're waiting for the driver to return to her seat so she can keep watch from the north while the first team moves in to unload the cargo. We'll only send one pair out at a time, so if there is an ambush, only two people will be at risk. Raven and I are the first pair up.

Once the driver settles down, Raven taps my shoulder twice and we move in. We duck low and step swiftly, covering ground faster than I expect. Raven is small and nimble, she climbs onto the truck without needing any help, despite the

5

platform being over her head. Tall as I am, I trip hopping onto the bed and curse as I nearly fall onto my face. Raven shoots me a look and I nod back with a sigh. She hates when I curse, but I can't help it. We started going to church while my foot was in a boot; neither of us knew how we felt about God, but we agreed to take that journey together. It wasn't fun or pretty. I remember bawling like a child during service one Sunday, Raven was there, rubbing circles on my back. I have no idea what overcame me. I can't describe the emotions that ran through my head in those moments, but I know they were real and so was the Voice I heard as I cried.

I love you.

Simple. Clean. Peaceful. I've been chasing after that Voice ever since, but there are times like now where I mess up. Cursing seems to be the one thing that gets me. For Raven, it's her temper. We hold each other accountable; she checks me whenever I swear, and I remind her to keep a cool head whenever her temper gets the worst of her. We work well together, even now as I wordlessly apologize for my language and sling my backpack to the floor.

Raven accepts my apology and starts passing me boxes to tuck away. We work in complete silence for about ten minutes until we hear a high-pitched whistle. The sound makes my blood freeze, but Raven's calm demeanor lets me know it's just our halfway point signal. We've got a few minutes and then the next team will move in. We've hardly packed as much as we need to, but we can't afford to stick around. I end up shoving things into my bag and then carrying a stack of boxes away in my arms. I'll load these into the wagon we've got.

As I'm loading the wagon, I hear the whistle for the next team to move in. Their footsteps resound around me while I stack boxes of Oreos on top of each other. Raven eyeballs the sugary snack but says nothing. When she touches my elbow, I smile, keenly aware of every little gesture she makes. *Good job.* Ruffling my hair, *hurry up*. Her hand on my cheek—*you ok?* I am. I feel great right now, loading my stash and then falling back into our defensive positions. We did our job and everything is running smoothly. I hope everyone noticed. I hope they saw how fast and smoothly we worked. I can only pray it makes a difference to Major Banks. Maybe after this mission I'll request to join her team again. She rejected me the first time and wouldn't hear a word of my request after my huge blunder, but this changes things.

I sigh as the next whistle splits the air. The last pair to approach the truck is Raven's sister Katia and her male counterpart. He's a tall blonde guy who protectively hovers over her as they crouch-walk to the truck. We wait in painful silence as they climb in and begin loading their things. The morning air is humid, I suck in deep breaths to clear my nerves, but just as I begin to calm myself down, I hear another whistle.

Too early. I glance toward Katia and her partner; they've stopped loading their gear and have poked their heads out the bed of the truck to see what's going on. The confusion on their faces confirms my suspicions.

Something's wrong. That whistle wasn't a signal—it was an alert.

I shouldn't be surprised. We drove a semi into a parking lot and really thought we could peacefully unload it while the world starves around us. When I think of it that way, I'm surprised we lasted this long without trouble.

A loud *pop!* fills the air and Raven and I both jump in response. I fight every instinct to duck and hide as I stare into the lot, gaping at our surroundings. In the distance, a ribbon of red smoke dances into the air. That isn't from us. We don't use smoke signals because it draws attention, the exact opposite of what we want, so when the smoke drifts above the buildings next door, I hear Keoni shout, "Bethel formation!" and we all leap into action.

We went over the possibility of an ambush before we ever set out on the mission, so when Major Banks gives the order, I move on instinct. My right hand unsheathes the hunting knife I keep strapped to my thigh and then I grab our wagon with my other hand. Raven takes point with a crossbow, an overstuffed pack on her back and another piled on top of that and tied down, so it doesn't sway as she crouch-walks to our escape route.

I try to follow her as best I can, but another *pop!* goes off and the entire lot is covered in a crimson cloud. At this point, I have to run to keep up with Raven because I don't want to lose her when I can barely see two feet in front of me, but I overestimate how quickly she's walking, and I end up stepping on the back of her foot. She turns to yell—that temper getting the best of her—but more *pops!* go off around us and I straight-up tackle her to the ground before she can even speak. Mercifully, Raven understands what's going on, so she doesn't complain about a six-foot-five body landing on top of her. Even if she was upset, there's no time for her to voice it. Gunfire erupts all around us, followed by screams and shouts in voices I don't recognize.

I have no idea what's going on. I have no idea where anyone is at, but I know I've got to do something.

I push off of Raven and drag her to her feet. "Do you know the way from here?" I shout.

She turns a circle, clutching my hand so we don't lose each other in the smoke. "I can't see anything!"

Okay, we'll do this the hard way, then.

I drag the wagon in front of us and turn it sideways, so it blocks us like a short wall. We have to duck to stay hidden behind it, but with all the supplies piled on top, it's better than having no protection at all.

"We'll push it together!" I shout to Raven.

Her reply is an angry scream as she shoves the wagon with me. We work slowly, ducking each time a spray of bullets fires into the air. I have no idea what direction the enemy is coming from, but I don't plan to stick around and find out. I know we've made it to the edge of the parking lot when the ground turns into dead grass. Quickly, I shove myself upright with a proud grin.

"We made it!"

Raven runs around the other side of the wagon and crouches in the grass, loading her crossbow. She starts firing into the red smoke without a word, so I cover her, scanning the area as I clutch my knife. We're a little further east than we need to be, but we've managed to land close to our escape route. Keoni is in charge of our return squad, but I have no idea where she's at—or if she's even alive. We can't leave without her because we need the van to get back. There's no way we can walk all the way back to Eternus with this haul. It took us a week to get here on foot without any packs. It'll be twice that time with all this stuff, not to mention any looters we might bump into.

"We've got to find Major Banks!" I shout to Raven.

A screaming man bursts from the red smoke and Raven shoots him in the chest without hesitation. Once he's twitching on the ground, she glances up. "You sure you want to go back in there?"

I don't *want* to at all, but I may not have a choice.

"Can you handle yourself?" I ask.

Raven nods but her face looks worried. She's thinking of her sister.

"I'll look for her," I promise, then I run into the smoke.

The parking lot is pure chaos. Men screaming, gunfire filling the air, and terror rushing in like an untamed fire. I can hardly think over all the noise, over the insanity I feel knocking at the door of my mind. It begs entrance, trying to take over every thought and instinct within, but I beat it back with a desperate prayer. *Please, God—*

"Caesar!" The voice belongs to Major Banks, loud and clear as the knife in my hand. I grip it as I change direction and sprint toward the woman I trust with my life. She's waiting by the loading truck with Claudius, Katia and her partner—a tall guy named Bobby. There's a gash over her eye leaking bloody tears down her face, but other than that, she looks more angry than afraid. I suppose that's a good thing. "Where's your partner?" she shouts in my face.

"She's safe! Waiting at the east side of the lot!"

A bullet *pings!* into the metal side of the truck and we all duck at once. Claudius throws his body over Keoni, she doesn't fight him until rapid footsteps approach us—then a screaming man bursts through the red smoke and Major Banks shoves Claudius away to raise her gun, but I'm faster.

I swing without thinking, shocked by how easily my blade cuts into the man's soft flesh. I stab him in the cheek which makes him shriek but he keeps pursuing. That's when Keoni releases three bullets: two to his head, one to his chest. He collapses on the ground right in front of her, blood staining the cracked pavement.

Keoni keeps talking like there isn't a dead man at her feet. "Grab whatever supplies you can and make it to the east side of the lot."

Claudius and Bobby hop into the truck while Katia catches the supplies they toss down and begins stacking it into the wagon on the ground. Keoni holds cover with her rifle, and I move to stand beside Katia to help load the wagon.

She passes me a backpack to fill. "Good job earlier. You saved Major Banks."

I glow with pride. "I was just doing my job."

"Your job is to be a Runner, but apparently you're a life saver, too."

"Think there's room on the Search-and-Rescue Team?"

She grunts as she catches a large box and slowly sets it on her neat pile. "Major Banks is tough to impress."

"Saving her life has got to be impressive."

"I won't complain if she keeps you with us. Raven needs someone by her side who'll protect her."

I am honored to have impressed Katia, I really am, but Mya is the one I want to protect, and I can't do that if I'm stuck here loading boxes. *One step at a time*, I tell myself.

Katia and I continue filling the wagon and the backpacks until Major Banks stops us with a raised fist. "We're moving out," she says. "Twenty seconds." She fires a few bullets into the smoke and keeps her vision forward as Claudius and Bobby hop down and strap bags to their backs. Once they're finished, Major Banks gives us a countdown and leads the group into the red cloud.

Some of the smoke has dissipated so I can see the bodies strewn throughout the lot. It's a gruesome sight that leaves me suddenly short of breath. I can't help but think of Orly Center and all the blood we found in that place, all the chaos those people must have endured. Now I've seen that chaos firsthand. I'd known nothing but chaos until I was brought to Eternus. I can only hope and pray that Mya is doing better than this. That she isn't screaming or crying or starving like these guys.

The wagon I'm pulling feels heavy with guilt instead of supplies. I should be thankful for everything I've experienced at Eternus, but my only goal is to leave. As quickly as possible. It isn't their fault that my friends were left behind. But I won't sit by and wonder about them any longer. I need to find my friends, and I think I've finally done enough to get on Keoni's good side. Once we make it back to camp, I'm asking her to let me join her team again. After saving her life, she won't refuse me—and if the bodies we're stepping over are any clue, I'm sure she'll have some vacant spots to fill.

2

Mya

I try very hard not to burn the food. Today is my day for breakfast so I've opened a can of sardines in olive oil and now I'm simmering them in a can of diced tomatoes from the cupboard. So much of Adrian's house was left intact, I can still use the dried dill and ground mustard I found as seasoning. I'm not very familiar with Russian spices, but I think Adrian will be proud of the sardines.

We left the library a few weeks ago, slowly making our way to Adrian's home. We stopped and looted as we travelled, hid from enemy soldiers, and even took the scenic route along the highway to see the city from above. It looks like a nightmare; nothing more than a red stain of blood, death, and Arizona dust.

Since Adrian's family was evacuated so early, their home was abandoned and never touched again. Adrian says looters overlooked it because it was a rickety white trash shack not worth the trouble of breaking into. I disagreed.

When we arrived, everything was dirty and covered in dust, but there was still food in the pantry and beds to sleep on. This place wasn't a 'white trash shack' it was a blessing from God.

We've been here for two weeks now, and I still can't believe this is where Adrian grew up. I never visited his place when we were in high school so seeing it now is like meeting a part of him for the very first time.

I try to imagine him walking down these dirty halls, bare feet padding over the stained carpet. I try to imagine him stealing snacks from the cracked ceramic cookie jar on the counter. And I try to imagine him washing laundry in the old machine they've got. It's a massive hunk of metal that scars the kitchen as it sits like a sore thumb in the corner, hooked to the sink. Thick rubber tubes run from the back, poking out from beneath the faded 1998 sticker, and snake into the same sink used to wash veggies and dishes. I don't know where the Nikols dried their clothes, I haven't spotted a dryer anywhere in the house, but there's a roll of twine and clothing pins in the counter drawer beside the gaudy washer, so I guess that's how they got the job done.

In the tiny living room, there's an outdated television and a ratty couch with cushions that weep stuffing every time you sit on it. The TV is older than both of us and only has one plug for power and another for the cable box. Adrian says his mother got it from a thrift store and paid for the cable with money from a boyfriend he can't remember. He never watched TV, so he didn't bother asking for details.

I look around this little house now and wonder how much of it was supplied with prostitution money. It's a small place, almost cramped for a family of five, but I can see signs of what used to be a vivid life, maybe even a happy one. There are lines drawn onto the wall of the kitchen entrance, marking the heights of two kids named Danya and Dinara. There are matching sets of bowls in the cabinets, one pink and one blue, the size a kid would use. There's even a plate with Spiderman's face in the center, it's faded, and his name has been scratched off by forks and spoons scraping along the plastic during family dinners. I wonder if that plate was Adrian's when he was younger.

I wonder if Adrian's mother called him to reach the jarred garlic on the top shelf of the cupboard like I had to when I started breakfast. I wonder if he helped her with family meals. I wonder which chair around the small round table was his. Or if he sat with his family at all.

There are clear signs of kids living here, but other than Adrian's actual bedroom, there's no real sign of *him* in this house. It's like he was a guest here, holed up in his room or out working and running. I haven't brought this up to him at all, I don't really know how and I'm positive it isn't something he wants to talk about. He'd always said he grew up poor but showing me his 'white trash shack' is much different from casually mentioning that he couldn't afford an iPhone at age 16. I mean, who could? If I had to buy all my own stuff as a *teenager*, I would've called myself poor too. But this is different. This wasn't Adrian complaining about missing out on the latest technology, this was his entire life. Stained carpets, canned food, and thrift store clothing. I wish I had known how bad it was. I wish I could have been there for him. I'm here now, but is it too late to reach him?

Adrian hasn't spoken much since we got here. He stays in his bedroom and I've taken the twins' room. Since I'm short, I fit in the bunk beds without a problem, and I've taken a liking to Dinara's stuffed animal collection. At night, I pile them up on my bed like pillows and as I fall asleep, I pretend they're my father sleeping beside me like when I was a little girl. Sometimes I pretend it isn't my father, it's a man years younger, much stronger, and dangerously handsome. A man with striking albino-blonde hair and a perfect mouth that I've kissed before…

I shake those thoughts away as I use a wooden spoon to gently flip the sardines. I shouldn't think of Adrian this way, but sometimes I can't help it. The shame I feel isn't just from a Christian sense of purity, it's from a place of guilt. I haven't been good to Adrian. He's been there for me from day one, loving me, reaching for me, doing everything he could to protect me. And each time I rejected him, he was patient enough to wait for me. Again and again.

I don't deserve Adrian, but he's here. He'll always be here. I think that's what makes this so difficult for me; I don't know how to approach him with these feelings now. Every time I see his serious face and his icy gaze, I feel my cheeks heat with shame, and I wonder if he sees right through me. Am I the pathetic girl who begged him for reprieve or the innocent Christian girl who holds his heart?

I still remember the night I went to his tent, asking him to take the pain away. Asking him to take *me* right there on his floor. And he nearly did until reality slapped me to my senses. We were both a mess that night; Adrian was desperate enough to tell me to imagine another man while he made love to me. And I was desperate enough to ask for his passion in the first place. I thank God every day that we didn't make such a mistake with each other, but there's no denying that we crossed the line.

We haven't touched each other since then, but I think that's only made my heart grow fonder. We have survived together, protected each other, walked side by side through abandoned and broken cities. We have shared each other's hope, pain, desperation, and prayers. This closeness, this dependency, has filled the sexual void of our relationship and made room for us to develop true intimacy. That's what is so dangerous here; intimacy is more powerful than sex.

Sleeping with Adrian would have stitched our bodies together, but spending these tiny moments with each other has stitched our hearts together. And now, only God can tie our souls. But would He do that? Adrian isn't a Christian. That's the exact same problem I had with Julius, and look how things ended with him.

I shut off the burner and sigh. I don't want to think about Julius any more than I want to think about Adrian. Julius is my best friend. My former lover. My world. And he was captured right in front of me. In many ways, it is Julie's absence that has made room for Adrian in my heart.

And there lies the guilt. Deep down, I wonder if Adrian has always been in my heart, or if he is simply the next best thing.

"Whatever," I mumble, fanning the ribbons of steam that snake up from the bubbling dish. "I don't have time to think about my pathetic love life."

Seriously, there are more important things to fuss over. Like our gas getting low. There's a gas stove in Adrian's house, but it doesn't work so we've been using a camp burner. But we're down to one last canister and I don't know what we're going to do once it's out. I suppose cold sardines aren't the end of the world, but I hope it won't come to that. We're planning to set out again soon. This place was only meant to be a pit stop but it's been weeks and Adrian doesn't seem interested in moving. He doesn't seem interested in doing *anything* except staring at his family photos and sleeping.

That's probably the *real* reason we haven't touched each other, and that scares me. What if Adrian has moved on?

I think of all our time together and it makes my heart ache. I don't want to be alone but right now I feel like no one in this world is with me except God. I remember the pain I felt when Julius left me to pursue Delilah not long ago, when I prayed to God about it, He said one word in reply: **Patience**.

At the time, I thought God wanted me to have patience to wait on Julius and his Christian transformation. Now, a small

19

part of me hopes that maybe He wanted me to wait for Adrian and his miraculous conversion to Christ. But I know, in my heart of hearts, God was telling me to be patient with myself. Stop trying to force relationships. Stop looking for love altogether, and focus on the love I've had all along.

That's the promise I made to myself back then and it's the promise that gives me strength to put myself last for once and think of Adrian as a person, not a replacement to help fill the void in my broken heart. He deserves better than that, and I promise I'm going to give it to him. The first thing I need to do is figure out how to get him out of this dark mood he's been swimming in for weeks now.

Maybe it's the stress of survival, maybe he's getting nervous about finding his family. I don't know. But I want to help him because I care about him and because I need him. I don't know what's come over Adrian, but if he doesn't snap out of it soon, we'll end up finishing off our supplies and then slowly starving to death.

The library had given us hope. We'd finally found proof that Adrian's family is alive, and we had proof that my father is alive. The next step is actually finding them, but we can't do that if we never leave here.

I grab Dinara's pink bowl and fix myself a serving then I pour the rest of the food onto the Spiderman plate for Adrian. It isn't the best food on earth, but it isn't awful, either. My father used to make sardines in spicy tomato sauce all the time when I was a kid. He used a Creole recipe and would serve it with toasted baguette slices. I'm sure his dish is totally different from how Adrian's Russian family would have made it, but I did my best. I hope it's at least edible. I need Adrian to be in a good mood because I've decided today will be the day I ask him a very important question.

What better way to get someone out of a funk than with a good meal, right?

I'm so desperate, I bow my head and pray over the food before I take it to his room. "God, please let this taste amazing. Let it lift Adrian's mood so we can have an easy conversation. I need this to work... In Jesus' name I pray, amen."

3

Adrian

It feels very strange to be back in my old bedroom. I honestly never thought I'd see this place again, and if I'm being honest, part of me hoped I didn't. I see my siblings in every part of this home, and it breaks me. The broken parts of me are held together by a false sense of hope that seems to do more harm than good. What is the honest chance I have of finding my family? And once I do, what happens then? We repeat the same miserable routine I've been living through all this time but with more mouths to feed.

Danya and Dinara are the reason I left campus to begin with. They're my sole reason for living. I can't turn my back on them now, but I don't know if I have the strength to keep going anymore.

"Get it together," I whisper, sitting on the edge of my bed, staring down at the stale pack of Oreos in my hands. Before

Mya moved into the twins' bedroom, I secured Dinara's hope chest. It's nothing but a shoebox she used to stash all of her favorite toys and keepsakes. I took it from their room because I couldn't let Mya snoop through it. I've given my heart to that woman; this one thing needs to be mine alone.

I don't know how old these Oreos are, but they're hard enough that I can squeeze them in my fist as tears burn in my eyes and they don't crack or crumble. I'm falling apart. It makes no sense, but the closer I get to finding my family, the more hopeless I feel. Like all of this will end the same way things have always ended for me. I can handle being passed over for captain of the track team. I can handle Mya tossing me aside for Julius. I can handle our friends leaving the group because they hate me. But I can't handle the disappointment of finding my family's bodies.

What if their new safehouse was attacked like Orly Center? What if they bumped into the thugs who took Julius? What if they arrived at the safehouse only to find it destroyed? Then they'd be left to the mercy of the unknown. If that's the case, I'd rather not find them at all. I'd rather hold on to the dream that they're together in a cozy little shelter like the library and they're doing okay. They're moving on—without me—but still moving. Still growing. Still searching for happiness, even in this bleak world we call home now.

"Please let that dream come true," I whisper, tucking the Oreos back into Dinara's shoebox. I don't know who I'm talking to. Wishes are worthless but I haven't been convinced that prayers are much better.

That isn't true… I shake my head, thinking of the fervent prayers I've whispered in my most desperate moments. God has saved my life multiple times; I owe Him the courtesy of acknowledging the power of prayer. But right now, I feel powerless.

My bitter tears turn into desperate panic, and I feel my chest tighten as my heart begins to race. *Not again*, I grind my teeth together. I've been having panic attacks again. They started as soon as we got here, passing me the shovel I needed to dig deeper into this hole of grief.

Worry.

Doubt.

Fear.

All of these things drive the shovel deeper, and I feel the muck of anxiety grab me by my ankles, holding me in place as I drown in my sorrows. But something smacks the shovel from my hand when I shift on the bed and knock Dinara's hope chest over.

A tiny kids' Bible tumbles out of the box and my breath hitches. I took the Bible from the twins' room when I packed up the hope chest; it's only got a few classic stories in it plus the first one-hundred chapters from the Book of Psalms, but I suppose that's good enough. It's more than I had before. I don't even know why I took it, but it's lying open on my floor now and I reach for it without even thinking.

I find **Psalms 100** and read it through blurry eyes as my mind slowly suffocates. The panic attack is in full swing now, I'm gasping, clutching my chest with my free hand, and my shoulders are shaking with dry sobs. This is a miserable experience. Sometimes it lasts for nearly twenty minutes, sometimes it passes in thirty seconds. No matter how long it goes on, every moment is agony.

My eyes land on the last verse, *For the Lord is good and His love endures forever; His faithfulness continues through all generations.*

Could that be true?

If You're so good, then protect my family! If you're so faithful, then stay with them until the end. If You actually love me, then make this stop!

A gentle knock interrupts my thoughts. It's so abrupt that I gasp and snap my head up, instantly breaking through the fuzz that'd gripped my mind. My thoughts clear with each teary blink, and I sniffle as someone knocks again. It takes me a moment to realize it's Mya (who else could it be?) and I clear my throat to say, "Come in."

She cracks the door but doesn't come in, just says, "Are you decent?"

I almost laugh. She's been exceptionally shy since that day in my tent. I remember every moment of that wonderful night, even the not-so-wonderful ending. But I don't care about the ending, I care that she came to me at all. I care that there was ever the slightest chance that I could make Mya feel good. That I could make her forget—or that she even wanted to forget in the first place. I think she finally has forgotten. I think Mya has moved on from Julius and this is my chance to get her to fall for me. Finally.

I haven't been very focused on our relationship since moving back into the house, but I can't say I haven't noticed how things have changed between us. We're closer now. Stronger now. But something has grown in the space we've given each other. Something foreign and awkward and unfamiliar. It's like Mya is uncomfortable around me now, and it makes me wonder if maybe she didn't just move on from Julius. What if she's moved on from me, too?

"Adrian?" she asks, still standing in the hall.

I cough, wipe my eyes, and then exhale my nerves and tension. "I'm good. Come in."

Mya enters my room with her eyes locked on my carpet. I hate that she can barely look at me now. What's gotten into her?

"Breakfast," she squeaks out, setting the tray on my desk. It's an old desk made of chipped wood and rusted nails; I painted it red when I got it, fully convinced that was a good idea, but the paint has peeled and flaked away so it looks patchy now. In my teenage years, I covered the patches on the side with swear words, so Mya has a good look at all the expletives I jotted down. The F-word is written smack in the middle; all caps and scribbled in black permanent marker so violently, it looks like an attack on the desk itself. Mya glances at it each time she enters my room but we both pretend it isn't there.

"What'd you make?" I put away Dinara's hope chest, even the little Bible, and then sit on my bed.

"Sardines in tomato sauce."

"Smells good."

"I hope you like it." She takes her serving and sits on my bed, criss-cross applesauce. "Want me to pray over the food?"

Mya asks to pray over every meal. I don't mind because I clearly need prayer, so I nod and then silently bow my head as she whispers things to God. I wonder if He listens to her more than He listens to me. Mya's been Christian all her life, I wouldn't blame God for giving her prayers precedence over mine. Maybe I should ask Mya to pray for my family. Or to pray for me.

"Adrian?"

I glance up to find her staring at me and I realize she's finished her prayer. "Sorry," I grunt. "I mean ... Amen—in *Jesus's name*, amen."

She smiles. "I wish we had toast to go with this."

"My mother served it with thick slices of bread."

"My father made crisp slices of baguettes."

"Fancy." I chuckle.

"How long has it been since I've heard you laugh?"

That wipes the tiny smile from my face. I hadn't realized how long it's been, or how good it feels to laugh. I'm not surprised that the first person who tugs a chuckle out of me in so long is Mya.

"You make me laugh." My voice is feather soft, catching both of us off guard.

After a moment, Mya replies, "I'm glad."

We fall into silence, and the room fills with the awkward sound of us scraping our plates with the dirty forks Mya found in my kitchen. This house is such crap, I don't have enough in me to be embarrassed about it. It is what it is. For once, the rest of the world is as crappy as the one I've lived in all along.

27

I open my mouth to ask Mya what she thinks of the place, but she cuts me off.

"Can I tell you something?"

I nod. Wipe tomato sauce from my mouth. "Of course."

"I was hoping this meal would put you in a better mood."

"I think it's working."

"That's good." She looks away and starts fiddling with her fork.

"What else, Mya?"

"There's a reason I wanted you to be in a good mood."

"What reason is that?"

"I have a question, and I'm not sure how you'll respond to it."

I swallow, wishing I had more food to stuff into my mouth so I wouldn't have to talk, but Mya is staring at me through her big, unblinking eyes, expecting me to give her permission to go on. I don't want to. I know whatever question she has will make me angry, and there's only one thing that pisses me off.

"Just tell me it's not about him," I say in a sigh.

"Not exactly."

Good God, she still hasn't let him go. Julius has been a thorn in my side for years. He was the reason Mya turned me down in high school, and the reason she refused to even look at me when she made it to college. Now, in an apocalypse, he is still the brick wall between us. And he isn't even here anymore!

I pinch my nose. "What is it?"

"We're heading to Koshen next, to find that shelter."

"Yes."

"But while we're still in Phoenix, can…" she pauses, and I glance up to see her licking her lips. They're full and shapely and had been sore from the friction of our kisses that night she came to my tent. But now they're slightly red from her pressing them together so hard. *She's nervous.* "While we're still in Pheonix, can we stop by Caesar's house?"

I suck in a little gasp through my nose. I knew her question had something to do with him, but I never expected this.

"Why?" I push from the bed and pace my floor.

"Because he lives here, and I want to see his home."

What on earth…

I start frantically cleaning things up just to give myself something to do. I've always kept my room meticulously clean. It's the only place in this garbage dump that isn't totally trashed. My bed is always made. My clothes neatly folded. My desk perfectly arranged. When I had a vacuum, I kept the carpet clean. For now, I resort to getting on my hands and knees and picking dust balls from the floor.

"You want to see his home," I repeat.

"Not for him. I want to see if his mother…" her voice trails off and guilt rushes in.

This isn't just about Julius, it's about his foster mom. She's an old Korean lady, I don't remember her name, but I do remember seeing her at track meets. I also saw her in some of the pictures hanging on the walls of Mya's home, which means they were close. Something of an aunt to Mya, maybe even a second mother after she lost her own.

29

I feel awful now. Mya doesn't want to see Julius's house because she's still clinging to him, she wants to see if his mother was evacuated or left for dead in her own home. I can't blame her for wondering, and if there is a chance Julius is alive out there somewhere, he deserves to know that someone cared enough to check on his family. That's the promise we all made to each other when we set out on this journey anyway.

"I'm sorry," Mya says.

I hear her climb from the bed and then I see her walk past me, carrying our empty plates as she heads to the door. I can't help but call out to her. "Wait…"

She stops. "It isn't about him—not in the way that you think."

"That's okay." Really, it is. The fact that she feels the need to explain things shows how much she cares about my feelings, something she honestly hasn't done very often. Her kindness warms me and makes me desperately want to kiss her, but I know if I do that, she'll get scared and never want to be alone with me again.

Baby steps, I tell myself. One brick at a time, I'll tear down the awkward wall she's built between us. I guess I'll start here by helping her with this silly little side mission.

"You know his address?" I ask.

She bobs her head in a nod.

"I'll take you there. Let's set out tomorrow."

Mya's smile lights up this entire Godforsaken home. "Thank you, Adrian."

"Don't worry about it."

4

Caesar

Eternus Camp is electrified with energy. We made it back to the settlement just two days ago, relatively intact and with wagons full of supplies. There were casualties. There was blood spilled. Lives lost. There are people at camp who will spend the next few days in mourning. But there are more who will spend it celebrating because, despite our setbacks, some of us *did* make it back alive and that's worth a toast.

With our generators, Eternus can produce electricity. Camp leaders are really strict about keeping it rationed so the clinic and kitchen are able to function properly. But there are times like today when we're allowed to drag old stereos out and plug them in to blast music throughout the camp. Rows and rows of tents and log cabins open as campers peer out in shock and curious surprise. It takes them a moment to realize they are not under attack. I can't blame them. How long has it been since any of us has gone to a *party*?

The celebration was my idea, but it didn't take much coaxing to get Keoni to agree to it. Took her a day or two to work out the details with Eternus leaders, and here we are. There's meat on the grill, rice steaming in the massive pots set up in the kitchen tent, and bread baking in our brick ovens. I hear the cook has enough supplies to make a cake. I can't wait. For now, I stand beside the drink table as Katia mixes something called a Pickle Nibble—apparently, she worked at a bar before the world ended. According to the shouting over the music, she spent more time on the pole than behind the bar, but she learned a thing or two on her day shift. Eternus Camp is a Christian settlement, so there isn't any alcohol here, but that hasn't slowed Katia down one bit. She's got these mini pickles in a jar and adds one to a tumbler, so it swims in the yellow liquid like a turd in pee.

I have no idea what the liquid is, but I'm about to find out as Katia passes me a drink with a smile. "Pickle Nibble!" she says proudly.

I sniff the glass and my eyes water. Smells like lemonade with mint and … pickle. "Really?" I ask.

"At the club, we added vodka to lemonade and then tossed in a pickle for fun."

"Without the pickle, that actually doesn't sound bad."

She grins and leans across the drink table. "I knew you would appreciate my talents."

"Why is that?"

"Heard you were a frat boy back in the day."

"Guilty as charged."

She bites her lower lip, and I'm transported back to my college days. If I were back on campus, nothing would have stopped me from taking Katia back to my room by the end of the night. But I'm not that guy anymore.

I toss back the drink and then bite into the pickle. Honestly, it's not bad. "So, you wanted to make me a drink because I used to party?"

"Nah." Katia winks. "I made you a drink because I wanted to watch you nibble on a pickle."

I *cannot* stop myself from snorting. A laugh bursts from my mouth so loud that heads turn, and I have to grab my stomach to keep from wheezing. Katia laughs too, shoulders shaking. This is the most fun I've had since my college dissolved into a miniature world war. I'm glad it's Katia whose made me laugh. I'd been so nervous about putting up a good-guy image to impress her, but it turns out she used to be just like me.

Obviously, she's not a stripper/bartender anymore, but it's cool to have something we can relate to. Make jokes about. Share stories with. In a way, her transformation gives me strength. Let's me know that life is still enjoyable without the things I used to do.

I motion for a refill and Katia beams. "Was it that good?"

"I want Raven to try one."

Her nose wrinkles in a silent laugh. "You've got to tell me what she says about it."

"Will do."

I raise the glass in salute before walking off to find my partner. She's at the music station, kneeling beside the huge stereos as she digs through a cardboard box of CDs. The 'DJ' setup is quite old, no Bluetooth speakers or smartphones, but that works for us. Eternus was entirely off-grid even before the fall, all this equipment—generators, old boomboxes and stereos, CDs—came with the camp for days like this. It's like a survivor's nightclub. Very retro. Very outdoorsy. I love it.

"Who is The Notorious B.I.G.?" Raven looks up at me with a wrinkle creasing her forehead. There's a faded bruise on her jaw that makes her innocent face seem out of place, but you can't fake the confusion in her eyes.

Her question makes me gag on a chuckle. I used to party hard before the fall, so this music isn't new to me at all, but it is a little dated. Then again, I'm shocked a Christian kids' camp has these sorts of CDs at all.

I squat beside her and take the CDs from her hands, noticing how small they are for the first time. As small as Mya's. There's no doubt she would be as confused as Raven right now, helplessly sorting through rap music in search of something wholesome to play. The thought of Mya attempting to throw a party makes me smile but the smile doesn't last very long. It's wiped away by a wave of pain that makes the backs of my eyes hurt.

I shuffle through the CDs for an extra second, just to keep busy. I can feel Raven staring at my profile, waiting for me to speak, so I say casually, "You think the camp will like hiphop?"

"Anything is better than this country music."

34

I snort. "Country music ain't so bad."

"When you're attending a hoedown."

I pick some pop artist from the 90s and pluck in the disc. A mellow beat thrums through the camp and I watch as faces light up in recognition. Music makes them smile. It brings back memories, reminding them of a time when the world hadn't fallen apart. Maybe giving them hope that we can put it back together again. I think we can, little by little. Brick by brick. Our success in that last run is the first step. But we were hit hard. There are as many teary eyes as there are smiles in the crowd, people who are suffering loss. People who are in pain. People who don't have the strength to keep hoping for better days.

A sigh slips from my lips as I lean against the makeshift DJ stand and watch the crowd move to the beat. Raven is still beside me, head bobbing along to the music. One of the cooks exits the kitchen tent and starts making rounds with skewers of meat and roasted vegetables. The crowd cheers.

"Looks like the party is going well," I say. Raven nods and I pass her Katia's drink. "Your sister wanted you to try this."

"There's a pickle in it."

"It's called the Pickle Nibble—that's the fun part."

She frowns.

"Just try it. I promise it's not as bad as it looks."

"You've had it?"

I nod, then a question tiptoes into my head. "You ever drink?"

She hesitates. "Yeah. Before all this."

"Me too."

Raven stares at me, waiting for more, but I don't have any more to give her. Raven doesn't like talking about her past very much. She wants to forget it and move on. New creature in Christ and all that. But I don't want to. I mean—*yes*—I want to move on and be a better guy than I was before. But I don't want to pretend I *wasn't* that guy before.

I settle against the cabin behind us, staring ahead as Raven shrugs and takes a tentative sip from the glass. She coughs and wipes her mouth, much to my amusement. "You said it wasn't bad!"

"Guess we have different tastes."

She shoves the glass at me. "This is gross."

"You aren't gonna eat the pickle?"

"I hate pickles."

I finish off her drink and eat the pickle in two bites. Raven stares at me like I've just swallowed a live snake. "Calm down, girl. It's just a drink."

"An awful drink."

I lift my arm, and she snuggles beside me, so it rests over both her thin shoulders. "I used to think you were the cool one between us," I say.

"Being cool does not mean I have to nibble on a pickle."

I crack up. Maybe it's the fifteen-year-old boy in me, but I can't hear that phrase without giggling.

"Gosh, I haven't heard you laugh since I met you."

"No way. I'm positive you've said something at least chuckle-worthy since we've met."

"Maybe."

"Definitely."

She pauses. "Well, we do spend a lot of time together."

That's true. Raven's my running mate, we're together every day; exercising, training, poring over maps and planning routes, then doing the runs. Not to mention all the time we've spent going to church together. Raven's been my partner in work and in righteousness. It's a bittersweet connection because now, finally, I see what Mya tried to offer me so long ago. The guilt of rejecting her eats away at me every day, but I'm going to make it up to her when I see her again. I'm going to show her how much I've changed. I'm going to prove to her that she's worth the wait. And I'm going to pray that she's been waiting for me.

"We spend all day together," I mutter, blinking away an image of Mya's smiling face.

Raven adjusts beside me, looking up with her large eyes and her pouting mouth. Her lips part like she wants to say something, but no words come out. She just stands there, body gently swaying to the music.

Oh...

My brain completely collapses on itself, and I stare at her without a single thought running through my head. I watch as she lifts her hand and runs the tips of her fingers along my jaw. My nostrils flare as I exhale, eyes fluttering shut. Was there alcohol in that pickle?

"Do you ... *like* spending every day with me?"

"Raven," I pause to lick my lips, scraping my brain for words—for *anything*—to say right now. In the distance, someone yelps and I glance up to see Major Banks walking through the crowd with Claudius right behind her. They're the heroes of the last mission, people practically line up to congratulate them. The sight of her fills my head with words and I vomit them out without thinking. "I'm going to join the Search-and-Rescue Team."

Raven's body stiffens beside me, she even pulls her hand away from my face. When I look down, her eyes are perfect circles, blinking her shock away. "Wh-What?"

"We lost a lot of good men and women on that last run. Keoni's team was hit hardest; she needs new recruits now."

"But, Caesar... You're a Runner."

"I know."

"So, you can't join the Search-and-Rescue Team unless..." her voice falters, and she clears her throat to gain confidence. "Unless you leave my team."

I know that. I've always known that, but Raven has always known that joining the SR Squad was my goal. If things had gone my way from the start, I never would've joined the Runners. Unfortunately, when I first arrived, Keoni didn't need any new members, so I was turned down when I asked to be placed on her team. But things are different now. Keoni's numbers are critically low; I'm positive if I ask to join her team, she'll let me. She's got to.

But...

I look at Raven, and I see the sadness on her face. I can't pretend it doesn't affect me, but I can't let my friendship with her get in the way of my love for Mya—or even for my friends. I have to put them first. They need me.

"Raven," I sigh and run my hand through my hair, "you know I've always wanted to join Keoni's team."

"I thought you'd let that go."

"I have to find my friends."

"Major Banks will find them!" she says desperately.

"What's wrong with me helping out?"

A flash of anger creases her brow, but she lets it go with a grunt. "If you have to ask, then never mind."

I don't have to ask; I just don't want to say it aloud. I don't want to go down that road with Raven. *Yes*, she's a pretty girl, I've known that since I met her, and it couldn't be more obvious now with her pouty lips and her body so close to mine that I can feel the heat rising from it. Or maybe that's just me. It'd be a lie to say I don't want anything to happen between us. But Raven is a girl I've considered off limits since I met her.

I was in a pretty messed-up place when I arrived at Eternus. Mentally, emotionally, spiritually, and then physically—after I fell off a building and busted my leg. I've never felt like I deserved Raven, and from the moment I met her, I've been openly obsessed with Mya. I've told Raven all about her, she's the only thing I talk about on runs or in training. So, how could she ever think that things would be different between us?

I gulp as I stare at the wrinkle between Raven's eyebrows, evidence of her anger toward me. That anger gives birth to understanding and I feel myself taking a step back from this girl.

She thought things would be different because she never believed I would find my friends. She never thought I'd ever see Mya again.

"You were just waiting, weren't you?" I ask in a quiet voice.

Her face pinches and then relaxes, her shoulders even droop as she realizes I've figured her out. "Caesar—"

"Don't," I cut her off, "don't say whatever excuse you've had waiting all this time." I shake my head. "You never had any hope that I would find her, did you?"

"What are the odds? Really, Caesar, be for real."

"I am!" I nearly shout.

A few people glance in our direction, but I ignore them. Hot with anger, confused by lust, overwhelmed by the mix of emotions swirling through me right now. I want to scream, cry, and kiss Raven all at once. But I don't do any of that; instead, I take a slow breath and close my eyes.

"What was the point of our friendship, Ray? Were you just waiting for me to finish grieving? To accept Mya's absence and get over her?" I open my eyes. "Did you drag me to church to *fix* me before you made your move?"

She bristles. "Get over yourself. Every moment I spent with you was honest and genuine. It was those genuine moments that made me realize you were just as lost as me. *That's* why I wanted you to start going to church with me." She presses her lips together and I see tears begin to fill her eyes. It's hard to ignore them, it's hard to keep myself from feeling like a huge jerk right now, but I won't let in the guilt or the pity. I don't know what to think of Raven. I don't know if I can trust or believe anything she's saying. Or maybe I just don't want to.

She pushes from the wall and laughs. "Gosh, Caesar. I have a *crush* on you, okay? I'm not confessing my love; I'm just asking if there's a chance for us to ever be more than friends."

She leaves that hanging in the silence between us. It stretches on, heartbeat by heartbeat. And then I crush it with a sigh, but Raven doesn't give me the chance to speak.

"Okay then," she mutters, turning away.

I take a step towards her, but someone calls my name behind me. It's Pastor Nicolette wearing a charming smile and holding a plate of grilled chicken. She offers me the meat as she says, "I'm happy you've got the music working."

"Thanks, Pastor." I take a slice of chicken breast, it's salty and juicy and makes my stomach growl as I stuff it into my mouth.

"Great. Great. The music is bumping, but this is a Christian settlement, Caesar. Would you mind playing something a bit more..." she pauses, glancing away to think. "Godly?"

"Sure." I hold in my sigh as I stoop to dig through the box of CDs. This is a *party*. Maybe the rap music was a bit too much earlier, but I've never heard of *Christian* party music, so I have no idea what anyone expects me to play. Still ... when the pastor asks you to do something, you just do it. So instead of complaining, I flip through the old CDs until I find a dusty one with permanent marker scribbled over it saying, **Worship Mix**. Not exactly what I'd grind to back at the frat house, but whatever. I quickly swap the discs in the boombox, punch the play button with my thumb and then stomp away to find more food.

5

Adrian

One thing I will never get used to in this new world is the silence. Everything is quiet. Everything is muted. It has to be. Too much noise could attract unwanted attention. While these last few months have been relatively peaceful, Mya and I have still had our fair share of trouble with strangers. Those troubles have left us scarred and paranoid; we're not taking any chances.

We left my place a few days ago, carefully crawling through the surrounding area, checking houses, and keeping our guard up. Julius doesn't live too far from me, but his neighborhood is noticeably better than mine. We haven't reached his house yet, but just entering this side of town has changed the scenery. The houses are all two-story family homes with driveways and garages; there aren't any picket fences, like in Mya's suburban community, but there also aren't any cracked sidewalks or pit bulls on rusty chains barking out front. This area is solidly blue collar, and it's still a neighborhood I would've fought to live in as a kid. I'd give my left arm to live in a place like this *now*.

Even with the busted windows and dust-covered cars in the driveways, even with the sour smell of dead bodies drifting in the air, this neighborhood is cleaner than my own. I count the houses as we pass them, taking note of each one, trying to commit them to memory. I've mastered the art of making mental maps since this whole thing started. It's amazing how an apocalyptic meltdown can cure all the bad habits of a tired college student.

I've memorized at least four blocks of this neighborhood today, that's about all I can take so I slow to a halt on the sidewalk and stare ahead, surveying the homes around us. Mya pauses, blinking back and forth.

"Something wrong?" she asks softly.

From my peripheral, I see her hand slide to the bulge under her hoodie. That's where she keeps the hunting knife she took from my house. I'm glad she's ready for anything, but I didn't stop because of danger.

I turn to her. "Let's call it a day."

"It's only mid-afternoon. We've still got plenty of sunlight left."

"There's no rush, Mya. Let's rest up and survey the area. We'll find his house tomorrow."

She pauses but agrees with a reluctant nod. Since she's clearly disappointed in our decision to stop, I let Mya pick the house we'll set up in tonight. She goes with a small family home at the end of the street. I don't like how exposed it is sitting on the corner, but it doesn't have many windows, and it looks like it's already been looted when we get inside, so I'm not too upset. But I'm still not taking any chances. While Mya checks all the kitchen cabinets for canned food, I step outside to walk the perimeter.

The backyard is small with a metal fence and dead yellow grass. There's a doghouse with a rusty metal bowl sitting on the ground in front of it. The way it's placed makes the little house seem like a memorial. I walk over and stare at it with my hands on my hips. The house has the name *Blue* carved into the front, and I can see a tattered cushion inside, along with a raggedy chew toy. Right beside the house is a pile of dirt, the sight of it breaks my heart a little. It's a grave.

I've never had any pets, and I honestly don't regret that. Pets are more mouths to feed. More crap to clean up. But this little grave makes me—

Wait.

I stare at the mound of turned soil, my eyes bulging, sweat traveling down the side of my face. The grave … it isn't small. I'm over six feet tall, but if I lay down on the ground, I could fit into the patch of dirt with my knees bent. That's far too big for a dog.

I take a step back in shock which only doubles when I see two more graves beside the first one. These are smaller, only half the size of the first one. But even if a dog could fit in one of them … why are there *two*?

My heart begins to race, and I take a gulp of air into my lungs, trying to keep myself from freaking out. This isn't the first time I've seen death out here. I've *killed* people out here. But for some reason, the sight of these graves makes my skin crawl. Maybe because they're in the back of a family home. Maybe because they're in different sizes, insinuating different *ages*. Or maybe because they're fresh.

The soil was recently turned. It's easy for me to tell because we dug graves back at the university for some of the students who died on campus. I helped dig those graves. I remember the stench of blood, the dry smell of earth and clay. I remember the dirt beneath my fingernails, the green smear of grass rubbing off on my t-shirt. Once you dig a grave, you don't forget any part of it. Every single detail is seared into your mind, into your nose, onto your tongue. Because you can taste the bitter flavor of your own tears on your cheeks, or the metallic twang of blood in the air. It doesn't leave you. Because the grave is for the person, but death still lurks among us.

Right now, death is right in front of me. It's fresh. Recent. And probably looking for me next.

Someone dug this grave.

I spin and run back to the front of the house. The second I cross the threshold, everything around me hushes. I can hear my own heartbeat. My own shaky breaths filling my lungs. Each footstep is a thump against the floor, wooden planks whining and crying out against my weight. I feel like I've just walked into a nightmare.

Where is Mya?

I close my eyes and reach up to clutch the crucifix she gave me long ago. This little necklace set fire to her relationship with

46

Julius, but I'm not thinking about my lost rival right now. I'm thinking about survival. My faith is razor thin, but it's enough to remember the God who's saved me twice before, and it's enough for me to pray that He'll save me again.

Please, I say inside, *at least let Mya be okay.* I don't care about myself, and even if I did, I don't think I deserve to be saved by God. So my prayers are preserved for Mya alone, the only good one between us.

My chest aches with fear as I tiptoe through the house. I can't decide if I should call out Mya's name or silently search. What if she's in trouble? What if she's hiding and I get her caught? I don't even know *what* could catch her. But if those fresh graves are any clue, its some psycho who's killed at least three people. Or two and a dog.

I shake my head as I enter the kitchen. Maybe the gravedigger didn't kill anyone. Maybe they all died of natural causes. Starvation. Dehydration. Illness. All those things are just as possible as violence and murder.

In the kitchen, all the cabinets are open. This is where I left Mya before heading outside, it looks like she searched the place and moved deeper into the house. But where did she go next?

I peek around the corner to find a dining room adjacent to the kitchen. Other than a wooden table, nothing else is here so I turn back and march through the kitchen. The front of the house is just as empty. A tattered sofa, pillows with the cushion spilling out, a lamp stand that's been knocked over. The lightbulb has been smashed on the floor, so it crackles beneath my feet as I try to step over it. I swallow thickly, choosing my footfalls as carefully as I can. The floor is dirty and stained with food or vomit. Who can tell? I try to step around that and the crushed glass, but as I raise my foot, I realize the stain I'm stepping over isn't food or vomit. It's dried blood.

Don't panic. The thought is instantaneous, and just to drive it home, I tug my gun from my waistband and squeeze it until my hand shakes. I can't believe this thing has made it all this way, but I'm so glad for it now. I've had to use it, and I don't regret it. In fact, I'm not afraid to use it again. I found a box of bullets in my house, tucked into the back of my stepfather's closet. I have more than I need, which gives me confidence as I head toward the stairs. My only thought is of Mya, but I shouldn't be so worried. Mya has never been the muscle of our group, but she's not a damsel in distress either. She's smart. She knows she's a small girl and probably doesn't stand a chance against most opponents, but she doesn't have to be the Terminator to survive out here. She just needs to stay calm.

The floorboards creak as I make it to the top of the stairs. There are three bedrooms up here, a modest home if I've ever seen one. The first door is open, revealing a bedroom that's been torn apart. The blankets have been ripped to ribbons and lay scattered across the floor, covered in dried blood. The sheets have been snatched from the bed; the pillows thrown in a corner. The mattress is askew, hanging halfway off the bed frame and sagging onto the floor.

Someone fought in this room. They fought for their lives. And I think they lost.

The second bedroom is the exact opposite of the first. It's completely put together; the bed is even made. I don't waste time opening the white dresser that's pushed against the wall, but if I checked, I'm sure the clothes inside would be folded. There are trinkets on top of the dresser; little figurines and plushy toys sitting up straight, none of them are out of place or knocked over. Even the family photo in the center display is perfectly aligned. In the picture, there are two teenage girls and a pair of smiling parents. Everyone looks happy. Content.

The only awry detail in this room is the massive bloodstain on the bed. It starts in the middle and bleeds to both sides, running a red stream down the blankets all the way to the floor. There's a trail of blood leading from the floor to the door, and into the hallway.

I turn around, staring at the floor, wondering what in God's Name happened here. The first room made my palms sweat, but this room makes me want to vomit. The blood trail isn't one massive line of blood. It's got streaks going through it.

Slowly, I kneel beside the blood and press my hand against the floor. My body goes numb. This blood is wet—*fresh*—and it goes through the spaces between my fingers. That means these stains are drag marks. Someone was *dragged* out of this room, their hands clawing at the smooth floorboards, trying to get a grip. To hold on.

Whoever was in the first room was killed a long time ago. Those stains weren't just dry, they were old. More black than red. But whoever was in this room was recently attacked. I would've heard screaming if Mya was the victim. And the stain starts in the bed; I don't see a reason why she would've been lying in bed. That means whoever was killed and dragged away died before we got here. Maybe just hours ago.

We picked an awful house to sleep in today. I should've listened to Mya earlier; she was right, we still had plenty of daylight left. If we would've kept walking, we wouldn't have encountered this horror. But we're here now, all we can do is survive and get through it. Like we always do.

With a breath, I stand and reenter the hallway. There's only one room left.

6

Adrian

The blood trail goes right to the last room, I'm guessing it's the master suite. As I walk, I take slow, deep breaths, squeezing my gun and trying hard to keep my nerves in check. My heartbeat is louder than the floorboards, but I pause each time they squeal in anger. Or maybe that's fear.

I'm halfway down the hall when I hear noise coming from the bedroom. It isn't a voice. It isn't a whimper. It … It sounds *gross*. Like slurping? Or maybe gagging? I can't describe it any other way except to say that it raises the hair on the back of my neck and makes me momentarily freeze. I tilt my head to the side as I listen, trying to place the noise but my mind draws a blank. If I want to find out what's going on, I've got to see for myself, so I take another step and then I hear tapping. Three soft taps, so delicate and quick, I imagine a woman tapping her fingernail on a table.

I glance to my left.

Across the master bedroom is an open door, another step lets me see that it's a bathroom and when I take another step, I hear the tapping again. It's louder now, almost persistent. But so is that gagging noise.

One more step—the tapping grows fervent. Am I being beckoned or warned?

I squint through the shadows of the dimming sunlight, it's almost evening now, but there's still enough light for me to make out the figure standing in the corner of the bathroom.

The tapping stops.

I lock eyes with the figure and my heart double thumps. It's Mya. She's pressed against the wall so I can barely see her, but I know that's her. And I know from her position and the panicked look in her eye that she's hiding. I can't see into the master suite. From this angle, part of the bathroom is visible, but I'd have to take a few more steps to peer into the bedroom. That's why Mya was tapping. If I take another step, I'll be able to see into the room, but I'll be in full view as well.

She doesn't want them to see me.

I lift my foot to take another step, but Mya holds up her hand and shakes her head. I pause. Her large eyes glance to the side, toward the bedroom, and I know what she's saying.

I take a step back.

What do I do? Should I take my chances and run past the room to get to Mya? Or should I charge into the bedroom and start shooting?

I look at Mya again, she's staring at me. Silent, yet screaming a thousand words.

Be careful. Don't panic. Help me.

She glances back at the bedroom and then at me, then she holds up her hand, signaling for me to stay still.

I get it now and I let her know with a nod, waiting for her next signal. The wait is pure agony. Standing perfectly still, listening to the awful noises coming from the room. I keep my eyes on Mya, trusting her timing. If I miss the cue, this will all fall apart.

And there it is.

She balls her hand into a fist, and I dart past the room, dashing into the bathroom and swiftly closing the door behind me. We wait in silence for a few seconds, making sure the coast is clear before we celebrate with a hug. Mya is trembling in my arms, but when I pull away, she doesn't show her fear. She presses her fingers to my lips to keep me quiet and then turns me so I can peer through the sliver as she slowly cracks the door again.

For a moment, I feel like I can't breathe. The trail of blood slithers from the hallway into the bedroom and ends in a puddle beneath the body of a young girl. No older than twelve. She's lying on her back with her head turned to the side so I can see her cold, unblinking eyes. She's dead, that much is obvious even from my distance. But it isn't the vacant look in her eye that gives this away, it's the man hunched over her.

He's on his knees with his back facing me, head bobbing, releasing that awful gagging sound from earlier. But he isn't vomiting. He … he's eating. He's eating that girl.

My eyes burn as I turn back to Mya. We stare at each other, unable to speak or make noise, but there aren't any words I can offer right now. My mind is void of thoughts, there's only room for raw emotion. Anger. Disgust. Fear.

What have we walked into?

"Mya," I whisper, but she quickly reaches up and covers my mouth with her hand.

I want to tell her that I'm sorry. That I shouldn't have left her in this awful house alone. I want to tell her that I'm going to get us out of this. That I'm here now. But all I can do is stare at her and hope she sees the resolve in my eyes. I see the same emotions in hers—the fear and anger, the disgust too. But as my eyes rove her face, I see something else enter her gaze.

Surprise.

Suddenly, Mya glances over my shoulder. Her eyes widen, and she sucks in a gasp. I waste no time pivoting, but it seems like I'm moving in slow motion. By the time I face the hallway, all I see is a red blur, but I get my hand up in time to block my face. A sharp pain heats up my arm, ripping a scream from my throat. The reaction makes me drop the gun, but I jerk forward to compensate, shoving the man away. We both trip and fall onto the floor; it's then that I see a knife slip from the man's hand and slide across the hallway. He stabbed me. But there's no time to think about that.

I'm on top of him now, which should give me an advantage, but the man slams his fist into my injured arm and my vision blurs for a moment. My mind goes blank. My breath hitches. All I register is pain, and in my momentary blindness, the man manages to squirm from under me. Now that he's standing two feet away, I can see how deranged he is. He must be insane if he's been reduced to eating children. He's completely naked, and so skinny that I can count his ribs. Every inch of his skin is covered in blood or pocked with scars, gross bubbles of sweaty flesh growing over infected gashes and poorly healed wounds. He looks like a walking dead man.

A loud *pop!* makes us both jump, but Mya's panicked scream snaps me into focus. She must have grabbed the gun, but the shot she fired missed by a mile. The crazy man is still on his feet, and now he's screaming as he charges me. I shove myself from the floor and ram him with my shoulder. I can *feel* his ribs bend inward, but he seems to feel no pain. We wrestle across the room; he tries to hit my injured arm again, but I shift away and dodge. Just when I expect another attack, a piercing cry fills the air. It's Mya again. She isn't shooting anymore, now she's sprinting into the room and doesn't hesitate to jump on the crazy man's back.

He spins in a circle, arms flailing, trying to reach around and grab her by the hair. I duck around them, making a dive for the gun which Mya abandoned on the floor by the door. The moment it's in my hand, I see why she tossed it away. It's jammed. No surprise there, Mya's experience with firearms is about as extensive as her experience with men. It takes me two seconds to tap the magazine and rack the gun again, effectively unjamming it. But Mya's still twirling around the room on the crazy man's back. I applaud her courage, she's given me the opening I need to finish this, but I can't shoot with the two of them moving like this. I could end up shooting Mya by accident.

I curse and lower the gun. "Mya!" My voice is like a whip cracking through the room. It earns me a mean glare from Mya, but I know the hatred in her eye isn't for me. It's for the monster she's doing her best to hold on to.

Once she sees the gun in my hand, Mya lets go and falls to the floor. I fire two rapid shots right into his chest, and the room goes silent.

The man stumbles forward, blood and spit dribbling from his mouth. He says something I don't hear or care about, then he coughs and falls face-first onto the floor. Mya and I sigh together, then we look at each other, we look at the room around us, we look at the little girl before us, and we wonder what the heck we're suppose to do next.

I drop to my knees and Mya crawls over the bloody floor to me. "Adrian!" she gasps, reaching for my bleeding arm.

"I'm fine. Just tired." I'm not trying to play tough. The wound hurts but it isn't very deep. I feel weak because the surge of adrenaline that gave me the strength to fight that guy has passed. I need to sit down or else I might faint.

"You're in shock," Mya says, cupping both my cheeks.

I want to argue with her and tell her I'm just fine, but when I open my mouth all I can do is sob. Mya pulls me into a hug, and I practically crush her, squeezing so tightly. I cry into the crook of her neck. Deep, heaving sobs that make my shoulders shake. Mya doesn't seem to mind. She just holds me and runs her hands through my hair, whispering, "It's okay."

I know it is. But I can't stop the stupid, awful panic I feel inside. I'm having another attack and this time I can't hide it. I can't find something to obsessively clean and distract myself. I can't leave the room and keep this all a secret from the woman I love. Instead, I'm breaking right in front of her, and I'm so scared it'll push her away.

This is the part of me I can't fix. The part I can't get rid of. And it gets worse every day. But Mya needs me to be better. My siblings need me to be better. *I* need to be better.

Anxiety rakes its claws down my back, sending tendrils of mindless fear into my head and heart. I feel weak with grief and confusion. I feel helplessly afraid of everything and nothing at all. I can't breathe. I can't stop my hands from shaking. I can't think. All I can do is hold on to Mya as I stare at the dead girl over her shoulder, waiting for this to pass.

What a gruesome sight.

The girl is wearing a nightgown that seems to drown her tiny body. I've had nights without food, but this child looks like she went the last few *weeks* without food. And then ended up as food. I remember the family photo in her bedroom. Two teenage girls and a mother and father. It's hard to believe this little girl had once been a smiling teen. She's so small. So fragile.

She's been stabbed multiple times, but I can still tell that her cheeks are sunken, her skin is like leather stretched over thin bones. Her arms are wires I'm sure I could snap, but her legs are the worst. Withered and shriveled. It dawns on me then that she might have been crippled. Her legs are skinnier than the rest of her, like she hadn't been walking. That would explain why her room wasn't torn apart.

She couldn't fight back.

Her father killed her in her bed, stabbed her to death and then dragged her bleeding body away to eat in private. I'm guessing Mya walked in on this but was quiet and quick enough to hide.

"Better?" she asks now, and I realize the attack has finally passed.

It's strange... thinking of death somehow calmed me.

I'm drenched in sweat now, so much that I'm surprised Mya doesn't stick to me when she pulls away from our embrace. She reaches up and uses both her hands to wipe the streaks of salty tears from my cheeks. I'm embarrassed, but I don't pull away. I just lower my eyes and mutter, "Sorry about that."

"Don't be."

"Mya—"

She shakes her head. "No. I won't let you apologize for being human."

Is that what this is? Me being human. But that crazy man was human, and he still ate his own family. Buried them in the backyard in little graves because he'd eaten most of their remains. And that girl was human, but she died at the hands of her own father. The people who kidnapped Julius were human, but they still took him from us. Being human isn't an excuse for all the things we've done. It doesn't change the fact that I can't fix the worst part of me.

Mya's hand touches my cheek. "Let's get out of here," she says.

I couldn't agree more.

7

Mya

We spend the night moving through the neighborhood. Neither of us wants to keep going like this, but we have no other choice. We weren't just spooked by that desperate cannibal; we were paranoid of bumping into other people. Adrian and I both fired shots from his gun. If anyone else was nearby, they were either frightened off or intrigued. We weren't about to stick around and see if anyone stopped by.

Traveling is slow and brutal. First of all, it's nighttime now and there aren't any streetlights, so we have to move by starlight. The power has been off for months, I'm used to living like a cavewoman, but I'm not used to dragging Adrian along.

He's 6'3 and one of the strongest guys I've ever met, but even he is not immune to the madness of this world. He's been having panic attacks again, and it seems like they've gotten worse. I'm not angry at him, but this is awful timing. He's barely recovered from his attack, plus he's bleeding from a stab wound. There's no time for him to get it together. There's no time for him to properly treat his wound. When we get downstairs, he uses a white rag from my bag to tie around his arm and then he grunts, "Let's go."

Yeah ... he sounds tough, but he spends the next two hours wheezing beside me as I practically drag him down the street. I take the lead because I'm the only one of us who knows Julie's address, but it's dark and we have to be more cautious than ever. It takes us hours just to cover a few blocks, and we didn't even get to loot along the way.

By the time we reach Julie's front steps, I'm exhausted. If the house were any further, I'm positive we wouldn't have made it. But we're here now, and Julie's house is a good distance from the cannibal home, so I think we're safe. I hope we're safe.

Somehow, Adrian musters the strength to kick the door in, but once we're inside, he succumbs to his injuries and collapses on the living room sofa. He doesn't even try checking the area for enemies or squatters. We're here and all we can do is pray the house is empty.

Silently, I close the front door and then tiptoe back to the sofa. There's no point in being quiet, if someone's inside, they've definitely heard us by now, but I take the time to check anyway. Adrian's gun is tucked into his waistband; it takes some maneuvering to get it from him, but once it's in my hand, I begin my quick search of the house. I'm not looting, there's no time for that. I just need to check for people, then I'm going back to Adrian so I can treat his injury.

Julie's house is small. It's only ever been him and his foster mom, so they've never needed much space. It's a two-bedroom home with a living room, a kitchen, a full bathroom, and a tiny den filled with dusty books. The house is torn apart, the cabinets stripped bare, the supplies taken by looters. Despite the mess, there's still a sense of beauty left behind.

The looters couldn't take the love that'd filled this home. They couldn't take the sense of comfort I felt every time I was here. They couldn't take my memories. They play out in my head as I walk through the little place; Julius running down the halls, me chasing him while his foster mom shouts for us to quiet down. In the den, I see us sharing a massive book; it's upside down and neither of us can figure out why the words look so funny. When I enter the kitchen, I see us sitting at the table repeating Korean vocabulary as Julie's mom quizzes us while she makes bibimbap. And as I enter his bedroom, I see us sitting on his bed together. We're wrapped in blankets and trying to make it through *Child's Play* during our weekend horror movie marathon. I always squealed first, but Julius couldn't make it through a single *Saw* movie if his life depended on it. He still can't today.

The last place to check is his mother's bedroom. That room is empty like the others, but it's oddly clean. There are clothes thrown onto the floor, but other than that, the room looks nice—almost like someone messed it up searching for an outfit to wear. I sit on the edge of the bed and blink around the empty space. It's still dark out, but the curtains have been torn down, letting in the pale moonlight. It casts a silver glow across the floor, like a twinkling shadow of light.

I exhale slowly. This room was barely touched because there wasn't much here in the first place. Julie's mother was a sweet, modest woman. Never taking more than she needed, but always offering her heart and some. She was my mother when I didn't have one anymore. Seeing her empty home now makes my heart break, but I can't afford to focus on the pain. I'll cry when there's time, but for now, I've got to worry about Adrian. He needs me.

I push from the bed and check the bathroom before returning downstairs. Adrian is exactly where I left him, his injured arm hanging over the edge of the couch, the other arm slung over his sweaty forehead.

"House is empty," I say softly.

He hums in response, making me wonder just how coherent he is.

"I'm going to clean your wound," I say.

He doesn't respond, but that's okay with me, the silence only keeps me focused. I set down the gun and dig out antiseptic and fresh gauze. We don't have much in the way of first aid, but neither of us has sustained any serious injuries since leaving my house, so we've got enough for now.

The strip of cloth Adrian used to tie around his arm is stained red and sagging from his arm from all the heavy blood. I peel it away with a grimace and then my frown deepens when I get a good look at the cut. It isn't very deep, but it's ugly—

I squeeze my eyes shut. How could I think such a thing? I've seen the rest of Adrian's body. His back and chest are full of scars, cuts, bruises. He's experienced more pain than this, more than I could ever imagine, and I'm wrinkling my nose about how *ugly* this is?

Grow up, I scold myself. I doubt Adrian cares about the scar anyway.

He winces as I pour water over the cut, then groans when I add the alcohol. "You're okay," I coo, trying to wipe the excess blood away. I try to be ginger, but Adrian's face wrinkles in pain and I suck in a gasp. "Sorry…"

He doesn't respond, but after I tie the gauze around his arm, his face relaxes, and he exhales a deep sigh. His version of thank you. My response is a peck to his dewy forehead, then I put the supplies away and stand in the middle of the room. I searched for survivors, but now I can loot and sort things out. Not supplies. I need to sort out my emotions.

There are so many of them and I don't know which ones I should let in. Adrian fought for me in that house. He took a stab wound for me in that house. But now I'm in Julie's house, surrounded by the memories of all that he's given me.

His time. His laughter. His joy. His heart. Things I can't put a price on. Things I'll never forget. Things I'm not sure I'll ever have again.

That's what helps me make my decision. The reality is that I may never see Julius again. I have to accept that. So it's okay to love him, but I can't let my love for him stop me from moving forward. Not just romantically, but in every other part of my life. My heart can't stop for Julius. My mind can't stop for Julius. My goals can't stop for Julius.

I want to find my father. I want to find Adrian's family. I want to find *love* again.

I feel so guilty…

I'm not just letting go of my best friend, I'm letting go of my boyfriend. The man I loved. The man I dreamed of marrying. All of that is gone now, and the only thing left is a painful emptiness that I cannot put into words.

Where do I go from here? I'm too embarrassed to crawl back to Adrian. I don't deserve another chance with him. But I can't even begin to entertain thoughts of Adri while I'm still grieving over Julius.

So, I decide to put this all to rest. Once and for all.

I march through the house, taking items as I go. My favorite plate from the kitchen, a book from the reading room, the television remote from the living room, a picture hanging on the wall in the bedroom of Julie's mother. Its hand drawn, something I made as a kid and gave to this kindhearted woman. I'm not surprised she kept it over the years, but I need it back now.

The last thing I take is a bracelet from Julie's room. We made friendship charms as kids; I lost mine along the way, but Julie still had his. All this time. I try not to let the weight of this revelation sink in, but I can't help it.

I have all this stuff, worthless things the looters didn't even take, but it means the world to me. In this empty house, missing both its occupants, all I have is leftovers. Echoes of the lives that'd once lived here. I wanted to get rid of these things. To say farewell and then move on, but now that I've got them all piled up... I can't.

I sink to the floor and cover my face with both hands as my body shakes with a sob. It's a silent cry, a voiceless scream with my mouth wide open and my eyes squeezed shut. My chest hurts. My head begins to pound. Even my ears ring. I'm in so much pain and I can't even let it out. If I scream, I'll wake Adrian or worse—someone else might hear me and come looking.

So instead of sobbing like an uncontrollable baby, I curl up on my side and hug my knees to my chest. My cries are muffled against the rough material of my jeans; my face rubs against it, my nose is smashed, my eyes are stinging, my cheeks begin to bruise, but the burning in my face is nothing compared to the ache in my heart. For the first and last time, I let it all out.

I cry. And I cry. And I cry.

8

Adrian

Waking up is like emerging from a pool of quicksand. I swim to the murky surface of my mind, fighting my way to consciousness so I can shake off the heavy remains of fatigue, fear, and injury. When I open my eyes, every part of me feels weak. Exhausted. I groan and lick my dry lips. My vision is blurry; the world around me morphs into clarity through watery-eyed ticks. It takes me a moment to realize that it's dark; for a second, I thought I'd lost my eyesight but there's a splash of pale moonlight that spotlights the floor just a few feet away from me. It pours in through the high windows on the top of the front door. That's when I realize I'm in a house. Lying on a couch.

Slowly, I sit up, muscles screaming out in protest. The room sways with the motion and my vision blurs again. I reach up to hold my head and feel a sting of pain travel from my wrist into my elbow. My arm is wrapped in bandages. The sight of them brings back memories that make me gasp. I suddenly remember the dead girl, the backyard, the small graves, and the wild man who stabbed me.

I killed him. Two shots to the chest.

I won't let myself dwell on that; if I'm being honest, that's not the first person I've killed and it likely won't be the last. I stopped caring about death and violence long ago. I only care about the next day. Surviving. Living. Making it to my family. If I have to take out a couple cannibals along the way, so be it.

My memories are foggy after killing that man. I had another panic attack and Mya helped me through it. We left the house together, afraid that the gunshots would attract drifters, and we'd have to fight again. After that... all I remember is walking and wheezing and praying to God to help me take just one more step. I was so tired, and even though the initial panic from that attack had passed, I was still swimming in the aftermath of it.

My chest hurt from my racing heart, my legs felt numb and quivered on every step, my vision was blurry, my head pounded with a migraine, and I was shivering from a cold sweat. Mya stayed with me through it all, practically dragging me down the street. I've no idea how far we walked. Julius's house was the goal, but I've never been there so I wouldn't know if the sofa I'm sitting on is his or not.

I blink around the room, trying to make out shapes and objects in this place I don't recognize. A sofa, an armchair, a shelf with more trinkets than books, and a TV stand without a

TV. I guess looters got to this place early, when there was still hope of the power coming back so people cared more about taking televisions than food. I wonder when they realized the TV was useless. I wonder when they regretted leaving the food and any medical supplies behind. Or maybe they took that, too. Greedy monsters.

At the foot of the sofa is my backpack, Mya's is sitting right beside it. I lean over and drag my bag into my lap. I have all the food, and Mya has all the medical supplies and extra clothes since it's lighter. It only takes me a moment to find a water bottle; I chug it in ten seconds flat and then gobble down a stale granola bar. It's not until I'm fed and watered that I begin to wonder about Mya. Her bag is here, and my stab wound has been treated, so, obviously, she's somewhere around. But I haven't seen her yet.

With a grunt, I push from the sofa and quickly grab my head as everything spins around me. I must've lost a lot of blood from getting stabbed, but I need to find Mya, so I push through the haze and stumble down the hall. There are pictures along the wall. Even in the dim moonlight, I instantly recognize Julius and his Korean foster mom. Unsurprisingly, Mya is in a few pictures too, but I don't have time to linger or reminisce.

The kitchen is empty. The little reading room I find is empty. Up the stairs, the bathroom is empty, but as I exit, I hear a muffled voice down the hall, and I know where to go. The voice is feminine but stressed, and I hear sniffles too. *She's crying...* the thought sends a stab of pain into my heart, and I don't know how to handle it.

Of course, Mya's crying. She's in Julius's house. Probably in his bedroom. And she isn't sure if he's alive—or his mother either. No matter how close we are, Julius will always have some sort of presence between us. Maybe not as her lover anymore, but still as a friend. A brother. Their connection is clear in the pictures on the walls. Clear in the sobs that travel from the room. It's clear in her heart, in the fact that she even cared enough to stop here. To bring *me* here, of all people.

I swallow my anger and inch toward the room, hand sliding over the dirty vinyl-covered wall. When I pass into the doorway, I freeze. Mya's lying on the floor in a heap, legs pulled into her chest, face tucked into her knees. She's sobbing so hard, she doesn't hear me. I can't get myself to speak. I just stand there and watch as she mourns Julius, and I wonder which part of him she misses the most right now.

The part of him who was her boyfriend, or the part who was only her friend.

There's a pile of things on the floor beside her tears. A book, a plate, a bracelet. Looks like junk, but I'm sure there's some significance. Who am I to question it? I don't even want to think about it, let alone try to figure it out. So instead of torturing myself any further, I turn and begin a slow walk down the hall.

I love Mya, I'll always love Mya, but I just can't be her emotional punching bag anymore. I can't sit back and watch her cry over another man. I can't be that man's substitute. I can't fill the void in her heart. I don't know what I can do, but it isn't this. Not any—

"Adrian?"

The sound of my name pulls me to a halt. I stand in the middle of the hall with my shoulders bunched and my eyes squeezed shut. I don't want to turn back. I don't want to put myself through this emotional torture any longer, but I also don't want to let Mya go. So, I turn back and when I reach her room, I stand there and wait for her to ask me to do something I know will break my heart.

She's sitting up when I reach the doorway, wiping away her tears. "I didn't see you until you turned away."

I nod.

"I'm sorry."

I nod again.

She swallows and stares at me. There are a hundred things I want to say to her right now, but I can't find the words. I don't even have the energy to try. Have I given up on any hope of ever being more than a friend to her? No. But I am fed up with being her crutch.

"You need a moment. I'll be in the living room." I turn away again, but she calls out to me.

"Wait. Adri, please."

"I can't do this!" I say quickly. Harshly. I whirl around so fast, I make myself dizzy, but I don't care. I'm hot with anger and the surge of frustration I feel only gives me the energy I need to focus and get this off my chest. "You know how I feel about you," I hiss. "So why on earth would you ask me to join you in whatever this is." I wave my hand at all the crap on the floor. Julius's crap. "I can't do this, Mya. I can't even be here right now."

"I love you," she says softly—so softly that I'm not sure I heard her.

I step into the room and squint at her.

"I love you," she repeats. "I've loved you for a while now, but I don't deserve you. So, I pushed you away and put a wall between us." She drops her gaze, running her hand over all the junk on the floor. "This stuff, I collected it because I wanted to burn it. But then I realized I couldn't. I still love Julie, I really do. But not the way I used to." She sniffles. "This is my goodbye, Adrian. I wanted you to be there when I say it. For the last time."

"Y-Your goodbye?"

"I'm letting him go. But I'm not strong enough to do it on my own." She looks hesitant, biting her lower lip and keeping her eyes on the floor. "Can you help me one last time?"

The sigh I release makes my bones ache. I'm so tired, but part of me believes every word Mya just said. She's done. She's letting Julius go. She's finally moving on.

And she loves me. ME. Adrian Nikols.

I can't think about her confession right now because I'm still pissed at her. I'm pissed that I'm in Julius's house, surrounded by his junk, and staring down at the girl I love who can't stop crying over him. But this is all about to end. These are the last of her tears, so if she truly means what she just told me, then fine. I can help her. One last time.

I walk over and kneel beside her. "What do you want me to do?"

"I want to bury this stuff out back."

I nod. "I'll see if I can find a shovel."

There's a shovel by the back door, I use it to dig a shallow grave and then I watch as Mya tosses each item inside. She kneels and touches them one last time, then she stands and heaves out a big breath.

"Any last words?" I ask after a moment of silence.

She shakes her head. "I have no idea what to say."

I have absolutely nothing to say, so I jam the shovel into the dirt and start covering the hole again. "That was an interesting goodbye."

"Technically, I said goodbye a little while ago," Mya says. "Back at the library."

"I don't understand."

"That was when I decided to move on from Julie. But it didn't feel right to just run back into your arms." She looks at me, but her gaze makes my face heat up, so I grunt and stare at the dirt as I keep shoveling. "You are not a rebound," Mya says. "You are not his replacement. You're a person who's been there for me, and you deserve every part of my heart, not just the parts untouched by Julius."

I grunt, stabbing the earth with the stupid shovel. The hole has been filled already, but I keep digging, keep adding more dirt. Because what the heck else am I supposed to do? I said I wasn't going to be Mya's emotional punching bag anymore, but I hadn't expected her to come out and admit that she's been a jerk to me and apologize for everything. This is what I've always wanted, but now that I've got it, I don't know what to do.

"I'm sorry," Mya says, voice feather soft. "You didn't deserve anything I did to you. I used you for my own pleasure. I played with your emotions. And you've loved me through it all." She hugs herself. "That's why I don't deserve you."

"I'm never going to stop loving you, Mya," I say, huffing for breath. I finally stop digging and lean against the shovel, watching her. Waiting for her. "You know that."

She nods. "But I needed you to hear me."

"Thank you."

She stands and walks over to me, standing so close, I could lean down and kiss her. But I don't. I just watch and wait.

"Do you forgive me?" she asks, and when I don't answer right away, she slowly nods. "I understand."

"Mya—"

"I'm willing to do anything to earn your forgiveness. And your trust again."

I blink. This is so unexpected. Almost overwhelming. I don't think Mya knows exactly what she put me through. I don't think she knows the extent of everything I feel for her, and how she trampled over it so easily. So publicly. She dated Julius for months. Sneaking around with him, sharing food together, giggling like children, rubbing all of their love in my face. I could only watch and let my anger and resentment fester. Then, the moment I thought I had a chance with Mya, she used me just to get over him. We've been apart ever since. And now she's opened that door again, and promised that the only thing waiting on the other side is her open heart.

But I'm not ready to go through that door again. I've been on the other side before, and it nearly broke me.

I sigh and step away from the shovel, digging the toe of my boot into the pile of dirt. Dirt that covers Julius's metaphorical body. This isn't just a goodbye, it's a funeral.

"We didn't find Julius's mother. Or any evidence of her whereabouts," I say slowly. "And we have no idea whether Julius is dead or alive either."

Mya nods, large eyes filled with confusion.

"That means he's dead to *us*. From this point forward."

She hesitates but still nods. I don't blame her hesitation, even though she's letting go of the romantic side of their relationship, Mya still loved Julius as a friend. I won't try to take that connection away from her, but I also won't leave any room for that connection to come between us again.

"From now on, we focus on ourselves," I say. "We focus on finding our families and finding each other again."

Somewhere, in the storm of all the anger, resentment, and confusion between us is the love we once had. The shy, innocent love we shared as high schoolers. Before things got complicated. Before Mya chose her faith over my heart. Before Julius weaseled his way between us. Before the complications of life outgrew our fanciful high school dreams. There was a time when all we had was love, and I think, if that love had prevailed, maybe things would be different. Maybe I would've been a better son to my mother. A better brother to my siblings. Maybe I would've been Julius's friend. Maybe I would've found God.

But as it stands, things suck, and I don't know if we can ever fix it. But we're going to try.

9

Caesar

I have two shirts, two pairs of pants, two and a half pairs of socks... I turn a circle in my room, searching for my other sock. I'm packing for a mission—a Search-and-Rescue mission. Yes, I spoke to Keoni and yes, she finally let me join the team. It wasn't as eventful as all that (or else you would have heard about it) but I was nervous when I approached her. As I suspected, the casualties we suffered had a heavier impact than that little celebration party let on.

We put on a proud face for the camp, but we were wringing our hands behind closed doors. The loss we suffered didn't just weigh heavy on our hearts and minds; it took a toll on our numbers. We need soldiers in every area now, but after being so brutally ambushed on that last run, no one is interested in joining. Except me.

Someone knocks on the post of my tent, and I grunt as I crawl on my floor to peer under my bed. "Come in!"

I recognize the disappointment in Raven's voice when she sighs. "What on earth are you doing?"

"Searching for my sock."

She walks across the room and bends to grab something from the corner, behind the desk pushed against the cloth tent wall. I used to share a small shack with Dr. Brown after getting out of the infirmary, but once my leg healed up, I decided I needed my own space. Since I'm a Runner, I get my own tent. It's on the far end of the camp near the dump holes but still, it's mine. And by 'dump holes' I mean the crappy graveyard where we dig holes in the desert sand and dump our waste.

In a camp totally dependent on trade and looting, there isn't much waste in terms of food and junk, but where there's people there's also poop. We have outhouses, but the camp is always growing. Always adding new people—new bowels to empty and butts to wipe. We started the graveyard about a month ago. Right next to my home. That's right; I live by the Eternus dumpsite, so my tent constantly smells of turds.

Raven fans the air as she passes me my sock. "I'm not going to question how that got behind your desk."

"I won't question how you knew it was there."

I take the sock and turn around to fold it with the other. Raven stands behind me, watching in silence. "When do you leave?" she finally asks.

"Tomorrow morning."

"Know where you're going?"

"Not yet. Major Banks likes to keep things quiet, so info doesn't get leaked to the wrong people."

"I see."

Raven appears beside me while I'm folding a pair of underwear. I'm not nervous or anything, but I'm fumbling around with the boxers, so it *looks* like I'm anxious. I just don't know how to behave around Raven anymore. We haven't spoken since that argument at the party, over a week ago. I'm not angry at her, I just don't know what to say.

She told me she had feelings for me, and she doesn't want me to leave, but I have to do this. She knows I have to do this.

"I guess this is goodbye," she mutters, taking the boxers and folding them for me. She neatly adds them to the pile of folded clothes on my bed and then grabs another pair. I should feel weird about a girl folding up my underwear, but I'm more focused on the conversation.

"This isn't goodbye." I chuckle to lighten the mood. "I'm coming back, Ray. Unless you think I'm going to die out there."

"I've never had a fear of you dying. But I don't think you're coming back."

I turn to her, and she quickly faces me. The motion is so fast that I pause, giving her time to press her palm to my chest. Right over my heart.

"This part of you isn't coming back."

"Stop it." I take a step back. "Stop making me feel guilty for this."

"I didn't come here to convince you to stay."

"You just came to make me feel bad."

"No." She faces the bed and stares down at my clothes. "I came to tell you that I'm sorry, Caesar. It was rude of me to throw my feelings onto you like that. And it was awful of me to have so little hope for your friends."

"I can't blame you for being realistic." I brush my hand through my hair, wishing for a haircut. "To be honest, I don't know if I'll ever see them again, but I couldn't live with myself if I didn't at least *try* to find them. I owe them that—because I know they've tried to find me." I think of Mya and how devastating this must have been for her. I know Mya. I know she would never stop looking for me. So, I can't give up on finding her either.

"Thanks for apologizing," I tell Raven.

She nods and then spins and flops onto my bed. "I just want you to be happy. And for a while, I thought you were happy here."

I am happy. But what is happiness if I can't share it with the person I love?

I feel like part of Raven will never understand this because she already has everyone she loves right here with her. Her older sister and her sister's boyfriend are here. Raven's lover never made it to the camp, but she's obviously moved on from him. She'd been estranged from her mother before the fall. Maybe there had been a time when she'd wanted to find her, too, but that time has long passed.

Raven is content with what she has; food, water, and the rest of her family. In this broken world, sometimes that's all you can ask for. Sometimes that's all you need. So, it must sound ridiculous for me to chase the wind and a dream when I've got people here to love and live with.

I've got plenty of supplies, access to generators—even a job. In Raven's eyes, there's nothing more I could want. But I *do* want more. I want all of this and my friends and my foster mother, too. I haven't given up on them, and until I find them, I won't be content.

"I'm coming back," I tell her.

Raven leans back on her elbows. "I know you are. I just had to make one last plea."

"I'm flattered." I wiggle my eyebrows, which makes her snort out a laugh.

"Oh please! I'm sure you had plenty of girls chasing you down before the world ended."

I don't respond to that. If Raven knew the sort of guy I used to be, I'm sure she wouldn't have any sort of crush on me at all. The old me wasn't worth her time. Still, I meant what I said earlier—I am flattered by her affection. It's been a while since someone genuinely liked me for me. Mya did, and I took her feelings for granted. Delilah liked me, but our relationship was shallow and built on nothing but sex. Raven has no real reason to like me except that I'm ridiculously tall and crazy handsome (aha).

Honestly, her affection is the sweetest thing that's happened to me in a long time. I hate that I have to turn her down, and I wonder if this is how Mya felt all the years I ignored her. The irony is bittersweet.

"You still there?" Raven says.

I know she's trying to lighten the air, but I want her to know that I still care for her. Even though I can't be her boyfriend.

"Raven," her name is a sigh, "listen, I wish things were different—"

"Oh no," she groans, covering her face with her hands. "Please don't start apologizing, that'll make me feel even more pathetic."

I laugh and she laughs too, and it suddenly feels like we just became best friends.

I flop onto the bed right beside her, staring up at the ceiling. I'm so much taller than Raven, my legs dangle off the bed and her feet don't even reach the end. She's small enough to curl up beside me, resting her head on my shoulder. I don't move away. I kind of like having her there.

"I'm coming back," I say, and then I feel her fingers slip between mine.

"You'd better."

10

Mya

I'll never get used to the silence that has engulfed this new world. Like a blanket set over us, the quiet laid down for a rest and we have no idea when it will awaken again. I miss the noise. The sound of music playing on a stereo as I studied in my bedroom. The sound of children laughing and playing... I haven't seen a child since the Fall, unless it was dead. I miss the sound of television playing in public places; the news, the latest action movies, Super Bowl commercials. I miss the sound of traffic. I miss the sound of birds singing outside my window each morning. I miss the sound of frat parties thumping too loudly as I tried to sleep in the dorms. A sound I only heard once. And I miss the sound of my father tinkering with a project in our basement.

That project was his own handmade generator. Something that kept me and my friends alive for months. Sound is just one thing I miss. But I have hope to hear it again—all of it. I pray every day that the world will get better, and I believe God hears my prayers. He's heard each one so far.

Patience. A word I had come to hate, but now I get it. Now I understand why that single word was God's only response to my fervent prayers.

It was patience that opened my eyes to what I was doing to myself and to those around me. In my haste, I'd forced a relationship with Caesar that was doomed from the start. In my haste, I'd thrown myself at Adrian, desperately hoping he could heal me. In my haste, I'd pushed Adrian away again, convinced that he was the source of my lustful desires. But my source was my own heart.

Patience taught me that Julius wasn't ready for a commitment to God or me. Patience taught me that I hadn't accepted my own heartbreak, and therefore could never fully overcome it. Patience taught me that someone had been by my side all along; and with a little more patience, he'd be there again.

I wasn't waiting for Adrian or Julius; I was waiting for myself. Because only the woman I am today would be strong enough to put Christ first. Though it hurt at the time, I've realized heartbreak was the only teacher I would yield to. Pain was the only lesson I could learn from. It was awful, but effective. And now that the lesson has been learned, I'll never have to experience that heartbreak again.

I sigh as I push to my feet and yank up my jeans and underwear. Yes, I've been squatting behind a building taking a dump all this time. For some odd reason, my deepest thinking happens when I'm completely exposed and vulnerable. Maybe it's the humility of the situation? I don't know. I mean, there is no greater reminder of how badly you need God than popping out a turd in a parking lot while praying that someone doesn't shoot you and take your toilet paper. Life is hard these days.

Another thing I miss? Praying for simple stuff. Like boys and making friends in college and passing my exams. One day we'll get back to the simplicities we took for granted, but for now, I've got to get back to camp before Adrian begins to worry.

I've managed to convince him that I don't need a chaperone for bathroom breaks but he'll flip out if I stay gone too long. So, I run around to the front of the post office we're camping in and find him setting up dinner inside. When I push the double doors open, he looks up and smiles. It's awkward and shy but it's the first shade of joy I've seen on him in months.

What color is joy?

For Adrian it's a gentle shade of red that blushes his cheeks, and I absolutely love it on him. We're not exactly dating right now, but we're closer than we've ever been. You've heard that line before, right? Something like it, at least. But I'm telling you the truth; everything has changed between us, but it also feels as if we're exactly what we've always been. Together.

"What's for dinner?" I say, setting the roll of tissue on top of our first aid box.

Adrian passes me a bowl of something with beans, vegetables, and mysterious pink hunks mixed together. "Slop," he says plainly.

"Well, I've had worse."

"Wanna pray first?"

Now it's my turn to smile shyly. "Of course."

Adrian takes my hands and waits for me to bless the food. He's been reminding me to pray ever since we buried Caesar's stuff in his backyard. That was the hardest day of my life, but I'm glad I did it. I'm glad I severed the ties of my soul. I still love him, but this love is different. This is a sort of love I can manage. It isn't obsessive, all-consuming, or desperate. It's just love. Love for my best friend and prayers that he's okay somewhere. Even prayers that I'll see him again. Until that happens, I'm going to focus on other things. Like surviving, finding my father, and being with Adrian. The last part seems almost natural, especially because we've been together all this time. But now we've made it unofficially official.

I say that because Adrian hasn't made a move on me at all. We haven't kissed, hugged, or so much as held hands outside of prayer since that funeral. Part of me is really bummed about it. I don't know why he's being so cautious or distant, but I don't want to push him and make him uncomfortable.

Still ...

In the silence, we sit together on the linoleum floor, our backs against the wall of office boxes. For a moment, the only noise is the sound of us chewing. As much as I hate smacking,

I feel okay listening to this. I could be listening to the sound of our stomachs growling.

Adrian nudges me with his elbow. "Not half bad."

I snort. "Told you I've had worse."

"I was not looking forward to cold meals, but this is alright."

We ran out of gas for the camp burner a few days ago. Neither of us were happy about that, but it is what it is. We've survived a good long time with hot meals and warm water for sponge-bathing. The warm water was the first thing we sacrificed when the gas began to dwindle; that gave us another week or two of hot food, but now the gas is completely gone, and I feel a bit guilty about complaining. In this world, the little things matter more than you think. Like I said, someone could shoot me for my toilet paper.

I wipe my mouth with the back of my hand and glance up at the wall of metal boxes. "You think any mail was left behind?"

Adrian sets down his bowl and then digs into his back pocket. When he holds up a massive set of keys, my mouth falls open.

"Let's find out," he says.

"Where did you get that from?"

"Found it when we checked the place for supplies."

"That was two days ago! Why didn't you mention it earlier?"

He looks guilty. "I was saving it for when we had some downtime. I thought it would be a fun surprise."

My heart melts. *Adrian* and *fun* don't really go together, so I can't stop myself from smiling or reaching for his hand when he confesses. He looks almost like a kid as he drops his gaze, a blonde boy with a gentle smile, paired with sharp eyes, and dangerously beautiful lashes. He's ridiculously tall with thick, heavy shoulders that bunch as he reaches up to palm the back of his neck. His dark shirt sticks to him from sweat, his jeans are stained with dirt and blood, his boots are worn out and covered with dust. But he's so perfect and handsome to me.

I'm still holding his hand, smiling and gazing at him as I think of how sweet it is that we're about to do something so simple. Something I'd honestly call boring if the world wasn't destroyed. But this moment is ours.

I lean toward him, glancing down at his full lips. "Thanks for thinking of me." The words are a gentle whisper, cut short when Adrian turns his head. I peck his cheek just to save myself some embarrassment, then I awkwardly pull away and fiddle with my bowl while he pulls his hand away and stands. He even pats the top of my hand and places it on my own lap, like I'm his grandmother.

What on earth is happening here?

"Let's start with this one." Adrian picks through the keys; each one is engraved with the number of its corresponding box, so he has no trouble finding the compartment he wants to unlock. He picks one at the end of the hall, far away from me, but as he's walking away, I call out to him.

"Adri, what's going on?"

Another beat of silence passes between us, then Adrian turns around with a confused look on his face. "What do you mean? We're checking the boxes, Mya."

"Don't play me for a fool." I fold my arms. "What was that a moment ago?"

The silence lasts longer this time. Adrian stares at the floor and I stare at him. We're experiencing two different emotions right now—anger and remorse—but each one is a storm and I'm not sure which will churn into chaos first. My anger is a growing fire, but Adrian's guilt is a rushing flood. Will we drown or burn?

"Talk to me," I demand, but I don't get to say or do anything more than that because the voice that responds back does not belong to the man I'm speaking to.

The words are unclear, but there's a voice speaking in the distance, inside the post office, which immediately makes us both drop everything and launch into action. I am not thinking about this argument anymore, I am not thinking about that embarrassing almost-kiss, I am not even thinking about my own emotions. My only train of thought is our carefully planned escape routine.

I pack the medical supplies and essentials. Adrian packs the food and water. If there's time, we grab the clothes and sleeping bags. Today there isn't.

The voice has now been joined by another three and they're all inching closer to our location. Inching is not an exaggeration, they're moving slowly enough that I can grab one of our blankets, but we don't want to waste any time so that's the only thing I get before Adrian tugs me to the back of the hallway. There's a room at the end with a door Adrian kicked in when we first arrived. The door doesn't lock anymore because of that, but we don't need it to. This room has an exit leading to the back of the post office, so once we pass through, we're dumped into the cracked parking lot with weeds growing all around us. It's not until we've made it through the back alley and across another street that I allow myself to breathe. Even then, I don't risk speaking. It's too dangerous.

Not only did we run into people, I'm pretty sure we ran into *soldiers* just then. Their words hadn't been clear, but that wasn't because of distance. I couldn't understand any of the voices because they were foreign. No one in that group had spoken a single word from the English language—or from any other language I've ever heard. As a Christian who's gone on missionary trips in other countries, I'm well-travelled enough to recognize a few different languages.

The one I heard in the post office is not one of them.

Besides that, they were all men wearing heavy boots. From the pattern of their footsteps, I could tell they were moving together. As one unit. That insinuates coordination. Adrian and I are certainly well coordinated, but we don't move in synchronized formation while walking through empty buildings. And it sounded like they were coming right toward us. Maybe they were just sweeping the area—or maybe they knew we were in there. I don't know, I can only speculate. But the point I'm making is that I have a lot of reasons to believe we were almost discovered by enemy soldiers.

Are they the same soldiers that took Julius? The question blooms in my head as Adrian checks an SUV in the parking lot we ran to; he turns and pats my shoulder then opens the back passenger door. I climb in without a word and quickly make room for him. Once the door is shut, the world outside hushes.

We stare at each other.

I can hear him breathing, each gulp for air is shaky and nervous. Mine are too.

"Soldiers," I whisper.

He nods.

"The ones who took Julius?"

He shakes his head.

"How do you know?"

"I saw soldiers when I first left Cross North campus, remember?"

I nod. He told us a horror story of watching a woman get raped in the middle of the street by a group of soldiers. Even today I try to forget about that awful event, I can't imagine the nightmares Adrian suffered having to watch it play out. Or hear it.

"The accents I heard in the post office sound the same as the soldiers I saw that day. Not the ones in Orly Center."

"Okay," I whisper. I've never seen any other soldiers except the ones who took Julius, but I trust Adrian enough not to push the issue. Besides, it's not like we're in a position to go back and ask them if they took my best friend. Whether they're from Orly Center or overseas, both groups of soldiers had weapons. We've got one gun and some canned food.

I shift and hold up the blanket. "Guess we should get comfy."

Adrian smiles. "Wanna stay here for the night?"

"I think it's too risky to travel. They could track us down."

Nothing is really stopping them from searching the cars in this parking lot, but I'm willing to bet they've already swept the nearby areas. We have no idea if there are more soldiers crawling through the streets, so it's better to stay here and move in the morning.

I spread the blanket over both our laps and Adrian leans back against the door. He opens his arms for me to snuggle against him, but I hesitate. He didn't want me to kiss him earlier, yet he's trying to cuddle like there isn't a wall building between us.

Should I confront this now?

We just ran from soldiers and now we have to spend the night sleeping in a dusty car. But it's not like there will ever be a good time for this conversation, so I take a breath and say, "Why didn't you kiss me earlier?"

He looks stunned and then quickly glances away. It's evening now, so the only light we have is waning, it leaves the car glowing in a beautiful mix of rusty orange and deep red. It's like a spotlight is being shined on Adrian but he won't step into it. He just sits there staring at the floor, waiting for the light to fade.

"You don't want to kiss me."

"It's complicated," he mutters.

"Then simplify it."

He doesn't speak.

"You told me you love me. That you would always love me—"

"I know that." His voice is a grunt, words on the edge of anger. "But things are complicated, Mya."

I shake my head. "This isn't fair. We agreed to start over and give us a chance."

"That's what I'm trying to do. I'm sorry that it isn't that simple or easy for me."

I stare at him. Is he telling the truth or just making excuses? It's so hard to believe that after all this time—years of waiting and confessing his love to me—*now* things are hard for him?

Maybe I'm just being selfish, expecting him to jump at the opportunity to make out with me now that *I'm* finally ready. It's so easy for me to climb onto my high horse as the virgin Christian girl, whispering that *I'm not ready* as soon as things get hot and heavy with a boy. But now the shoe is on the other foot, and I feel angered by this rejection.

Was this how Julius felt while we were together? Is this how it feels to be told to wait?

I don't like it. But what choice do I have except to respect it?

"Okay," I say, voice a trembling whisper. "I'm sorry for pushing you."

"I do love you, Mya," he whispers back.

I move closer and let him pull me against his broad chest. We snuggle up until I'm comfy, wrapped in his arms. My head fits perfectly against his shoulder, he rests his chin on my head and sighs. We're both tired.

"I love you too," I murmur.

He hums in response, and I leave it at that.

11

Adrian

I want to kiss Mya. I'm sure she's filled your head with her doubts about me and my intentions, but I promise I'm not having second thoughts about our relationship. If anything, I'm even more in love with her now. But things are still complicated.

I'm not Christian.

Believe me, I've taken huge steps lately: asking Mya to pray, respecting her faith, even sending up my own desperate prayers to God. As an atheist, it takes incredible strength and humility to admit that there is a God—and to acknowledge that this God is the Almighty of the Holy Bible is even crazier. But that's just the beginning.

Giving my life to Christ is a step I'm not ready to take yet. That means I'll be turning my back on everything I've ever believed in. Everything I thought to be true. And once I do that, every part of my life will change. It won't be a bad change, but it will be different. I'm not against it, I promise I'm not. I'm just not ready.

The reason I'm not ready is because of Mya. I have no problems praying with her, if we lived in a better world, I'd even go to church with her sometimes. I love her that much. But changing for Mya isn't enough.

I want to make sure the change I make is for me alone. I want to convert because I'm truly convinced that there is no other truth in this world except that of Christ. I want to convert because I've discovered what faith truly means, not a desperate hope to survive, but an honest revelation that love is real. That *God* is love.

I haven't had that yet. I've had a few miraculous encounters; I'm not denying or diminishing that. But the awe of a miracle only lasts as long as the problem. *Love* lasts forever. Love is what I need to discover, not another inexplicable event.

So … I'm holding back when it comes to Mya because I know how much my faith means to her. Or lack thereof. This is the whole reason her relationship with Julius fell apart. I'm not foolish enough to think the same couldn't happen with me; because the only thing Mya loves more than the man beside her is the Man who died for her. Jesus Christ. She's made a lot of mistakes—dumb ones, crazy ones, lust-driven ones, but she's always known that God is right beside her. That He loves her enough to wash away the filth of her mistakes. So, when it comes down to it, I have no doubts that Mya will choose her faith over her feelings. As any good Christian should.

That's why I haven't kissed her yet. That's why I haven't made any moves. Because once I open that door, I am not going back. I won't be able to stop at just a kiss, and neither of us would recover from the fallout of that mistake. Mya would never speak to me again once the guilt of her sins caught up, and I'd never be able to live with myself once it truly sank in that I took something so precious from her. Something she could never get back.

So, as we snuggle together in the back of a dusty truck, I try to ignore the twisting in my chest. It starts as adrenaline, the rush of escaping those guys in the post office, then it settles into anxiety. Nerves that prickle at the prospect of being caught. But once that worry passes, I'm left in the silence of our pain. We're no longer focused on those soldiers. They could snatch this car door open right now and I'd still be wondering what Mya's thinking. How could I think of anything else? She's right here in my arms, after that awful conversation. I thought she wouldn't want to touch me, but here she is. All mine. I could run my hand down her waist, over the curve of her hip, cup her thigh and drape her leg over my middle so she could straddle me and—

I close my eyes. I promised myself I'd be a gentleman with her, and I'm *trying* to, but I can't ignore the heat growing in my stomach, swelling, pouring into my groin—which Mya is pressed against.

Crap.

I exhale slowly. It's been a long time. A *very* long time. Because, unlike my dumb friends, I wasn't focused on getting laid these last few months. I didn't have a cute girlfriend to sneak off with like Julius, and I didn't get a piece of Delilah, which everyone else seemed to have enjoyed along the way. I mean ... *yes*, I have slept with Delilah, but that was a long time ago before the world ended. Last year at some party, an encounter that didn't amount to anything more than two people moaning for an hour. I've never liked her much, but she's always been... well ... *you know*. When you're interested in having relations but not in a relation*ship*, Delilah is the type of girl you turn to. So, she helped me out a few times last year. That's it. I haven't touched her since.

I haven't touched *anyone* since that awful mistake with Daniella in the back of a car on the highway. Connor was there. And thanks to his heavy-handed criticism, I've been alone ever since. Waiting for Mya.

So here I am, with the best opportunity I'll ever have with the woman I love, and I'm not going to take it. It isn't the right time. And it isn't like I haven't kissed her before, held her before, or done far more than that. I haven't forgotten the night she came to my tent. We almost made love on my bedroom floor, and—gosh—it would've been the best night of my life. But it also would've been the most desperate night of my life. The most regretful night of my life. The one night that Mya realized I wasn't any better than Julius. And I'm still not sure if that's the case or not. But I want to figure it out.

God... I pray inside. *I want Your permission to date Your daughter. But I know I'm not good enough right now. So, if there is any chance for me and Mya to be together, then please help me. Help me let go of the things that aren't of You and Your goodness. In Jesus' Name I pray, amen.*

Slowly, I close my eyes, fill my lungs, and exhale every ounce of breath. With that breath goes every worry and fear and uncontrollable desire I have inside. I feel the tightness in my chest loosen and melt away, I feel my muscles relax, I even feel the shadows of anxiety unhook its ugly claws and retract from the very vestiges of my mind. In that moment, I feel set free. But the joy doesn't last long. Before I can celebrate the strange switch that has been flipped, I glance up to see a beam of pale light pierce the darkness veiling the parking lot.

"Crap," I whisper, shifting to get a better look. The movement is jarring enough to wake Mya who sleepily lifts her head and blinks at me. My face must be filled with panic because she immediately snaps to attention and wipes the sleep from her eyes.

"People," I whisper, jerking my chin toward the windshield.

She looks forward and I see her eyes widen and her lower lip tremble, but by the time she looks back at me, she's already swallowed her fears. This world is unkind to the weak, there is no place for tears. Not anymore.

"I don't think they're the people from the post office," I whisper. We've been cuddled up for at least two hours now. If those guys were still around, they would've found us a long time ago. Whoever is waving around that flashlight now is someone else entirely, but I doubt they're friendly.

"We've got to go," Mya whispers. "We can sneak out my door and head south."

That'll work if the enemy is only approaching from one direction. As it stands, there's no way for us to tell exactly how many people are moving toward us or from which directions. But we've still got to move, so I quickly slide my stiff arms back into the straps of my bag and cue Mya to open her door.

She turns around and reaches for the handle—then she screams.

Someone's at the window already, staring in at us. I gasp and jerk backwards, expecting my back to hit the door behind me, but it's suddenly snatched open and I fall out onto the concrete. I'm momentarily stunned, but I fight through the daze anyway. My long legs are still halfway inside the truck, so all I can do is flail with my arms. It's dark out, I have no idea how many people are around or where they're positioned. I'm still on my back, twisting like a drunken turtle as I swing my arms and try to get my legs out of the vehicle.

I hit nothing but air. But I can hear voices gathered around me. Some of them are telling me to calm down. Others are yelling for someone to grab me. Then I hear Mya's voice. She's screaming, letting out all the panicky fear I've got bottled up in my chest right now, clogging my throat. As long as she's screaming, I don't stop swinging.

My fist collides with something hard, and I hear a man curse. I swing in that direction again. This time, I miss, but I've got the gun in my other hand. I fire a shot, and the thunderous sound leaves my ears ringing, so I don't hear anyone's voice. Not even Mya's anymore.

Suddenly, someone shines a blinding light in my eyes and then kicks my hand, so the gun skitters across the lot. Then my vision erupts into a burst of stars as my head heats with pain.

I see nothing but darkness.

The pain in my head is what wakes me. I peel my eyes open to stare at a dusty cement floor, blinking away the blurriness in my vision. My hearing isn't any better, like listening to someone speak through a pillow. Still, I recognize the voice as Mya's, and I'm suddenly alert.

I jerk upright and immediately realize I'm restrained. There are ropes tied around my wrists, sending biting pain up my injured arm. I have more rope tied around my ankles, and another around my chest. I'm tied down to a large wooden chair, it creaks as I thrash back and forth, panicking.

What the heck...

WHAT THE HECK!?

My mind sinks into a black hole, but before it drifts beyond the edge of infinity, I hear Mya say my name loudly. "Adrian!"

I snap my head to the side to find her smiling, though she is also tied to a chair. The smile is forced, there's even sweat riding the curve of her face, dripping off the tip of her round chin.

"Wh-What's going on?" my voice is nothing more than incoherent noise falling from my mouth, but Mya seems to understand.

She swallows and says, "We're safe. It's okay."

"*Safe?*"

"You're only restrained because you tried to shoot us."

I look up to see three figures standing across the room; one man and two women. The man is tall and slim, but he looks healthy and confident. He's got on clean clothes and his shirt sleeves are rolled up to his elbows, showing off smooth skin totally free of dirt and scars. The ladies are the same; a woman with short blonde hair and another lady with light brown skin and one thick braid that goes down her back.

No one offers smiles or greetings. For a moment, we just stare at each other until the man clears his throat. "We've been waiting for you to wake up."

It's at that moment that a sharp pain cuts through the back of my head. I squeeze my eyes shut and try to focus. "What did you hit me with?"

"My boot." The man steps forward and squats in front of me. "I kicked you. Twice."

I want to spit at him, but I bite down on my tongue instead. This guy has me tied to a chair, and I'm sure he's got my gun now. Spitting at him could get me killed. But Mya said we were safe.

I glance over at her, ignoring the smirking man in front of me. She stares at me, and I try to find meaning behind the look on her face, but all I see is her forced smile. She's trying to be strong for my sake. After all the panic attacks, I'm sure she thinks I'm on the verge of cracking. I think I am, too.

"What's going on?" I ask. "Who are you and what do you want?"

"We just want answers," the man says calmly.

"You didn't have to kick me and tie me up to get them."

He scoffs. "You think I trust a guy who almost shot me?"

"I fired the gun because you ambushed us!"

He pushes to his feet. "It wasn't an ambush, kid. Our radio station intercepted a transmission about possible drifters holed up in a post office. That was all we could hear before the signal was cut and we were locked out of that channel." He sighs. "But it was enough information for us to find you."

I raise an eyebrow. "Are you saying you're some sort of rescue team?"

"I know it's hard to believe while you're in this state, but yes. We're a team that finds survivors and gives them a place to stay."

"Yeah, right."

He takes a deep breath. "Over the months, we've learned that our enemies are much better at finding people than we are. So, we focus our efforts on hacking their radio signals and tracking down the folks *they* are tracking. When you don't have to go through military protocol, you tend to get things done much faster."

"So, you're not military?"

He shakes his head. "Nope. Just survivors who want to help others."

I seriously doubt that last part, but I do believe he isn't in the military. The people who ambushed us at Orly Center were organized. They had uniforms and weapons, and they were merciless. They took Julius without compromise. Probably killed him, too.

These guys don't look or operate the same as the ones who took Julius, but that doesn't mean I trust anything this guy is saying. He must sense my doubts because he waves his hands around and says, "We're in the backroom of a church, not an army HQ—"

"A church?" Mya interrupts. She looks at me and we silently exchange a thousand words and questions.

We've been looking for a church, one that's been converted into a shelter. Just like this. But is it safe to reveal that? Are these guys the ones we've been trying to find all along?

"What city are we in?" I ask.

The man raises an eyebrow. "Why?"

"Please … We've been trying to find our families," Mya says. "We found clues that they might've been taken to a church in Koshen." She glances from the man to the silent women across the room. When no one replies to her statement, she gets frantic, jerking forward against her restraints. "Please just tell us if we've found the right place!"

"What sort of clues?" the man asks.

"A letter in a library—"

The blonde girl shifts from one foot to the other, and I zero in on the gesture. "You know something," I say.

"Please…" Mya begs. "You told me you weren't enemy soldiers. You said you would keep us safe. You said you would *help* us once Adrian woke up."

I stare at her profile. How long was I out? Apparently, long enough for them to fill Mya's head with empty promises.

"Listen," the man says, "we found you before the soldiers did. We've helped enough."

"Hayden," the Black woman steps forward, but Hayden shakes his head.

"He shot at us, Lori. That makes him hostile. You know we can't take in dangerous drifters, that's our number one rule."

"We aren't dangerous!" Mya shouts. "We thought you were attacking us!"

"They were defending themselves," Lori argues, but Hayden shakes his head again. The gesture makes Mya sob, and the sound breaks my heart.

I feel hollow. Like I've lost everything, and maybe I have. Mya was the hopeful one between the two of us, if she's broken—if she ever loses faith that we'll find our families—then we're doomed. *I'm* doomed. Because I can't go on without any hope to live for. I need someone to believe my family is out there. Mya's tears say they aren't. Mya's tears say this is the end for us. We just lost any chance we might have had of finding them.

We can't lose it all here…

"My name is Adrian Nikols!" I say loudly. That cuts off Mya's crying and interrupts the conversation going on between

Hayden and Lori. They all look over at me like I've just lost my mind. "I'm looking for my twin siblings, Danya and Dinara, as well as my mother. They're young, no older than nine. All three are natural blondes. My mother was born in Russia; she's bilingual and has a slight accent."

They blink at me. Hayden looks annoyed, Lori looks sympathetic. The blonde woman looks like she's in shock. Her eyes are wide open, her jaw is screwed shut, lips pressed together. She knows exactly who I'm describing. She's seen my family.

"You know who I'm talking about," I say directly to her. "You know my family is alive!"

No one speaks. All I can hear is the sound of my pounding heart and the muffled noise of my own voice as I beg them to help me. "You don't have to let me into your shelter," I say, voice cracking. "Just ... please tell them I'm alive. Tell them I've been searching for them." Tears fill my eyes, so I don't see anyone nod or smile. But I do hear them.

I hear Lori sigh. "Hayden, look at them," she insists.

I hear Hayden groan. "We have rules—"

"Forget the rules!"

Pounding footsteps approach me, then I feel something tug at my restraints before relief floods through my swollen wrists. I lift my hands to wipe away my tears and find Lori kneeling in front of me. She uses a pocketknife to slice through the ropes tied around my ankles, then she walks behind me and cuts the ones wrapped around my chest. As she moves to untie

Mya, she finally speaks again. "We're taking them to the base. I'll take full responsibility for whatever problems they cause."

Hayden takes a deep breath. "Oh, that goes without saying."

12

Caesar

The first time I rode in a van with Major Banks, I thought she was going to kill me. That's because I was tied up and had a bag over my head, and also because Claudius had kicked me in the ribs. I'm riding in a van with both of them yet again, but this experience is entirely different.

I'm not blindfolded. I'm not tied up. I'm not bawling my eyes out, desperately praying to God for protection. This time, I'm part of the team.

The inside of the van has been remodeled so the seats are against the walls and we're all facing each other instead of staring forward toward the windshield. That means I get to smirk at Claudius throughout the entire ride, which goes on for days. He does his best to ignore me, but after the third day, he finally switches seats with another soldier, Katia's blonde boyfriend, Bobby. Bobby creeps me out because he smiles right back at me, so I stop smirking and force myself to be serious.

During the ride, Keoni slowly gives us more and more information on our objective. Our radio station picked up a signal coming from an area that we've been assigned to search. Radio signals come from radios. People have radios. So, if there's a signal, there's a survivor, and we're going to find them.

Or we'll find a battalion of enemy soldiers who've lured us out to ambush us and take our supplies. Or torture us until we give them the camp's location.

"That's certainly a possibility," Keoni says, swaying as the van makes a turn. "We must be prepared for all outcomes, which is why we assign bullet buddies for each mission."

I blink. "Bullet what?"

"If you get caught by the enemy, one of us gets to put a bullet in you to keep you from talking." Claudius folds his meaty arms and grins. His teeth are crooked.

"Claudius and I are bullet buddies," Keoni says, touching his arm. "But since you're new, you don't have one." She looks at me, and then at Bobby.

I groan. "Shouldn't *I* get to choose the person who's gonna kill me?"

"Normally, that's the case. But we don't have time to let teammates bond and get to know each other anymore. Things are serious now."

"Shooting me is serious."

"Treachery is serious," Bobby inserts. He folds his arms to mimic Claudius, and I have to stop myself from rolling my eyes.

"Bobby's right." Keoni nods. "This world is full of treachery now. We trust no one, and we take no chances. If you're caught, you're shot. We refuse to give the enemy the chance to find Eternus."

"Yet, we're risking our lives to find survivors and take them back to our secret place."

"Everyone deserves a chance. That's why we took you in."

"You could've taken in my friends, too," I grumble.

Major Banks reaches up and bangs her fist on the ceiling three times. I feel the van begin to slow. "Congratulations," she says, turning to pull the window curtain aside, "this might be the day we finally make up for that blunder."

I lean over to peer out the window, and my jaw drops open.

I don't believe it... We've just pulled up to Orly Center. Is this where that rogue radio signal came from? Maybe my friends really are here. Maybe they got ahold of a radio and hunkered down here, hoping I would come back for them. It's a longshot, but I've got to have hope, no matter how small.

When the van pulls to a complete stop, I nearly jump from my seat, but Claudius stands in my way. We're both sinfully tall, but he's built like a ram and itching to knock me down. I flick my gaze over his bulging muscles and decide not to take my chances. Fighting him isn't worth it anyway.

"Wait for orders," he says.

I turn back to Major Banks. "Can we go now?"

She shakes her head. "This isn't the Runners, Caesar. We move slowly and safely on this team."

She's right about the slow part. Runners are meant to run. As soon as we get to our destination, we take off. Our missions depend on our speed, how quickly we can get in, get our supplies, and get out. The Search-and-Rescue Team is the exact opposite. Success is built on stealth and carefully organized routines. We've got to follow orders and put our trust in Keoni's leadership. If she says to stay in this van for the next eight hours, we're going to do just that.

This is the worst part of our routine. Waiting for the enemy—if there is one. Enrique parks the van somewhere inconspicuous, and we use ourselves as bait, trying to see if anyone approaches or tries to attack. We cut the engine and leave the curtains pulled over the windows, so we can't see out and they can't see in. Only Enrique knows what's going on since he's in the driver's seat. For now, all we can do is wait until he gives us the all-clear, but who knows how long that will take? It could be hours from now.

Enrique said one mission they stayed in the van for three days before Keoni gave them the OK. I don't know what she uses to determine whether we're safe or not. Instinct? Gut feeling? *GOD?* Whatever the case, no one is leaving this van until Major Banks says we can, so instead of working up my nerves, I settle down in my seat and close my eyes for a nap.

Pain shoots up my leg and I jerk forward to find Claudius glaring at me like he wants to fight. "Get up, kid. This ain't nap time."

Now I get it… He kicked me.

I blink at him, slightly confused and also slightly annoyed, so I don't make any motion to move just to tick him off.

He lifts his big, heavy boot again. "I said *get up.*"

"Don't be so rough," Keoni interrupts. "It's his first mission."

Claudius's voice is a growl. "You think other looters will care that he's a virgin?"

"I'm not a virgin." I smirk at him as I stretch out my arms, and then I let go of an exaggerated yawn. "I promise my experience makes me *more* than qualified—"

"Alright, let's get ready to leave before this conversation takes an awful turn." Major Banks stands and then turns to lift the cushions on her seat. Inside is a compartment filled with guns which she begins passing around. Claudius gets an assault rifle, Bobby takes a handgun, Enrique has a sniper rifle since he'll be staying with the van, and I get … nothing.

"What about me?" I whine as Keoni closes the compartment and adjusts the cushions.

"Virgins don't get guns." Claudius laughs like that's actually funny.

"You don't need one," Keoni says.

"Or maybe you just don't trust me with one."

"Not yet."

The truth hurts, but I swallow it like a man and jerk my chin down to nod. "Roger that."

"I'll take point, Claudius will hold our six." Major Banks shoves the door open as she continues giving orders. "Bobby and Caesar, follow my lead and wait for my cue to take the flank. Enrique—" she taps her earpiece, and we all hear Enrique fumble around in the front of the van. "You there?"

"Ready!" he calls from the front, but we can all hear his voice a second time in our earpieces which lets us know they're connected and working.

"You're our overwatch," Keoni says. "We're counting on you."

"You know I've got your back, mama."

She nods and hops out onto the gravelly concrete of the Orly Center parking lot. The moment I exit the van behind her, my heart begins to race. I haven't been here in what feels like ages. Without smartphones or watches, I stopped telling time by the hour. Every part of my life is now marked by a major event.

The Fall is when the grid went down. The great Exodus is when we finally left campus. The *second* Exodus is when we finally left Mya's house. Then there was Orly Center and discovering Eternus Camp. After that, breaking my ankle was the next big event, and the last major thing that's happened to me is this moment right now. Returning to Orly Center.

I'm not entirely sure how much time has passed since the Fall, but the scribes at Eternus say we've been without power for nearly a year now. Can you believe it? It feels like it's been so much longer, but then it also feels like I was taken from Orly Center just yesterday.

The place looks exactly the way I left it, except there's another layer of dust covering everything.

Keoni guides us through the foyer and into the main lobby; we see the same large room with rows and rows of cots for survivors to sleep on. Some are overturned, others are still perfectly in place, like I could lie down and sleep in them now. Except for the blood stains covering everything. I already know this blood is old, so it doesn't faze me, but I see Bobby shrink away from a pile of bloody clothes as we pass through the room.

The hallways are dark, so Keoni uses her flashlight as she checks corners and then leads us through the area. I feel a dark wave of nostalgia hit me like a nightmare and I have to gulp back a scream. The last time I was here, Major Banks and her men held me hostage and chased my friends through these rooms. People died that day. I was taken that day, and even though things turned out alright for me, I still have no idea what became of my friends.

Something buzzes ahead, in one of the rooms at the end of the hall. Everyone freezes as soon as we hear the noise. It isn't very loud, but in the silence, the smallest whisper sounds like a shriek. That little buzz might as well have been an earthquake shaking the walls of the building. Keoni holds up a fist and we all hold our breath until she glances over her shoulder.

Claudius says, "Didn't sound human."

No, it didn't. But I can't place my finger on what it did sound like—until I hear it again. A distant buzzing that seems to flicker on and off. The sound is so odd, I take a subconscious step forward and immediately face the wrath of my leader.

Keoni pivots and punches me in the chest, her fist hits me with a thud, and I stumble back with an *oomph* slipping from my lips. My shoulder hits the wall beside me, and I suck in a deep breath, clutching my heart.

"Wait for orders," Keoni growls. "We don't know what we're dealing—"

The buzzing happens again, this time it's accompanied by a high-pitched whistle, and I instantly recognize the noise. It's the crackle of a radio, likely reacting to the radios we're all wearing.

Keoni comes to the same conclusion and reaches up to tap her earpiece, but the interference picks up and sends a sharp shriek through the radios that makes all of us cringe. Keoni even yanks her earpiece from her ear.

We're all left standing in a still silence that seems to eat away my patience. With a grunt, I march past Keoni, heading toward the buzzing radio we all know we heard. If there was anyone lying in wait, they would have come out by now. I'm tired of waiting around. I need answers.

I ignore Keoni's hissing voice behind me, I even shove Claudius away when he grabs me roughly by the arm. Bobby doesn't try me. The only thing that pulls me to a halt is the click of a gun.

Slowly, I turn to find Keoni with her weapon raised. Her face is dead calm, her voice clear and firm. "Do not move."

"Are you serious?" I ask.

"I will not let you risk this team or this mission so you can chase your own endeavors."

"That's why you brought me here!" I shout. "My friends were left here!"

"But we don't know if that radio signal is from them."

"We don't have to explain ourselves to you," Claudius interrupts. He brushes by Major Banks, letting go of his rifle so it swings from the strap over his shoulder. As he walks, he cracks his knuckles and then stops right in front of me like a white-haired bear. "You have your orders," he growls, "now stand down. Or I'll make you stand down."

I cannot beat Claudius in a fight. I'm smart enough to know that. I'm also smart enough to know that I'm walking on thin ice here; no matter what we find on this mission, Keoni will probably never let me leave Eternus with her again. So, I might as well go check for my friends because this will be my last chance.

I sigh, knowing that I'm about to make a huge mistake, but before I can make a fool of myself, Bobby speaks up. "I'll check," he says, pushing his way to the front of the group. He walks over and stands beside me, facing Claudius and Keoni. "The last time he was here, his friends were with him. Cut him some slack."

"This *is* us cutting him some slack," Claudius says.

"Tell me you wouldn't lose your mind over your daughter?"

Claudius freezes, eyes bulging, nostrils flaring. He opens his mouth, but nothing comes out. He looks like a fish, gulping for breath and words.

Bobby looks at Keoni. "Tell me you wouldn't lose your mind over finding Zion."

"Leave my husband out of this!" Keoni shouts, shaking the gun at him.

What have I just started?

I've been at Eternus long enough to hear rumors about everyone, they aren't even juicy rumors. This is an apocalyptic world war; we've all lost someone. We're all looking for someone. But through all that gossip, I've never heard anything about Keoni or Claudius, except that they were sort of together. Heavy on the *sort of.* And maybe this is why. Keoni's still married, and she's probably not sure if her husband is dead or alive. That makes things a little complicated between her and Claudius, who may still have a daughter out there somewhere.

This world is so cruel. *I'm* cruel for acting so selfishly. I thought I was the only one at Eternus who had someone out there to find, someone who needed me. But the truth is that I've been chasing a lost relationship, not a lost person. I want to find Mya so I can ask her out again, but Claudius's daughter needs him. Keoni's husband needs her. And what about Bobby? I know he's with Raven's sister now, but what was his life like before the world fell apart? Who did he lose? Who is he hoping to find?

We all want to find people we love, but I'm the only one acting like a jerk about it.

"I'm sorry," I whisper pathetically. The sound of my words catches everyone off guard, even Claudius snaps out of his silent rage to blink at me. "I'm sorry for disobeying orders. I'll stand down."

Bobby looks like I've betrayed him, but he gives me a solemn nod as I step back and make room for Keoni to take the lead again. She doesn't move. She's still holding her rifle, pointing it at Bobby now, trembling.

Bobby lifts his hands. "I'm sorry—"

"Shut up!" Keoni barks, then she curses and drops the gun. "I'm not going to shoot you."

"Could have fooled me."

She wipes her hand over her face, she's got battle stripes across her cheeks and one of them smears when she swipes her fingers over it. "Both of you were out of line," she says.

"We're sorry," Bobby replies.

"Don't say sorry. Just do better." Keoni puts her earpiece back in and then taps it. "Enrique, you there?"

"Yeah, but our connection was cut due to frequency interference earlier. If there's a radio in that building, you're right on top of it."

I tap my earpiece just to lower the volume. "We should move in now."

"That's not your call," Claudius says.

Keoni steps forward, walking past all of us. "Let's move."

She rounds the corner into a small room, one of the burned-up offices I remember checking the first time I was here. Mya and I were left in one of these rooms together when Keoni's group showed up. That's when everything fell apart.

Even though it's been months, this room still smells faintly of smoke. I wrinkle my nose as I step inside, but then I take a deep breath and begin to cough. There's another scent in the room, and it's darker than the smoke. Heavier. Dirtier.

It smells of decay.

"Found a body," Keoni calls from the corner of the room. "And the radio, too."

I pull the collar of my t-shirt over my nose and inhale my own sweaty scent as I cross the room and freeze. The body is of a young woman, curled up on a makeshift bed stuffed into the corner of the room. She's lying on her side, the radio clutched in her frail hands, they're so skinny I can see her bony knuckles pushing through her paper-thin skin. She looks like she starved to death with her hollowed cheeks and sunken eyes. But even in this awful state, I recognize her.

It's Delilah.

I drop to my knees as a wet sob bubbles out of my throat. My eyes immediately blur with tears, and I can't stop myself from falling apart. I wasn't friends with Delilah. I didn't even like her very much, but I can't say she meant nothing to me. I can't say she deserved to die—especially like this.

She's all alone. Hidden in the corner of a dark room, clutching a radio she thought would give her hope. The way it's positioned in her stiff hands, it looks like she died holding it to her ear. Listening for a voice that never answered. For help that never came.

How long had she been waiting?

Until she starved to death.

"Lilah…" I blubber, pulling her body into my chest. I'm sobbing like a child, choking on my tears and sniffing back trails of snot that run from my nose. My shoulders tremble as I wail, it's an awful, ugly noise that fills the room and travels down the hall. I can hear my own cries coming back to me in an endless echo of pain. I am absolutely miserable right now.

It's not just that Delilah is dead, it's not that she died waiting for help, it's that my hopes have died with her. Until now, I hadn't accepted the death of my friends as a possibility. They couldn't die. They were invincible characters waiting for their rescue arc to happen. But that isn't the case. My friends are real people living in a real world that doesn't care how badly I want to see them again. The truth is that we may be separated for good. For eternity.

All of that hits me right now, as I hold Delilah's dead body in my arms and cry like a child. My grief overwhelms me, and I hear my wails turn to screams. Uncontrollable sobs that leave my mouth in deafening shrieks. I'm not holding Delilah anymore, I'm clutching her, squeezing her, shaking her by the shoulders as if I could call her soul back to her body.

"No!" I scream, though I'm not sure why. I don't even know who I'm talking to. Or what I'm talking about. But I deny it all the same.

No, she can't be dead.

No, this can't be true.

No, I won't accept it.

Someone grabs my arm, but I turn and shove them away. "Leave me!" I shout.

"Get it together!" The voice belongs to Claudius, and that makes me even angrier for some reason.

"Stay away from us!" I kick at him, pulling Delilah's body close as I crawl backwards into the corner where we found her. I drag her body with me, cradling it, like I need to protect her corpse. Everyone stares at us. No one knows what to say. No one knows how to react.

"Stay away," I say again.

"Kid…" Claudius lifts his hands in mock surrender, but he keeps inching closer.

"Be careful," Keoni says behind him, like I'm some feral animal.

"We're not your enemy," Claudius says. "We know you're hurt, okay?"

I shake my head, hugging Delilah closer.

"Just let us bury her. She deserves a burial." He takes another step, and I lunge at him, but Claudius is quicker. He raises his fist, and I feel my jaw *click* before the lights go out.

13

Adrian

I didn't sleep much last night. I haven't slept much this week, to be honest. Those guys who picked us up agreed to take us to their camp; it was a three-day trek with ropes around our wrists and a bag on our head so we couldn't report our location if we managed to escape. We didn't want to escape. We were finally heading exactly where we wanted to go. There was no way Mya or I would cause any trouble and get ourselves left behind or locked out.

We walked quietly and tried our best not to complain. Hayden found fault in everything we did—never walking fast enough, taking too many bathroom breaks, eating too much of their food, even though we had our own. Lori insisted on sharing with us, and the other girl with them seemed content to help us out. Everyone except Hayden was welcoming, but I couldn't blame him for his apprehension. I've seen the enemy soldiers up close. I've come face to face with crazy drifters. I walked in on a cannibal eating his own child. The world is too cruel to take any chances. So, even though I can't stand Hayden, I don't hold his anger against him. After all, we found our way here.

The church camp is better than I thought it would be. It isn't just an old cathedral with people sleeping on the pews, it's an entire network of underground bunkers connected through tunnels. Don't get me wrong, there are people sleeping in the pews, but those are just the guys who guard the underground entrance.

When we first arrived, we spent a full day in the sanctuary getting drilled with questions. There was a camp scribe who wrote everything down and said she would check with survivors to see if there was anyone who could recognize our names and descriptions to verify our identity or story. It was a very rough way of figuring out who we are, but it's not like anyone was still walking around with a driver's license these days. I didn't even know my birthday was coming up soon. I'll be 23. Crazy, right?

The church scribe says we're somewhere in late May. I would've graduated from college earlier this month. For some reason, that news makes my chest ache. Because I was so close to achieving a goal I'd worked so hard at. And it all crumbled. Like I never had a chance.

I would be the first one in my family to graduate and earn a degree. I would be the first one to give my siblings a dream. To show them that we could do great things, too. They wouldn't have to see me in that stupid Karty Mart uniform forever. They wouldn't have to worry about being hungry ever again. They would know that anything was possible.

Now, I just wonder if I'll make it to my next meal.

I sigh as I stare at the ceiling. I got to sleep on a comfortable bed with a warm blanket and a belly full of food. But I'm still anxious and prickly. The church camp let us move into the basement after the first night because someone inside did recognize our names and descriptions. Two people recognized us, actually.

Benson Kovac and Jupiter Star.

When I heard Bunny's stupid name, I burst into tears. What were the odds that the two of them would have ended up here? Yes, they were headed to Koshen—which is where this church is located—but it never fully registered that they might also find this place or settle down here. They could've rested for a few weeks and then moved on to find Jupe's family. Maybe they did find her family here. Who knows?

"You up?" Bunny kicks my mattress before flopping onto his own. He stares at me from across the room.

"I'm up," I say slowly. I moved in with Bunny, and Mya moved in with Jupiter. The church is still a church, so it's pretty strict about co-ed roomies. Only married couples get to snuggle up together; Bunny says there were some complaints about the arrangements but when the option is to separate or leave, people get in line pretty quickly.

"Sleep well?" Bunny asks.

I shake my head.

"I couldn't sleep much when I first arrived either."

"What was that like?"

"Crazy." He chuckles. "Weird. I hated it here for the first few weeks."

"Why?"

"I'm not really religious. So, all the people thanking God and praying really got on my nerves. It seemed weird to thank God when there was nothing here to thank Him for. People are dying. Starving. You know?"

I nodded because I really did know what he meant. I wondered the same thing every day, but even in the chaos I faced, I knew there were moments where I felt God's presence. Slowly, I've learned that God never promised us a cushy life, He only promised to be here with us through the problems we face in this life. And, honestly, He has been.

I found my friends again. I've got Mya to love me again. And I found my family, too.

Yes, they're here. I haven't seen them yet because the twins are so young, church counselors wanted to tell them about me first and then reintroduce us later, once the news sank in. I hated the wait, but I understood the process. Sometimes reuniting could be overwhelming, even for adults. I can't imagine what my kid siblings must be going through. Or what they went through to get here in the first place. To be honest, I don't want to know what's happened. I don't want to think of the twins running from cannibals or hiding from soldiers or eating crap just to stay alive. I want to hope and pray that their journey was nothing like mine. In this case, the mystery gives me peace. Ignorance is bliss, right?

I turn onto my side and watch Bunny make his bed. "I'm guessing you eventually warmed up to the church, right?"

He chuckles. "They give me food, water, and a bed to sleep in. Of course, I warmed up to them."

The room falls silent, and I watch as Bunny stares at his pillows. He's still clutching his blanket, knuckles red, grip tight. I wonder what else he wants to say, and I wonder why he feels like he can't. There's a gap between us now, a hole that extends for months where Bunny and Jupiter had to fight alone. Fend for themselves. Watch each other's backs. Make decisions that could have ended with one of them dead.

They made it out of that wilderness alive, but it's clear neither of them is unscathed. Their scars are hidden beneath their forced smiles and pursed lips. The same as mine and even more for Mya. Because I found my family, but she did not.

Still, Bunny finds the strength to smile up at me and when he speaks, his words sound sincere. "There's more to it than that. Besides, the food, I mean. I like it here."

"It's a good place." I can tell just from a few days here. The place is organized, clean, and even provides chores and jobs for survivors. It gives us a sense of normalcy, waking up to go to work, walking the kids down to the education sector so they can go to 'school.' Life down here is nothing like what it was a year ago, but it's far better than living on the streets.

This church is named He Walked On Water Ministries, a miracle I was unfamiliar with before showing up here. They hold services multiple times a week, so on my second day, I moseyed down to the underground sanctuary. Honestly, I was just there to see if I could catch a glimpse of my family, or even Mya. The male and female living quarters are separate, so I only get to see Mya in public spaces, but she's been holed up in her room since we got here. Jupiter says she isn't coping well with not finding her father. I get it... I just wish she'd let me be there for her.

Anyway, I went to the church and didn't see my family or Mya, but I did learn about the miracle the church is named after. Jesus walked on water. My mind can't even begin to comprehend what that must have been like. If I could put it into terms that I *can* understand, it's like finding peace in a storm. Maintaining control. Kind of like what we're doing here. Except Jesus's miracle wasn't a fancy metaphor. He really did walk over the waves of the sea.

Like Bunny, I'm not a convert or anything, but I sat through that little Bible study with my heart pounding in my chest. I haven't slept well all week, but when I do manage to get a wink of sleep, my dreams are filled with rushing water.

"Their hope is infectious." Bunny sits on the edge of his bed now. He looks good, like he's been eating regularly. His hair is long enough to pull into a little bun, which he does as he smiles and says, "I'm still not religious, but I like being around religious people. Sometimes their hope seems pointless, even annoying, but it's better than being angry and bitter." He sighs. "Sometimes I catch myself having hope too, you know? Like maybe one day I might find my family, too."

I forgot Bunny isn't from Arizona. I had to travel for months and fight for my life to find my family, and we were only separated by a few hours' drive across two cities. I can't imagine the hopelessness he must feel when his folks are in an entirely different state. But, like Bunny alluded, it's better to have hope for your faraway future, than to be angry at the emptiness of your present.

"Maybe you can find them," I say. "Doesn't the church have a group they send out to find survivors?"

He nods. "Yeah, but they don't cross state lines. Not yet at least. Besides, I'm thinking of joining the Strike Team."

I raise my eyebrows as I finally get out of bed.

"You know the church is connected to other shelters and camps, right?"

I nod.

"Well, there are rumors that officials are saying it's time for us to focus our efforts on reclaiming lost territory. It's time for us to strike back."

The world is at war. I hadn't forgotten, I'd just gotten used to losing. Every soldier I've ever seen has had weapons and gear, meanwhile, American citizens are running for their lives. The only evidence of our military presence was those burned records from the National Guard we found at Orly Center. I'd convinced myself that this was it. America wasn't fighting back anywhere; we were just trying to survive. Maybe now we can turn the tides.

"So, the church is forming an army?" I ask.

Bunny nods, changing into a clean shirt. "Nothing is set in stone, but I'm sure it's only a matter of time."

I snort. "You're not a fighter, Bun."

"I can learn!" He sounds offended but still manages to smile. It's weird that we're even joking around like this. I used to hate Bunny. But something about seeing him after all these months, after realizing that he was capable of carrying his own weight out there, it's made me respect him—maybe even regret underestimating him before.

Bunny tosses me a clean shirt. "No more talking. You've got a big day, remember?"

I do. Today is the day I get to see my family. The wait has been agonizing, but now that it's here, I'm nervous. I kind of want to crawl back under my covers and wait a little longer.

Is this really happening? Am I really about to see my siblings after all this time?

Bunny catches my hesitation and throws it out the door. "They've missed you, too," he says kindly.

"How do you know?"

"I've seen them."

That catches me off guard. Bunny has never mentioned seeing them before. He only said he was happy that I finally found them.

"What do you mean?" I rise from the bed, and he shrinks away, even lifts his hands like he thinks I might punch him. I don't mean to intimidate him, but I forget Bunny is as small and fragile as Mya. I could slap him around like a child if I wanted to. I don't, but still. I could.

"I mean, they were here when I arrived with Jupe!" Bunny confesses quickly. "I didn't know who they were, so I didn't bother talking to them. I *still* haven't spoken to them! That's all."

I don't know what else I expected from Bun. Of course he's never seen my family before. No one from college has except Mya. I lived over an hour away from campus, and my family never attended any of my track meets. It wasn't like I ever invited anyone from the team or the fraternity over to meet them anyway. It's totally understandable that Bunny or Jupiter would live in the same shelter as them for so long and never know it.

"I—I'm not angry," I say, sitting back down on my bed.

"You sure?"

I roll my eyes. "Positive."

"I think it's definitely time for you to meet them."

"You're just saying that."

He snorts and opens the door. "You're excited either way, right?"

Excited, nervous, scared—all of the above—but I find my feet and march out the door as confidently as I can.

The underground church is huge, but Bunny has been here long enough to know his way around. He leads me to the meeting room in just a few minutes, only slowing down to wave and greet other campers we pass by. He seems popular, which isn't surprising considering he's still the prettiest boy I've ever seen and has a smile that could put even Mya to shame. The women here treat Bunny like their loving son, the girls fawn over him like a little brother, and a few even blush as he walks by.

"You've gotten to know a lot of people here," I say casually.

He glances over his shoulder and winks. "Well, what can I say?"

"I guess you haven't changed."

"I have a little." Bunny stops at a large door and knocks twice before turning the handle. He opens it with a grin and says, "I've got a girlfriend down here."

I raise my eyebrows, but he steps into the room before I can ask any questions, forcing me to follow. Once I enter the room, all thoughts of Bunny and his new squeeze fall away from my mind.

The first person I see is my mother. We've never had a great relationship, but the sight of her brings tears to my eyes. I can't even speak, but I open my mouth to try and all that comes out is a blubbering sob. I take a step forward and my legs buckle, making me trip and fall to my knees. My shoulders shake as I sit there and sob, but something warm touches my shoulder and I look up to see my mom. She looks like the woman from my childhood, not the one who frowned and slapped me around, but the woman who hummed as she made pelmeni by hand and told Russian folktales to my siblings. That woman was my mother, and for years, I'd lost her. But somehow in this wilderness, she's found herself again, and she's found her way back to me.

"Mom?" I whisper through my tears.

She nods and falls to her knees in front of me. I wrap my arms around her so tightly, she grunts in my grasp, and I have to let her go. We both laugh, and she reaches up to wipe my cheeks with her small hands. That's when I notice two figures over her shoulder. They're slightly taller than I remember. And heavier too, like they've been eating good food—something they didn't get to do even before the Fall.

"D-Danya? Dinara?" Somehow, they look more alike now than when they were smaller. I've always been able to tell them apart, but now I don't know if they're scruffy twin sisters or cute twin brothers. And I can't pick out which is which until one of them speaks.

"Ari!" The voice is high-pitched and shamelessly warbles, so I know it's little Dinara. She's always been open with her emotions, never afraid to allow herself to feel everything that passes through her.

Danya is more reserved, always trying to be a brave brother to his gentle sister. He hovers in the background for a few moments longer as Dinara runs and hugs me. But he's still a kid who missed his brother, so after a moment, I hear his small feet scurry across the room, and I'm crushed in another hug.

We're a family again. Finally. Despite all my hopes and dreams and wishes, I didn't truly believe this was possible. Not for me. Not when so many other things in my life had gone so terribly wrong. This one thing went right.

I'm large enough to hold all three of them in my arms, the twins and my mother cling to me and we cry like four kids until someone moves closer. I hear whispering and then the door opens and closes, people are leaving to give us space and privacy. I would say thank you, but I can't speak—I can barely even think. I am, however, coherent enough to make out a familiar face as a womanly figure passes me by.

It's Mya, smiling at me with tears in her eyes. Of course she's here for this moment. I wouldn't have it any other way, and neither would she. It's the first time I've seen her since we arrived here, and after the heartbreak of not finding her father, I wasn't sure how she would feel about me finding my family. But she's here, and she's moving closer, and the next moment her arms are around me, too.

Now, it feels perfect. It feels complete. This is my family, and I'm going to do everything in my power to keep us together.

14

Caesar

Last night I dreamt of Mya. I see her a lot in my dreams. She's happy, and she's smiling, and she's telling me not to worry. But that's just a dream. The reality is so much darker. The reality is Delilah's dead body, curled up in the corner of a dark room. Lifeless. Hopeless.

Her body was so thin, malnourished and shriveled. She'd starved to death. Alone. That's what bothers me most. That she was all alone. Where are the rest of our friends? I didn't see any other bodies nearby, then again, I didn't have time to search since I was knocked out and have been locked in the van ever since.

I don't remember anything except screaming and sobbing. I know Claudius lunged at me, but after that, I only recall pain and darkness. He must have hit me hard because that was days ago and I'm still sore. My head is pounding, but compared to the pain of Delilah's death, this is nothing.

What I feel inside is a confusing mix of emotions I can't even name. Grief. Heartbreak. Misery. I'm mourning someone I wasn't even close to. It wasn't just the death of this person, it was the death of everything I thought possible. I won't be reunited with all of my friends. I won't end this story happily ever after. Delilah wasn't my world—she was barely my friend. But she did mean something to me. Not just because we'd been involved, honestly that's what I miss the least about her. I miss having someone in my life who knew me before.

Other than Delilah, I have Dr. Brown. And that's it. Everyone around me is a stranger brought into my life through a series of unfortunate events. I'm glad to be here with people like Major Banks, Pastor Nicolette, and even Claudius. But those are people I have learned to live with. Delilah was someone I chose to be with. We'd fought together. Survived together. Planned together. And before all that, we'd partied together. Studied together. And, yes, we did more than that on occasion, too.

The point is that I miss the people I started this story with, and now that one of them is gone for good, it feels like this story will never truly end. I'll always be right here, wondering what went wrong. Why didn't I make it in time. Why couldn't I be there when she needed me. And worst of all, now I'm wondering if the rest of my friends have met the same fate.

That's what drove me mad in that room, clutching a corpse and screaming in terror. That's what brought on the panic and the fear and the doubt. It wasn't the fact that Delilah was dead, it was the mystery behind it. What happened? Is everyone else dead, too? Was she here alone?

WHY? Why was Delilah all alone?

We'd made a vow to stay together, but I found her here by herself. Did she leave the group? Or did they abandon her? Maybe everyone was separated… that means Mya could be *anywhere* and any hope I had of finding her goes out the window now.

That's why I feel helpless. Hopeless. And just as dead as Delilah. I feel myself slipping into a dark place that has no exit. Major Banks probably sensed the same thing, or she just doesn't trust me. She's had me locked in the van since Claudius rocked me. Enrique keeps guard with his gun and a radio to update Major Banks on my condition once every hour. I'm here with all our camping gear and food, so I can feed myself when it's time and then knock whenever I need to use the bathroom. Enrique walks me out and lets me handle my business while he keeps his back turned and his finger on the trigger. I don't think he'll shoot me, but the fact that he's got his weapon out in the first place makes me want to curl up and die.

I totally ruined everything. Just when I'd finally gotten Keoni to trust me, I went wild and got myself sentenced to isolation. I haven't even seen Keoni except when she comes back to collect their food or gear for the day. She doesn't speak to me or even acknowledge my presence, but that doesn't stop me from trying to plead my case.

I sit up from the cushioned van seats and stare out the window. It's midday and I can already see Major Banks in the distance. She comes back for lunch and dinner every day; sometimes Claudius comes with her to help haul their gear back out. The rest of the team is camping somewhere in the distance, too far for me to see. They're either in the surrounding area or camped out in Orly Center. I have no clue and Keoni won't tell me. Neither will Enrique. No one will talk to me and it's driving me nuts.

Keoni doesn't knock when she reaches the van, just yanks the door open and stomps inside with a sigh. I immediately stand and straighten my wrinkled shirt. Clear my throat.

"Major Banks." I nod and contemplate saluting her but I doubt that will make much difference, so I settle for standing awkwardly in the middle of the van with my arms stiffly at my sides. Major Banks busies herself with loading a rucksack full of supplies.

"How was the search?" I ask.

She doesn't respond.

"I know we're still at Orly Center. It's a big place, I think I could be of some assistance—" I pause when she brushes by me, reaching for a sleeping bag. She doesn't even look at me. If I hadn't stepped to the side, I'm sure she would have reached *through* me if possible. The way she ignores me makes my nostrils flare in anger. "Major Banks," I say, deliberately placing my body in front of the cardboard box full of canned goods she needs for lunch. Only then does she look at me. Her head snaps up and her eyes lock with mine in a glare that makes me hesitate—but only for a moment.

"I know I freaked out in there, but I'm past that now," I say. I'm speaking fast so I can get it all out before she inevitably cuts me off and shoves me out of the way. "You don't have to guard me. You don't have to worry about me losing it—"

"Yes, I do," she says firmly. Her voice is set in stone, but there's also a sense of warmth behind her words. It throws me off, a small bit of kindness I wasn't expecting. But it doesn't take away the blow she's just dealt.

I rock back on my heels. "You can't blame me for reacting to the death of my friend that way."

"I don't. I blame myself, Caesar. Anyone would have reacted the way you did back there. I'm not punishing you for being human."

I glance around and chuckle. "Could have fooled me."

"You didn't see yourself." Her tone is soft and motherly. I don't like the way it so easily rolls off her tongue. It makes me uncomfortable. Knowing that she cares. Knowing that she *needs* to care. "You were feral," she says, and I shake my head, if only to keep the images of Delilah's body from resurfacing.

"I'm sorry," I whisper.

Keoni reaches out and gently touches my arm. "Don't be. If I had found one of my friends or loved ones like that, I probably would have flown off the rails, too."

"Then why lock me up like this?"

"Because we're still searching Orly Center, and we don't know what else we'll find. I don't trust you in there." She nearly whispers that last part which makes me feel even more ashamed. I must have acted like a caged animal for her to take these sorts of precautions.

"I screwed up, didn't I?"

Keoni sighs. "It's my fault. I knew it was your first mission with us, and while you might have been ready for that, you weren't ready to return to Orly Center. It's too personal for you, but I made the call to bring you along anyway. Now I'm dealing with the consequences."

"Seems like I'm dealing with the consequences," I grumble.

"I know this seems cruel but keeping you away from Orly Center is the best way to protect you from yourself and others." She wears a sad frown. "When we get back to Eternus—"

"You're kicking me off the team."

Keoni just waits quietly, neither denying nor agreeing. That only makes me angry but there's no point in lashing out. That will only make things worse.

"When we get back to Eternus," Major Banks says again, "I'm ordering you to take a few weeks off. No missions with Search-and-Rescue or the Runners. You will undergo a full psych evaluation and begin counseling with someone from the Grief and Comfort Committee. Understand?"

"A psych evaluation?" I can understand why she wants me to take some time away from missions. I can even understand the grief and comfort crap. But a psychological evaluation? "That's a bit extreme, don't you think?"

She shakes her head. "You were feral, Caesar. You could have hurt yourself and others. I will not allow you to participate in any mission on any team so long as you are a risk."

"I'm not a risk!"

"The psych evaluation will prove that."

I turn away and run my hand through my hair. There's no point in fighting this, but I want to anyway. I've never liked therapy or any form of silly conversation involving a stranger telling me my own thoughts and feelings. Coach Noble made us see a counselor on campus three times a season. It was mandatory for all athletes or else we couldn't compete. The only reason none of us complained was because Dr. Amalia Glenn was hot. But she was serious. She made us talk and she made us look our wins and losses in the face and go over every frustrating detail.

What went wrong? Why weren't you good enough? Will you be better next time? Why do you hate losing? That question always stumped me because it was so simple. Why does anyone hate losing? Because it sucks. But I'm not talking about a game now. I've just lost my friend. A human being. And the way I feel about that can't be explained away in one-hour sessions with a hot doctor I secretly wanted to bang.

I don't want to talk about Delilah. I want to get back out there and find the rest of my friends. But how can I do that? Should I rush Major Banks and run screaming through Orly Center?

That would be pointless. Keoni said they've been searching the center for the last few days. If they found any of my friends, they would've let me know by now. Which means my friends aren't there. Or Major Banks did find them and they're dead.

Defeated, I flop onto the cushioned seat of the van and take a deep breath. "A few weeks off and a psych evaluation. That's it, right?"

"Plus, grief counseling."

I grind my teeth but nod anyway. "I agree to that, and I can stay on the team?"

"If you pass the psych evaluation and the grief counselor says you aren't a risk or a danger anymore, then yes."

I don't want to do this, but I also don't see any way around it, so I reluctantly hold out my hand. "Okay. I'll do whatever it takes to earn your trust back."

"It's not about trust, Caesar. It's not even about me. It's about your heart and mind. Get yourself together, and then come back."

I really don't think I'm falling apart, but Keoni will never believe me if I say that, so I just smile and shrug. "I'll try my best."

15

Mya

For the first time in a very long time, I wake up with a smile. The church is called He Walks On Water Ministries and the shelters they've built are amazing. I love this place, and I love my roommate, too. I'm sharing a room with Jupiter!

I'll be honest, it was weird at first. Jupiter and Bunny vouched for me and Adrian; because of them, we were allowed to enter the camp so I knew there couldn't be much bad blood remaining between us if they were willing to do that. But just because Jupe wasn't willing to let me starve to death doesn't mean she was ready to be friends again.

Looks like I was wrong.

The first day they finally let us into the underground bunker, I thought we would spend our days in silence. Existing beside and around each other but never truly interacting. That was so far from the truth. With my box of clothes and personal supplies issued from the shelter in hand, Jupiter led me to her room without speaking, but once she closed the door behind her, she crushed me in a hug.

I started sobbing right away. It was like all the drama and anger between us completely melted away. This time apart made me realize how petty we'd both been. I missed Jupiter, and seeing her again, knowing that she was alive and okay trumped everything else. I couldn't let her go for nearly an hour once she hugged me.

We cried together, wiping each other's tears and laughing like girls—like best friends. Now we're roomies again, just like we were in college, and I'm certain nothing can tear us apart again. But despite my quickness to forgive her, Jupiter went out of her way to apologize. That was the first thing she said to me through her blubbery tears.

"I'm so sorry! I can't believe how childish I was!"

"I'm sorry, too!" I'd sobbed. And I was. I was sorry that I'd let my emotions lead me into bad decisions, decisions that'd impacted our friendship, and even worse, decisions that'd impacted my faith. But I'm back on the right track now, and we're back together again.

Speaking of getting back together, Adrian and his family have been reunited! I was so excited, I could barely contain myself. It took everything within me not to run across the room and kiss him when I saw him with his siblings and mother. And then he held open his arms and welcomed me into his family. I could've stayed there like that forever. I want to be with him forever. But I haven't seen Adrian since that day nearly a week ago.

I'm not really avoiding him. At first, I was bummed about my father, and then after seeing him with his family, I thought it would be a good idea to give him space. Yes, he welcomed me into that intimate circle of emotions, but this is still a precious time for him. He needs to enjoy this, cherish these moments as much as he can. There will be plenty of time for us. I can wait. He's worth it.

"Breakfast won't last forever!" Jupiter tosses me a washcloth, her way of telling me to get up and get dressed.

I groan as I toss my covers back, stretching my arms above my head and listening to my back pop. It's so easy to sleep here. Having a bed is like having a piece of heaven these days, but Jupiter has been here for a few months, I doubt she even remembers what it was like to sleep outside. She says the journey here wasn't fun or pretty, but I've gotten no more details than that. I won't press her on it, I'm just happy she's alive and even happier that she gives God the credit for keeping her safe and leading her here.

Jupiter found her older brother and her grandfather when she got here, but no one else. I don't know how she feels about not finding her mother or father, but the way she talks makes me think she never expected to since she was raised by her grandparents and never really saw her mom or dad to begin with. Still ... no one has seen her little sister since the fall. She was at school when everything happened, her grandfather and grandmother split up to find each of them. Grandpa went to grab her brother from his job while grandma raced to grab her little sister from elementary school. The two of them never made it back.

Jupiter's grandfather and older brother travelled together until they found this shelter, and after months of prayer, God brought them Jupe. They're praying He'll bring the rest of their family together. Until I see a body, I'm believing with them. And even after I see one, I'll believe God will raise them from the dead. He's done it before, who says He wouldn't do it for us?

That's the sort of faith I'm living on now. Truly believing that anything is possible, just like Jesus said. Only faith got me here, and faith will keep me going. Without that, I have nothing.

After washing up, I change into a fresh pair of jeans and grab a t-shirt from the little drawer under my bed. Both of them are black, my sneakers too. I feel like I'm slowly getting back to my old self. Jupiter even helped me wash my hair and pick it out into a large afro. This is the version of myself I've missed.

Jupe grins across the room. "You're just missing a pound of eyeliner and about two dozen chains."

"I miss being goth," I whine, poking out my bottom lip.

She snorts and hooks her arm through mine. "And I miss being a pixie."

I remember her bright pink hair. When I met her, she had about an inch of it styled into finger waves, so she looked like a Black version of Betty Boop with bubblegum pink hair. Now, nearly a year later, she's got a few inches of a curly afro growing with pink tips. It's still super cute, and the pop of color is so exciting in this drab grey world, but the grey around us just makes me miss my dark fashion even more.

"At least you've still got a little pink," I say as we leave our room together.

"Yeah, but no makeup! No eyeshadow, no glitter, no sparkles. I feel so out of place."

It's funny the little things we miss and complain about once we're done worrying over survival and food. I haven't thought about gothic clothes or makeup or my Doc Marten boots until now. Before that, my mind was consumed with food, water, toilet paper, and Adrian...

I take a deep breath as we round the corner into the cafeteria. I do this every time I enter a public space, expecting him to be there. He is. Sitting at a round table near the center of the room. I watch him scoop oatmeal into his mouth and smile as his little sister shows him her half-eaten bowl. She feeds him a spoonful and then giggles. My heart melts from how cute they are. I've never seen this side of Adrian before. He looks so happy. So peaceful. It's like he's become a different person overnight. I love this. I love him.

"You should really go sit with him." Jupiter nudges me.

I startle and clear my throat. "What are you talking about?"

"You're staring at him. You always stare at him whenever we see him, but you don't talk to him."

"That isn't true." I hope it isn't true. I mean, I don't talk to Adrian much, nothing more than a wave hello or a nod goodbye, but I don't *stare* at him. Do I?

Jupiter laughs as she takes her place in the food line. Today is oatmeal or a boiled egg with toast. I take the egg, Jupe grabs a bowl of oatmeal and flirts her way into an extra scoop while I busy myself with choosing between powdered milk or powdered orange juice. There's also instant coffee but with no cream or sugar, I pass and reach for the orange juice.

"You wanna sit with him?" Jupiter asks.

I feel my hands begin to sweat, but I'm holding my tray of food so I can't wipe them off. "Uh ..." Mercifully, I spot Bunny across the room and make a beeline for him. "Let's join Bun today!" I call over my shoulder.

"Mornin'!" he says when I set my tray down.

I grin at him and then immediately bow my head to say grace over my food just so Jupiter can't question me the moment she sits down. Like a good Christian, she politely waits for me to finish my prayer before hounding me in questions.

"You know you can't avoid him forever, right?"

Bunny and I roll our eyes together but for different reasons. "Is this about Adrian?" he asks in an exasperated voice. "It's too early for their lovebird drama."

"This isn't lovebird drama!" I cram half my boiled egg into my mouth. Somehow, I've become a nervous eater. It takes me two bites to finish my egg and three for my toast, then I down my glass of orange juice and anxiously glance around for more things to eat. Like most places, no matter how well off they

147

are, we are still on rations, so I have nothing else to stuff into my mouth and stop me from answering these awful questions.

Bunny raises his coffee and says, "I don't understand why you two don't just talk to each other. He's going crazy for you, but he won't say anything either."

He's going crazy for me?

I don't realize I've asked this aloud until Bunny sighs. "He's like a lovesick puppy. I can't stand it! And he hangs around me so much since he's got nothing else to do when he isn't with his family, now I've got no alone time with Ae-cha!"

Ae-cha is Bunny's new girlfriend. She's a cute little Korean girl who's tiny enough to be shorter than Bunny, like me and Jupiter, but sweet enough to claim every other thought in his head. We've heard about Ae-cha as much as we've heard about my complicated relationship with Adrian.

"And this is why I'm still single." Jupiter scoops oatmeal into her mouth and talks around it. "Seems like love is a lot of hard work."

"It isn't hard." Bunny points his spoon at me. "Some people make it hard by not talking for no reason."

There is a reason, but these two wouldn't get it. Adrian and I have been through so much and everything between us is crazy complicated and fragile. One wrong word and I feel like everything between us could unravel.

I wipe my face with my hands. "I'll talk to him later."

"After breakfast," Jupiter says.

"That's too soon!"

148

"Well, you should speak soon, even if it isn't about your romance. You need to at least discuss whether you're going with the caravan." Jupe says this so casually, she doesn't notice me staring at her as she scoops the last of her oatmeal from her bowl.

"Caravan?" I glance at Bunny.

"You haven't heard? There have been a lot of reports coming in about soldiers in the area."

Like the ones who found us in the post office that night? They're the reason I'm even here now. Hayden said his team intercepted a radio call about those soldiers finding us. They managed to get to us before them—thank God—but now it seems those soldiers are closing in on this place.

I gulp. "So, what's going to happen if those soldiers find the shelter?"

"Obviously, we're going to defend the place," Bunny replies. He's been talking about joining the Strike Team a lot lately, but none of us have taken him seriously. Until now. I thought he was only interested in joining because Ae-cha's father is on the team. I figured he saw it as a good opportunity to impress him. Apparently, he had other reasons for joining, like the fact that we could be invaded soon.

I just got here. I just settled in. I just started to feel safe. And now it might all fall apart.

"Even if we fight," Bunny continues, "we don't have the manpower to hold out for long. Not with the numbers those reports are saying."

"How do you know all this?" Jupe asks.

149

"Ae-cha's father keeps her informed. And she keeps me informed." Bunny winks. "Perks of love, baby."

"Too bad those perks don't include breakfast with your lover."

He frowns. "Ae-cha is on a fast, she's skipping breakfast all this week."

Most people in this camp are Christian since almost all of them were members of the church before it became a fallout shelter. Ae-cha and her father have been here since the Fall. Literally. They were in a church service together when the lights went out and never left. In the city, things became chaotic much faster than on campus, so Ae-cha and her father never felt safe leaving, and since the rest of their family still lives in South Korea, they thought it was best to stay here. To stay safe.

Good call.

I think of my father and feel my heart begin to ache. "So, anyone who doesn't want to fight is leaving with this caravan?" I ask.

Bunny and Jupiter both nod. "Camp leaders haven't made any official statements, but the rumor mill is spinning," Jupe says. "I'll be packing up as soon as the decision and destination are announced."

"I'm staying here." Bunny fiddles with his empty bowl. "Ae-cha's father is staying. So, she's staying, too. I won't leave them."

I wonder what Adrian will do. I'm positive his mother isn't on the Strike Team, and even if she is, there's no way that family would agree to separate after just being united. Either all of them are staying or all of them are going. But what does that mean for me? I can't stay here. Even though I'm safe and settled, I have to eventually go because my father isn't here. He's out there somewhere. And I'm going to find him. That means I'm leaving with the caravan. But I don't want to leave without Adrian.

I close my eyes. I guess I do have to talk to him soon.

16

Adrian

It felt strange when the world fell apart and we were all forced to live like cavemen, but we adapted. Now, somehow, it feels just as strange to go back to electricity and warm food and clean clothes. But I'm adapting.

Life at the church shelter is nice. It's comfortable. My family is here, my friends are here, and Mya is here, too. We haven't spoken much, but I see her around every now and then, and lately I've been working up the courage to actually say something to her. I think she's giving me space and time to spend with my family and adjust to life here, but I want to do all that *with* her. She is my family. And she's the one I want to settle down with. So, if I'm adjusting to anything, it's life with Mya.

I sigh for the third time as I line up my ax on the splintered wood. I've got a job at the shelter, woodworking. It doesn't pay much, but I'm not really here for the extra rations, I'm here because it's something productive that keeps me busy and also helps me get to know the layout of this place. My mother helped me land the job; she works in the church library, giving Russian lessons to kids and any adults who are interested. When I told her I wanted to help out with the twins more, she spoke to some people and got me this job, though I'm sure she lined it up for me just to keep me from moping around her place so much.

I'm still rooming with Bunny, but he's made it abundantly clear that my presence has started to get on his nerves. Apparently, I hover a lot, and pace a lot, and sigh all the time. But what annoys him most is that I'm always there. He's got a girlfriend now, so he likes to have her over during visiting hours, which are very short and very strict since the church doesn't allow men and women to mingle in the dorms much.

"You ruin the mood!" he'd groaned one evening when Ae-cha came over for dinner. She'd brought homemade dumplings and barley tea, enough to share with me, but the thought of sharing his girlfriend's home cooking ticked Bunny off and he put me out before she served dessert. I don't even know what it was, but I suppose it was something special to Bun because he refused to let me have any. I spent that evening at my mother's apartment, enjoying her cooking and listening to stories about the twins and their life here so far. Since then, I've visited my mother every day and spend any free time with my family. But now I'm getting on their nerves too, so my mom got me this job to get me out of everyone's hair.

"You need a girlfriend!" my mother complained this morning when she opened her apartment door and found me moseying in the hall. Waiting for her. "You are handsome and tall. A beautiful Russian boy should not be moping around his mother's house like a loser."

Yep, good old fashioned Russian parenting. With her job as a tutor, she speaks more Russian than English these days, so her accent is in full glorious force now. She never spoke Russian when I was a kid, so I like to hear her speak now, even when she's insulting me.

"I have a job," I'd replied, picking up Dinara and carrying her down the hall. Danya liked to pretend he was too big to be carried so I left him to walk beside our mother. "I don't see you as often since I started working. With a girlfriend, I'll never see you guys."

"Good." Mom made a lewd gesture with her hands. "With a girlfriend you will soon have a wife. Then you can have great sex and bring me grandchildren."

"Mom!"

She'd giggled, and I'd pretended it wasn't the most beautiful sound I'd ever heard. I wished I could make her giggle again in that moment. My mother had changed completely while in the church shelter. Partly because she was finally sober now; there are no drugs or alcohol in the church, but also because she'd gotten saved down here. Most of the survivors were already members of the ministry, with such a warm and cheery environment going on, it was no surprise other people began converting over time. Mom even got the twins baptized and got me to attend service with them last week. I haven't converted yet, but I can't express how happy I am for all the progress she's made.

I wish she would make progress in one other area, though.

Slowly, I'd chewed on my words, contemplating if now was a good time to bring this up. "Mom, you don't need grandchildren so early. You're still young enough to have more kids on your own. If you were dating."

She'd cut her eyes at me, and I knew I'd crossed into dangerous territory. "I am not interested in dating. You know that."

"Mom—"

"No men!"

I'd let it go after that, especially since she was yelling in the middle of the breakfast line by then. Mom refused to even speak about romance when it came to her own life. I didn't get it. She was still young and still beautiful, you'd never know she was a former addict or prostitute just from looking at her. But maybe that's why she was so reserved. She felt guilty for her past. Or guilty because my stepfather was down here, too.

I didn't find out Ryan was living in the shelter until days after reuniting with my siblings and mother. He didn't come see me; we bumped into each other by chance when I was on my way to work. That was when I realized how many secrets my mother had been keeping from me. She never mentioned Ryan's presence, nor did she mention that he also had a job in the wood shop. He's probably the reason I got hired, but I never pressed my mother on the issue. I'm sure she had her reasons for never bringing him up, considering how much I've always hated him. Getting me a job at the same shop was probably her way of giving us the chance to see each other. To decide for ourselves what to make of our odd new relationship.

Nothing about this connection is new, not to me at least. I still hate him, and he still can't stand me. But we manage to get along at work. We're cordial enough to greet each other, but no more than that. I have no idea why he isn't with my mother anymore, but I don't care enough to ask. As far as I can tell, Mom is better off without him. Every time I pass him in the shop, he reeks of alcohol and body odor. There's no alcohol in the church so I'm guessing he's got connections above ground, helping him smuggle things in that shouldn't be here.

I haven't snitched on him because he's still the father of the twins. That's the extent of my kindness. I don't want to be his friend. I don't want to be his stepson. But I can be polite enough to make sure he doesn't get kicked out, just so my siblings can still have their father in their lives. A luxury I didn't get. A luxury Mya still doesn't have.

Dr. Brown's absence has devastated her, I can tell by the look in her eye when I catch her across the cafeteria at breakfast. But lately she's been looking better. Smiling more. Chatting with Jupiter and Bunny who tells me that she misses me as much as I miss her. He says we're both crazy for torturing ourselves like this, but I can't explain the strange desire I have to be by her side and simultaneously run away whenever she's around.

Maybe this is what love is truly like. A desperate desire to be with her, but also a desperate fear of losing her. So, the only solution in mind is to stay away altogether.

I grunt as I bring the ax down on the stump of wood now, it splits on the first try. I've gotten good at this; my first few days were so pathetic the shop owner had to give me lessons in woodchopping because I couldn't split any logs myself. I kept getting the ax head stuck in the wood.

Just as I toss my log onto my pile of chopped wood, Saloso, the shop manager, rounds the corner and smiles. She's a tall woman with tan skin and silky brown hair she keeps in a tight ponytail. She always wears a tank top so I can see her carved arms and a pair of blue jeans that are either stained or torn. We spend our days cutting and carving wood, so it's not like she needs to look professional, but I do wonder if she owns any clean clothes. She even wears jeans to church services.

Saloso slaps my shoulder hard enough to make me grunt. She's so strong I'm actually jealous. "My favorite servant!" She laughs.

I'm not sure if her English is bad or if she actually thinks of me as a servant. Saloso was born and raised in Peru, moved here to marry her American lover two years ago and then lost him in the Fall. He was stabbed when they were looting a Karty Mart together. Saloso found her way to the church on her own and has been here for six months running this shop.

"Afternoon, Ma'am," I say with a grunt.

"How is the wood slicing?"

"Good. I'll be done with my pile before lunch."

157

"Good. Good. I am searching for Ryan?"

"Haven't seen him."

She clicks her tongue. "That is bad. If he does not show up, you will have to slice his logs."

I pause, ax raised above my head. "Why me?"

"You are instead son, no?"

I'm guessing *'instead son'* is supposed to mean stepson. "Yeah," I admit. "But we aren't close. I don't want to pick up his slack."

"Someone must."

"It doesn't have to be me." I drop the ax and glare at Saloso. "I don't like him. I'm not covering his crap."

"Crap?" She tilts her head to the side which makes me sigh.

"Poop," I say. I doubt that makes much more sense, but some part of me feels like the vulgar alternative will be completely lost on her.

She wrinkles her nose. "You do not have to wipe Ryan's butt, servant. I just need his wood sliced. Can you help me?"

I really don't want to help this man out in any capacity, but I can't leave my manager hanging. I need this job and I'm positive my mother will fly off the rails if I have to tell her I got fired because of Ryan.

"Fine," I groan, yanking off my thick safety gloves. "But I'm taking my break early, and I get another fifteen minutes on my lunch."

She grins. "Fair enough."

With a huff, I step outside the shop and lean against the wall. I'm not very tired, I've only been working for an hour or

158

so but I'm in a bad mood knowing that I'll have to cover Ryan's sorry butt. I would wonder where he is, but the truth is that I don't care. I hope he's dead.

Guilt runs through my mind, and I take the thought back. I don't like Ryan, but his death would devastate the twins. They're still innocent enough to see him as a good man, despite everything he's done that they witnessed firsthand. The love of a child is so strong and precious, it makes me hate Ryan even more. My siblings will always love him, and he deserves none of it.

I grunt and push off the wall. I'm done giving my attention to that scumbag, but I don't really have anywhere to go so I find myself wandering the halls until I end up near the library. I know better than to go inside, my mother works here and if she sees me, she will go on a very loud and very long rant about how I shouldn't be visiting her in my free time. I should be having great sex with my girlfriend to give her grandchildren. The thought makes me laugh out loud until someone startles me.

"Someone tell a joke?"

I whirl around to find Mya idling near the library entrance. She looks shy but approaches me with a smile and a little wave. "Sorry. Didn't mean to scare you."

I … I don't know what to say, so I just stand there and stare at her like she's an alien creature. In a way, she is. I've only seen Mya up close once since we got here, nearly three weeks ago. Somehow, in that short time, she's become a different person. She's gained a little weight, but in a good way.

She doesn't look half-starved like before, and there aren't any dark circles under her eyes. She's always kept her hair neat, braided back or twisted into a simple bun, but now it's flared out in a puffy afro that frames her face really well. And she's back to wearing all black now, even has black liner rimming her eyes.

Before the Fall, I thought her fashion was weird, especially for a Christian. But seeing her in these dark colors with a bit of liner on makes me want to grab her and kiss her. This is the Mya I fell for, with all her weird clothes and crazy hair. I never lost her, but I did miss the view.

"You look great," I blurt.

She smiles. "Thanks. You look good, too."

"Well, three meals a day will do that to you."

"How's your family?"

"Good." I pause. "My mom works here in the library."

"Yeah, I heard she was giving Russian lessons."

"Were you looking for her?"

"No." She hesitates, and then steps closer to me. "Actually, I was looking for you. I heard you hang out with your mom a lot."

Every part of me deflates and I let go of an embarrassed sigh. "Gosh, who'd you hear that from?"

"Bunny."

I want to groan but Mya laughs and immediately disarms me. "I'm glad you're here," I say instead.

"Me too."

"What did you need?"

Mya chews her lip and then shakes her head like she's annoyed. "You sound so formal, Adrian. Stop talking to me like a stranger."

I blink.

"It's me." Mya presses a hand to her chest. "Mya Brown. The girl you said you loved. Remember?"

"Of course I remember."

How could I forget?

"Then why haven't we spoken to each other?"

I could point out the fact that communication is a two-way street, but Mya is the one who was looking for me and initiated this entire conversation, so I guess she technically has the moral high ground right now. Great.

"I'm sorry." I run my hand through my hair. "I should've said something sooner. I thought you needed space to cope with everything."

She nods. "I guess I felt the same."

"Then why are you so angry?"

"Because I've missed you." She smiles and it melts my heart. Without thinking, I step forward and she does too, we share a hug for a long moment. Mya is small enough that she has to stand on her tiptoes for me to rest my chin on her head, I feel her humming against my chest and realize she's laughing.

I pull away. "You've always been short."

"You're just abnormally tall."

Julius and I have always been tall—we were tallest on the track team all four years, but I don't say that. Mya's already dealing with a lot since she didn't find her father, bringing up her childhood best friend would only make things worse.

"Listen," I say, but at the same time, Mya calls my name, and I pause.

We both blush.

"Sorry. Go ahead," I tell her, but she shakes her head.

"You first."

I swallow. The truth is that I don't really have anything to say. Mya is the one who sought me out, but I'm not sure she has any news either. We both just wanted to see each other, and now that we're finally speaking, neither of us has any words.

"Want to come over for dinner?" I ask suddenly. The request surprises both of us and leaves us staring at each other in a shocked hush. I'm distantly aware of the fact that we're standing in the middle of the hall and anyone walking by can see or hear us. I bet there are ears inside the library who've probably overheard everything and will report this back to my eager mother. The thought drags a sigh out of me, and I palm the back of my neck. "My mom would love to meet you. But no pressure."

I won't dare mention the grandkids thing.

It takes her another moment of silent surprise, but Mya eventually smiles and nods. "I'd love to have dinner with your family."

"Great. I've got to get back to work now." I turn to leave but she calls out to me.

"When will you give me details? Like, what time or date?"

"I'll find you!" I shout, then I wink and jog back to the wood shop, smiling all the way.

17

Caesar

"Do you still dream of her?" Pastor Marcos leans forward and places his elbows on his knees.

The question annoys me, but I answer respectfully anyway. I like Pastor Marcos, even though I think he's pushy and tries a little too hard to get me to open up. He's a relatively new pastor, ordained by Pastor Nicolette less than a month ago. I like talking to her, she's the pastor who delivered the sermon that left me weeping in the wooden pews like a baby. But when Major Banks dropped me off for grief counseling sessions, I was assigned to this guy.

I have to respect him because he's a pastor. I might be new to Christianity but even I remember what God did to the Israelites who disrespected Moses. Moses wasn't perfect, he made mistakes and even murdered someone, but God refused to let his followers badmouth him. That's one of the perks of wearing the burden of leadership, God has your back.

I mean, sure, He's got my back, too, but I don't think He'll open the earth to swallow my enemies just for talking about me. Probably because He knows I'd end up throwing the first punch if someone talked smack about me, whereas a humble pastor would just turn the other cheek. When you're a pastor, God is your defender. And He's fierce about it, if the story of Moses is anything to learn from.

That's why I'm not a leader in the church. I'm not humble like Moses. Not anointed like Aaron. Not wise like Miriam. Three of the most incredible prophets of the Old Testament are just figures I dream about on good nights. I'm nothing like them. If I were, then I wouldn't be here in grief counseling with Pastor Marcos.

He's not so bad. Honestly, he's good at his job and takes his faith seriously. I'm just never in a good enough mood to talk to him. I hate counseling as it is and to be paired with anyone other than Pastor Nicolette feels like a betrayal. I would've preferred Dr. Brown over Pastor Marcos, but beggars can't be choosers.

I sigh. "Yes, I still dream of Mya."

"Do you think those dreams have meaning?"

I shrug. "Dunno. Probably not."

"Do you think dreams have meaning at all?"

"They're dreams." I shrug again.

To be honest, the only dreams I've ever really had were nightmares or fantasies. The best ones came after sex; passed out beside a babe, lost in a drunken stupor of ecstasy. Can't get better dreams than that. Those dreams never meant anything. But I know if I say any of the thoughts that just drifted through my head, Pastor Marcos would start rebuking me.

"Maybe some dreams have meaning," I mutter.

He nods and sits back in his chair. We're in his office, a room barely large enough to fit his desk and two chairs. There's also a tiny bookshelf crammed into the corner with all of six lonely books sitting on display. Pastor Marcos himself is the opposite of his dull office; he's wearing a yellow t-shirt and fresh blue jeans with a creased pair of Converse All Stars on his feet. His smile is big and shows off white Chiclet-size teeth. His hair is longer than mine, a chocolatey brown ponytail that hangs over his left shoulder, which is meatier than a pork roast. Pastor Marcos is big, like *Adrian* big, with the same size muscles and same length legs.

I've always been a few inches taller than my Russian rival, but I'm not too shame to admit Adrian has always been stronger than me. I'm lean and slender while he's bulk and weight. It's a wonder he manages to be so fast. Should've been a boxer, if you ask me, but I digress.

"You're right." Pastor Marcos flashes that winning smile. "Some dreams do have meaning. In the Bible, God spoke to multiple prophets through dreams and visions. Who is to say He can't do the same today?"

"Right." I mostly agree because I don't want him to launch into a Bible study lesson if I disagree, but I do see his point.

"So, tell me about your latest dream. Was Delilah in it, too, or just Mya?"

"They were both there."

"And?"

I take a deep breath. "The dream starts with me walking through a dark tunnel. I can hear someone crying at the end of the tunnel, and when I finally get close enough, I realize the person crying is Delilah."

"Why do you think she's crying?"

"Because she's dead."

"Dead people don't cry."

"Because she died in pain."

"What sort of pain?"

I lean over and hug myself, tucking my chin against my chest. I don't want to talk about this anymore. I don't want to think about Delilah. I don't want to imagine the sort of pain she experienced as she slowly withered away.

Did she know she would die alone? Or did she hold on to hope until the end? Blindly believing that we would come for her. That *I* would come for her.

"Caesar," Pastor Marcos isn't smiling anymore, he looks concerned which makes me angry. If I don't keep it together, I'll never be able to leave and find Mya. I can't let her end up like Delilah. I *won't* let her end up that way.

I clear my throat. "I think Lilah experienced a lot of physical and emotional pain before she died."

"Was her body beaten?"

I shake my head, but then I stop and shrug. "I don't think so, but I didn't get a good look at her before I was taken away."

"And you understand why you were taken away, right?"

"Yes," I say truthfully. "I was out of control. But I'm better now."

"Why is that?"

"Counseling. Prayer. I'm doing the things I need to do to get better. It's working."

Pastor Marcos chuckles. "The way you word that is funny. *It's working.*"

I shift in my seat.

"God is not a system that works or malfunctions. God is a person. Faith is what connects us to Him. So, *it* isn't working, your faith is. God is. The Holy Spirit is. Jesus Christ is."

I nod, somewhat understanding what he means. I don't think Pastor Nicolette has broken this down yet; I'll have to pay attention at the next Bible study session.

"Right, sorry," I say, but he waves me off.

"You're still new at all this. No worries. We're both here to learn."

That surprises me, that a Pastor could learn anything from a baby Christian like me, but I take that as a compliment before I look too deeply and realize it isn't personal at all. He's probably just learning how to counsel better from doing these sessions.

"Continue." Pastor Marcos waves.

"Well, after I found Delilah crying, I ran to hug her, but she stopped crying before I got there. And she changed."

"Changed how?"

"She wasn't Delilah anymore. She became Mya."

Pastor Marcos raises his eyebrows. "Are you sure?"

"I'm positive. Delilah turned into Mya. But I still moved closer because I wanted to hug her all the same."

"You care a lot for Mya, don't you?"

"I love her," I say quickly. "She's the reason I'm alive. She's the reason I'm a Christian."

Pastor Marcos looks like he wants to say something but chooses not to. I wonder if he disagrees with what I said, that Mya is the reason I'm saved. Is it bad that I found my faith in God because I was chasing after her? Or am I looking at it wrong? I found my faith after I got my butt handed to me, it had nothing to do with Mya, honestly. But now that I'm saved, I have a real chance to be with her, so I can't ignore the fact that my faith has helped me in more ways than one.

"What happened after Delilah turned into Mya?" Pastor Marcos asks. "You still went to her to show her comfort."

"Yes, but I didn't get to hug her."

"Why not?"

"Because she faded away before I could reach her."

He's silent for a moment, rubbing his chin with his large hand. "I see."

"Does that mean anything?"

"It could mean a lot of things, Caesar, but I don't want to fill your head with false interpretation. Let me pray about it first and ask God what it means, then I'll get back to you in our next session."

I blink as he stands, I hadn't even realized how much time had passed. It's over already. One hour. That quick.

"Right." I stand and shake his hand as he guides me to his door.

"You did good today. I look forward to seeing you again."

"In two days, right?"

He nods. "Two days."

Outside, the afternoon sun is in full force which means it's the perfect time for a run. I have nothing else to do since I can't take on missions and the kitchen doesn't need any extra hands. I try to volunteer when I'm free, but not even Dr. Brown needs help today. He's in a meeting with Pastor Nicolette and Major Banks, something about him building an alarm system for the camp. Raven is working out with her sister, undoubtedly Bobby is with them, so I'm free to do as I please.

I haven't forgotten the joy of running. The rush of adrenaline and the intensity of my heightened senses. When I'm running, I feel invincible, like if I go fast enough, I could take off into the sky. It's a crazy, childish dream, but I can't stop myself from grinning at the wind whipping against my cheeks as I sprint through the Arizona desert.

The trail I'm running is beaten down by the steps of other runners, men and women who want to blow off steam or stay in shape. It doesn't matter, we've all answered the call of the trail for one reason or another. It's nothing like the track at the university with dust kicking up after each step, tumbleweed skittering by, and the ever-present danger of looters or soldiers.

It isn't the same track at all. But somehow, I've come to enjoy this trail for the beauty it does hold.

It was carved by the tired feet of the Eternus campers, it is protected by the same God who called us all together, and it is the place that keeps me calm when all else fails. Out here, I don't have to worry about answering questions or impressing Pastor Marcos. I don't have to think about Delilah or worry about Mya. All I have to do is place one foot in front of the other.

It's just me and God now. No one will see the tears that trail my cheeks, marking my path as they fall. No one will hear me scream in frustration when I crest the hilltop at the end of the path. And no one will witness me unravel as I drop to my knees and sob.

This is so unfair. I shouldn't be running a trail, I should be out there. Pastor Marcos says he doesn't want to fill my head with false interpretation, but I already know what my dream means. I'm losing Mya. She's fading away from me. Every day that I'm here, she moves a little further from my grasp. The only thing I can't figure out is if she's fading the way Delilah did or if it's just her heart that's gone.

Is she dying or moving on?

I don't think I can handle either outcome, which is why I wipe my tears and sprint back to camp with a new sense of determination. I can't wait for Pastor Marcos to tell Major Banks that I'm all clear. I've got to get out of here now.

I burst into my tent and run to my cardboard drawers. I grab my rucksack from beneath my bed and then start throwing clothes into it. I have two water bottles in a box near my clothes, I can pack those and stop by the kitchen to get more supplies before—

"What's the rush?"

I glance up to find Raven entering my tent without knocking. Normally, that wouldn't bother me, but she's just caught me packing for a mission I don't have permission to go on, so her presence sends a ripple of anger up my spine.

"Can't you knock?" I snap.

She raises one eyebrow. "Am I interrupting something?"

"Yeah. Actually, you are."

"Well, what's the rush?" she asks again, this time with more attitude. She even sets one of her hands on her hip and marches over to me to peer into my rucksack. "I thought you weren't cleared for any missions until you finished your counseling sessions with Pastor Marcos?"

"I'm not." I snatch my rucksack off my bed.

"Then what are you packing for?"

"This isn't a mission."

"Then what is it?"

"Do you always ask so many questions?" I turn away and set my bag on the floor but Raven storms over and kicks it away. It tumbles across my room, spilling clothes and water bottles with each roll.

We both watch it in silence until she says, "Tell me what the heck is going on, Caesar."

I stand. "I'm leaving, Ray. Don't bother trying to talk me out of it."

"Are you insane?" She follows me through the room as I collect my spilled things. "You're forbidden from leaving. Sneaking out will get you in big trouble. It might even get you banished from the camp!"

"She's worth it!" I spin so fast, I don't realize how close Raven is and I end up shoving her backwards with my bag. She yelps and trips over her own feet, tumbling to the floor. "Crap, I'm sorry!" I gasp, dropping to my knees beside her.

She's rubbing her ankle, but her face doesn't show any signs of pain. Not serious pain, at least. "You jerk," she whispers.

"You know I didn't mean to hurt you."

She slowly gets to her feet, swatting away my hands when I try to help her. "You're willing to get yourself killed for this girl. But the worst part is that you expect me to just sit back and watch."

I swallow. It'd never crossed my mind that Raven would ever betray me. She wouldn't do that. She would never turn me in.

Right?

"Raven—"

"Calm down," she says, rolling her eyes. "I'm not going to snitch on you. I'm coming with you, Caesar."

I ... was not expecting that.

"You know you'll also get in trouble if you do this, right?"

"What choice do I have? Don't you remember what happened the last time you tried to run off?"

I busted my leg and got a concussion.

"Someone has to look out for you," Raven says. "I can't stop you. So, I'm going with you. At the very least, I'll make sure you don't get yourself killed. And if you don't find her, I'll take you back home."

I grind my teeth. She's still hoping I don't find Mya. I can't fault her for that, it isn't easy watching someone you like chase after another person. I know because I've been stuck in a revolving love triangle since this story started. It sucks. Miserably.

"Okay." I grip my rucksack. "I'm leaving this evening, right before sunset."

We'll need at least an hour of sunlight to give us a head start. It's possible no one will notice my absence for a while, but Raven has a loving sister who spends all her free time with her. If Ray disappears unexpectedly, people will go looking for her. But they won't look at night. Chances are, they'll hold off on the search until morning, giving us plenty of time to rise early and set out before them yet again.

Raven nods like she already understands my plan. "I'll meet you here."

That's a good idea. My tent is right beside the poop graveyard, it'll suck, but we can leave through there since no one in their right mind would ever suspect us of braving the field of crap just to get out.

This is exactly why I'm happy Raven is joining me. She always knows what I'm thinking and has a plan to make it better. I need her by my side.

"I'll see you soon," I say with a nod.

She smiles before she leaves, but it's the saddest smile I've ever seen.

18

Mya

Adrian wants me to have dinner with his family. His mother and his twin siblings are the sole reason he breathes, and he wants me to join them. Do you have any idea how important this is for me?

Despite surviving together for months, fighting for each other, even seeing each other at our worst, despite kissing each other, and nearly having sex, I am nervous.

I got caught up in the grim details of this world and forgot what it was like to be a 19-year-old with a crush. If the Fall hadn't happened, I'd still be in college. I'd be studying for exams, rushing through a paper that's already two days late. Getting into silly fights with my dorm parents, sneaking out with Jupiter, and probably making really dumb mistakes with boys. I've done that last part already, but everything else has fallen away. I'll probably never get to do those things in this life now. But no matter how much the world outside changes, some things still remain the same.

Like falling in love. And meeting your lover's family.

Really, what's the point of this dinner? I wonder as I toss clothes around the room I share with Jupiter. Everything I have is black and torn or faded—perfect for my grunge/goth style, but not good enough to impress Adrian's mother.

"This is so stupid," I groan.

It's not like Adrian needs his mother's approval to date me, right? I mean, that's so old fashioned. I'm just having dinner to be polite and spend time with the family.

Right?

"What if I'm wrong?" The words leave my mouth in a childish whine, like I'm on the verge of tears. Just to be dramatic, I drop my head into my hands and flop onto the end of my small bed. It's at that exact moment that Jupiter emerges from our shared bathroom and clicks her tongue at me.

"You really are in love."

"What?" I snap my head up.

"You must love him if you're stressing this hard over having dinner at his place."

"It's dinner with his family, Jupe. This is huge."

"Yeah, in its own way. But I don't think you have to worry." She walks over and kneels in front of me. "Adrian loves you. He's always loved you, that's why he wants you to meet his family." She laughs. "He wants you to approve of them, not the other way around."

177

My heart skips a beat. Could she be right? Adrian has always been shy about his personal life, especially his family. I always thought he was secretive because his family was precious to him. But after seeing his home and learning more about the way he was living, I think Jupiter is right. Adrian never spoke much about his family because he was somewhat embarrassed.

From what I know, his mother wasn't great and it's no huge secret that he's never liked his stepfather. In comparison, life with my father, and even Julie's stepmother, probably seemed idyllic. It wasn't perfect, but my house didn't have holes smashed into the walls from anyone except looters.

Suddenly, my nerves and anxiety seem to melt away. I don't need to worry about making a good impression, but that doesn't mean I won't put any effort into this dinner. I want Adrian to know that he doesn't have to impress me. I love him and I don't care how good (or bad) his family is. I've technically met them already, and that one encounter was enough for me to know that they love him dearly. That's all I need.

I exhale slowly and then smile at Jupiter. "Thanks. You really are my best friend."

She reaches forward and squeezes my hands. "Of course, I am."

From the look on her face, I know she's about to apologize *again*. Jupe has been doing that a lot lately. She feels so guilty for all the fighting we did before she left me and Adrian to go to Koshen. I've told her a hundred times that I've forgiven her.

I've apologized, too, but it seems like she can't go a day or two without saying sorry yet again.

I shake my head before she can speak. "Forget all the stuff from the past."

"I just want you to know that I'm sorry, Mya. Truly sorry, and even embarrassed for my behavior."

I nod because that's the polite thing to do, but I'm not angry at Jupiter. I couldn't care any less about the petty fights we suffered through. We're together again, and the time apart made our connection even stronger. Jupiter is more like my sister now than anything. So, in a way, I'm thankful for the troubles we faced, and I praise God that our friendship endured.

Our story reminds me of one of my favorite scriptures, Luke 6:32, *If you love those who love you, what credit is that to you? Even sinners love those who love them.* Meaning, it is easy to be kind to the people who are kind to you, that's nothing special. Even sinners without the love of Christ in them can do that. But to survive the trials of jealousy, anger, and bitterness that Jupiter and I went through, and remain friends through it all, that's a true blessing.

It wasn't easy to love Jupiter when she was fighting with me. Pointing fingers at me. Or letting Delilah slap me in the face. But I loved her through it anyway, because as Christians, I wasn't loving *Jupiter*, I loved the Spirit within her. I loved the part of her that came from God, the part that mercifully loved me back even when I was being just as angry, selfish, and petty.

That's the love that brought us back together and it's the love that will keep us together now.

I want to share that love with Adrian. I've seen his mother at church services, and I've seen him going with them recently. But I don't know if he's retaining anything. Maybe I'll find out soon.

I squeeze Jupe's hands. "If you really want to make it up to me, let me borrow something nice to wear to this dinner."

She grins. "Only if you let me do your makeup."

She managed to find me some eyeliner last week, I have no idea how she got ahold of it, but I'm not passing it up now. "And my hair?" I add.

Jupe nods. "You're gonna look amazing. And even if you don't, the world is so crappy right now, it's not like there are better girls lining up for Adrian to choose from."

That makes me snort because it's kind of true. When people are dropping like flies and you don't know if you'll see tomorrow, love becomes much less complicated.

When Jupiter is done, I look *almost* normal. I've been gaining weight since I'm eating more food now, but I still look very skinny which makes my eyes seem like they're about to pop out of my head. My hair has dulled a little, losing most of its natural luster, but it's still curly as all get out, so it fluffs out nicely with some water and olive oil which Jupiter worked two weeks in the kitchen to trade her rations for. As a Black woman, I totally understand. It isn't coconut oil or shea butter, but it's better than nothing.

Jupe uses liner and black eyeshadow to hide some of the bulginess in my eyes, then she gives me a braided crown and fluffs the rest of my hair into an afro. She lets me wear a black t-shirt dress which I pair with my own black combat boots. I think I look pretty good. This isn't something I normally would've worn to meet my boyfriend's family, but it is something I would've put on for anything else. That alone makes me feel confident. It makes me feel like the world hasn't completely ended. I mean, who would've thought I'd be getting dressed for a date today? A few months ago, a few *weeks* ago, that seemed like a silly fantasy. But now it's happening.

Jupiter hugs me before I leave, and I spend the entire walk to Adrian's place wondering if I should've tried to bring something for the table. We're on strict rations down here, so there isn't much I could have brought. I've started working in the indoor garden, sometimes they let senior members take extra vegetables home, but I haven't been working long enough to qualify as a senior, so I have nothing but my smile to offer when I knock on the door.

Adrian answers with a smile, too. Seems like an even exchange.

"You came," he breathes.

"Of course, I did."

We stand there staring at each other, not really knowing what to say. It's been three days since I've seen him, even though he promised to get back to me with details later that afternoon when we first spoke. He got caught up with work and then I started my own job, so we weren't able to make arrangements until yesterday. We might as well be strangers with a crush right now because I have absolutely no idea what to say to Adrian, so I blurt out the first thing that comes to mind.

"You look good."

He blushes, pale skin turning pink and then red as he fumbles for words. "I—gosh—th-thanks. I mean, you look amazing, too." He palms the back of his neck. "You always look amazing. Even when we weren't bathing regularly."

His eyes bulge when I make a face.

"Well, I didn't care about you bathing! No one could bathe. The smell never bothered me."

"The *smell?*" My voice is a horrible squeak. I can't even maintain eye contact anymore.

Adrian doesn't fare much better. He pales and then starts sputtering apologies. He's so large that he hovers over me, wearing a grey pair of jeans and a faded blue dress shirt. His clothes don't match, but I do appreciate the effort he put into dressing up. It's not like it's easy to find new clothes around here, especially for a guy his size. Any other time, I'd be over the moon about how handsome he looks, but right now I want to crawl away and die in my dorm.

Mercifully, Adrian's mother interrupts us with a loud laugh. "Adri! You are ruining your date night before it has even begun!"

Adrian submits to defeat with a sigh. His shoulders sag and he gazes sheepishly at me through his blonde bangs. "I'm sorry," he mutters.

"Let's start over," I say.

He manages a smile. "Hey, thanks for coming."

"Hey, thanks for having me."

Then, with a nervous smile on both our faces, Adrian lets me through the door.

The entire family has dressed up for dinner. The twins wear matching clothes, a red dress for Dinara and a red sweater for Danya. It's a little warm for the sweater, Danya even wipes his forehead a few times during dinner, but he never complains. The fact that the kids were willing to wear nice clothes just for this melts my heart. Plus, Adrian's mother is an excellent cook and a great host. She made Russian classics using ingredients she could trade for. She apologized that she had to replace certain seasonings or vegetables, but I've never really had Russian food so I wouldn't know the difference. Everything tasted great, and it made Adrian swell with pride each time she mentioned that he'd helped her cook.

Apparently, he's a wonderful assistant in the kitchen, which is funny because he never helped me cook while we lived together but I don't comment on this. Instead, I enjoy the beet and potato salad, I slurp down my cabbage soup, and then I devour the meatballs he helped make. They're served in a creamy tomato sauce made of canned tomatoes and cream of chicken soup—not entirely traditional, but still tasty. Adrian got his hands on a few heels of bread. They're stale and probably would've been thrown out if he hadn't taken them, but they go down easily after I soak them in the flavorful sauce.

For dessert, the twins serve sweet pancakes with jarred applesauce. It's the homiest, most heartwarming meal I've had since before I left for college. My father went all out the week before I packed up, making one of my favorite foods each night. We had Salisbury steaks with mashed potatoes, simmered mustard greens and cornbread, jambalaya with shrimp, and even homemade chicken pot pies. I helped with most of the food, but my father dominated desserts since I can't bake for my life.

This dinner reminds me so much of that week. Not the food, but the emotions. The joy, the humorous conversations, the love. The peace. Adrian's family loves each other, every single one of them. When I stayed in his house, I saw little evidence of Adrian's happiness, but it's here now. It's heavy and seems to make up for all the lack he faced in his childhood. He can't stop smiling when his siblings speak, cheeks filled with food. And even though his mother says some crazy things, she makes us all laugh and dotes on each of her children. She even makes me feel welcome, asking about my life before the Fall, even promising to make Salisbury steaks for me next time I come over.

"Because there will definitely be a next time, yes?" She raises her glass and winks, it's full of mint tea, I watched her make it before she poured it into her glass, but even I still wonder if it's spiked. Adrian's mother is so full of life, it's almost overwhelming but it's also charming. She's a breath of fresh air in this dreary world. And so is her apartment.

Since she's got two little ones, she was given one of the few rooms with a tiny kitchenette which allows her to cook such great food. She even has a little fridge filled with cold water; we all have a glass after dessert like we're drinking a delicacy. In a world without much power or electricity, cold beverages are the closest thing to fine wine.

I savor the ice-cold chill of my water as it slides over my tongue. I squeeze my chilled glass, feeling the condensation wet the tips of my fingers. This is heaven. I could do this every night. I *want* to live like this every night.

"Of course, there will be a next time," I say.

Adrian exhales which makes us all laugh.

"My son is so nervous." His mother winks at me. "You have his heart. Special woman."

"*Mom*," Adrian mutters.

"What? She needs a confidence boost after you told her she stinks."

The twins giggle, even I let go of a little chuckle, but I reach over and squeeze Adrian's bicep to make him feel better. And to make me feel better, too; his arm is firm and solid, a stark reminder of the handsome guy he was before the Fall. He's still that guy, just shier, more subdued now.

No … not subdued. This is Adrian without the anger. Adrian when he isn't having panic attacks. Adrian when he isn't filled with hate. Or frustration. Or rage. This is the real Adri, and he's shy because he isn't sure if he'll be accepted in this form. As himself.

I trace my hand down his arm and reach for his hand under the table. Our fingers interlock. Adrian looks up at me, we don't speak, we don't even smile at each other, but in that moment, we exchange a hundred different things. We whisper a hundred different words, and I catch each one, hold them in my heart.

"Are you fondling under the table?" His mother raises her eyebrows and we both jerk away from each other.

"*Mom!*" Adrian cries.

I laugh with his mother who lifts her glass. "As a mother who wants grandkids, I say go for it. Use my bedroom tonight if you must." She sighs solemnly. "But as a Christian, I have to say, please wait until you get married."

"Married?" I whisper and that little word silences the room. Everyone is staring at me, even Adrian, like he isn't sure how I'm going to react.

"Why not?" his mother asks. "You are in love. It's not like you have much better to do. I approve."

"I didn't bring Mya here to propose, Mom." Adrian pushes from the table and starts angrily collecting dishes. "You're going to scare her away if you keep talking like that."

"Love has no fear!" His mother slams her teacup down like a Viking. "That's in the Bible."

It is, but still. Neither Adrian nor I are ready for marriage. We haven't even made our relationship as boyfriend and girlfriend official yet, even though it's obvious that we are together. Marriage just seems like a huge step.

"I'm not afraid," I say quietly.

Adrian jerks his head up, he's leaning over the sink in the kitchen, about to start the dishes. His eyes find mine and I see a question swirling in them. *What do you mean?*

"I love your son," I say aloud.

His mother looks surprised, then her face grows serious.

"I'm *in* love with Adrian," I say more confidently, "but I don't want to rush into something I'm not ready for. I want to enjoy every step of our relationship."

His mother sighs. "Kids are so sure they have forever."

"Mom," Adrian starts but she shakes her head.

"Love hard and love with everything you've got." She stands. "Tomorrow is not guaranteed."

No one speaks for a long time, the only noise that fills the room is the sound of Adrian slamming dishes around. Eventually, the twins retreat to their rooms and Adri's mother begins to clear the rest of the table.

I reach for my cup to help her. "I'm sorry," I say softly, "I didn't mean to cause trouble."

"It's not you," she says. "It's the news of the soldiers."

Adrian walks over and slowly lowers himself into a chair beside me. "There have been sightings."

"I've heard. That was what I initially wanted to speak to you about."

Shock passes over Adrian's face, it makes me feel guilty. I guess he thought I'd wanted to talk about our relationship and plan dates like he did. But this is serious. If these soldiers are a real threat, we won't have a future to enjoy a relationship.

Now, I understand his mother's eagerness. She doesn't want us to rush, but she knows we may not have much time left. In this world, each day is a 50/50 chance of starvation, battle, or illness. Nothing is guaranteed, especially not tomorrow.

Adrian's hand finds mine beneath the table again. "There's a caravan forming for the people who want to leave. But there's also a Strike Team forming for those who want to fight for this place."

When I look at him, I see a man who doesn't know what to do. It scares me.

"My family wants to go. But I want to fight."

"Adrian," I whisper.

"This place saved me—"

"You belong with your family!" His mother nearly explodes, her Russian accent sharp and strong. I understand her emotion, the soldiers we've seen haven't been a joke. They are trained killers. If they've got their eyes set on taking this shelter, they won't show any mercy.

I squeeze Adrian's hand. "You're not serious, are you?"

"Someone must defend this place. We can't just lay down and let those guys take it."

"We were just reunited," his mother says. "You just found a woman who loves you."

Another reason she's so eager. She probably thinks settling down with me will influence Adrian to leave with the caravan instead of joining the Strike Team. Now I feel used, but I don't let it bother me. It's not like I want Adrian to fight any more than his mother does. I don't even understand why he's doing this.

"You know I have to leave, right?" I place my free hand on his cheek. "I want to find my father."

"That means she's leaving in the caravan. Like we are." His mother glares at him. "Like you should be."

Adrian pulls away from me. "I haven't decided what I want to do."

"Well, every day those soldier get closer," his mother says, "choose soon. And choose wisely."

I couldn't agree more.

19

Caesar

It takes us a few days to get to Orly Center—I say *us* because Raven came with me. I appreciate her more than she knows. She's risked so much for me, being here could get her banned from Eternus as much as me. On top of that, her older sister is back at camp. We both know she's probably worried sick. Even worse, we both know it's only a matter of time before we're hunted down. That's why we moved without stopping, barely getting any sleep, barely taking any rests. But we're here now.

I stare up at Orly Center, my chest pumping, my heart thudding in my rib cage. I'm out of breath because we sprinted the last mile here, true runners if I've ever seen any. Raven is just as tired as me, yet a huge grin splits her face as she looks over at me.

"We made it," she says, like she can't believe it. I can hardly believe it. We're only standing outside the building but just being here fills me with hope, the sort of hope I didn't realize I'd so desperately needed.

I've been living my life in quasi peace for months now, holding on to faded hope that I would find my friends. But what I had wasn't truly hope, it was just wishful thinking. I didn't really have faith. I had a desperate plea. But this, leaving the camp, chasing after my goals, *this* is real faith. Right? I mean, the Bible says faith without works is dead. So, what's the point in sitting around at camp *hoping* that things work out? *Hoping* that one day my friends will magically appear.

I had to leave; I had to *do* something to truly activate my faith.

At least that's the excuse I feed myself as I step forward and grasp the front door handles. Raven takes my free hand, and we enter the building together, glancing around with big, gaping eyes. I forgot she's never been here before. She's a Runner, so she's been to a bunch of different places outside of Eternus, but not Orly Center. A place this large is always considered too dangerous for drops because of the potential for looters to already be here. So, this place is new to Ray, but it's the background of my personal nightmares.

I take a deep breath, trying to exhale the images of Delilah that plague me. As much as I wanted to get back here, I didn't think that it might be difficult for me. I feel myself choking with emotion as I venture into the ghostly halls of this building.

With all the lives lost, all the screaming deaths that've taken place here, Orly Center is nothing more than a massive grave.

Connor died here. His neck broken by one of Major Banks' men.

Delilah starved to death here, clutching one of Major Banks' radios, hoping for help that never came. Help that could've come from Major Banks if she had cared enough to help me find my friends. Now, I've got to find them myself.

There must be clues here. That's the courage I swallow as I tamper the anxiety and fear that threatens me. I can't lose control here. I didn't come all this way to break down into tears.

"Caesar…"

I glance sideways to see Raven looking up at me. She's been walking silently beside me all this time but now she's stopped, tugging me to a halt along with her. Her face is full of concern, maybe even a little fear. That's when I realize I've been squeezing her hand. Hard.

"I'm sorry." Frustrated, I reach up and yank out my little ponytail with a grunt. My hair is long enough to brush my shoulders now, if I were still in college, I'd call it lazily stylish. But now it's just annoying.

"You okay?" Raven asks.

I nod. Swallow. Then shake my head.

"No. I'm not okay."

Raven hugs me and I nearly collapse, squeezing her, gasping into her hair. "What if they're dead just like her?" My voice shakes and then I surrender to the tears I'd tried to defeat. This is a lost battle.

"What if they're all dead?" I sob.

"We won't know until we try to find them. We deserve to know the truth and they deserve peace."

I pull back and look at her, *really* look at Raven, at the girl who's loved me enough to run away for me, even though my only intentions have been to find another woman. She's still here, knowing where my heart lies. And she's willing to keep going with me. For me. Because of me.

How could I drag her along like this?

"I'm sorry, Ray," I whisper. "I didn't realize this might be hard on you."

She shakes her head. "Before I ever had a crush on you, I cared. I still care, no matter what happens between us."

I smile, though it feels forced. There is nothing happy about this conversation, her willingness to continue helping me only makes me feel even worse.

"If I don't find them," I say slowly, "if I don't find *her*... Maybe—I mean—I think there could be room ... for us."

Raven gives me a slow blink. Her mouth parts, lips puckering to form words, but nothing comes out. I don't know what to say any more than she does. I don't know if she's offended or excited by what I just told her, but I can't take it back. So we stare at each other, swimming through this confusing mix of emotions. Ignoring the death and darkness around us, just to hold on to the tiny flicker of light I just ignited. A light of romance, a gift I thought I'd lost.

Now that it's back in my life, I don't want it to be snuffed out. I don't want the shadows to claim the only light I've had in a long time. So I feed it, fan it, let it grow. And I watch it burn.

Without thinking, I lean down and kiss Raven. She kisses me back, slowly at first, and then something breaks between us. With a gasp, I pull back and Raven reaches for my shirt, tugging me close again. My hands go to her waist, and I run them over her body, slipping beneath her shirt. She leans away and lets me pull it over her head, never breaking eye contact. As soon as the shirt is gone, she tugs at mine and I take that off, too, then I kiss her again, hotly, messily, desperately.

We find ourselves on the floor, gasping and groping in the lobby of Orly Center, pretending the tiles beneath us aren't stained with old blood or charred from a long past fire. We ignore all that and focus on the passion burning between us. At least that's what it starts as, but very quickly, the passion burns into something darker, twisting into uncontrollable lust.

I don't try to stop it.

She unzips my pants, and I lift my hips so she can pull them down. I don't stop her when she straddles me, and she doesn't protest when I grip her hips. My teeth snap shut with a hiss, and I swallow a grunt, eyes watering in ecstasy. I don't remember the last time I felt this good, felt this unbothered by everything around me. This dance isn't just lust, it's freedom. I let go of my stress, let go of my pain, let go of my anxieties, burying them in the storm crashing around us. The fire I fanned earlier is an inferno now, and it's burning everything in its wake. Somehow, we find each other through the flames and put them out together.

Body trembling, Raven rolls of off me, lying on her side so she's gazing at my profile. I stare at the ceiling. Stunned.

What the heck did we just do?

"I don't regret it," Raven whispers.

Her pronouncement shocks me. I haven't decided how I feel yet. We just had sex on the floor—my first time in a *long* time. It had been embarrassingly fast, but it was sex, nonetheless. Outside of marriage. With a woman I know has deep feelings for me. Feelings I know I don't share. If I felt guilty before, I feel like a monster now. But I don't want to think about that. So I don't. I block out the lust and the sin and the grave mistake I just made as I sit up with a sigh.

"We should search the building," I mutter.

Raven sits up, too, blinking at me. "What?"

"We should search the building."

"So, that's it?" She stands, hands balled into fists that tremble with emotion. "You're gonna screw me and then leave?"

"Ray—"

She turns away, hugging herself. "Just go."

I don't argue with her. There isn't much to say here, and I get the feeling that Raven needs the time alone as much as I do. I need to cope. Pray. Repent. I need to accept that I've made yet *another* mistake. I need to figure out what happens next, not just between us but with this entire mission. I came here for a reason, and it wasn't to sleep with Raven.

I grab my clothes and leave Ray in the lobby as I walk barefoot to the nearest room. It's a storage closet still stocked with a broom, a mop, and a dusty bucket. With a sigh, I get dressed and then set out to find clues I know probably don't exist.

"Don't lose faith now," I whisper, like the biggest hypocrite on earth. How could I talk about faith after that raunchy hookup?

I sigh. I've been going to church for months, chasing after the Voice I heard so long ago. I thought I had a handle on things. I thought I had my faith in check. But the truth is that I barely understand my faith. It's held together by desperate prayers and the torn pages of my tattered Bible. The Bible I barely touch unless I'm taking it to church with me.

I'm not ready to find Mya. Sex was exactly what tore us apart, and it's exactly what shatters me now.

"I still don't deserve her," I whisper angrily.

The proof is in the dance I just did with Raven. It's in the footsteps I take back to the lobby in search of her. It's in the way I know exactly what I found her for and how I don't really care that I'm about to mess up again. Just twenty minutes after the first time.

Raven stares at me when I walk up to her, she's still getting dressed, slowly sliding her arms through the sleeves of her shirt. Her mouth opens, but I speak over her.

"I'm sorry I used you. But please don't think I felt nothing, Raven. Things are complicated."

She doesn't speak, which makes me squirm uncomfortably.

"I'm sorry," I mutter again.

"You're an awful jerk, and I'm a fool for ever trusting you." She stops to shake her head. "Despite that, I meant what I said earlier. I don't regret what we did."

"Raven, we sinned—"

"I know!" she nearly shouts. "But … I thought you were worth it. I know that makes me a terrible Christian, but I can own up to my weaknesses. I'm weak…" She swipes at a tear. "I'm a weak woman who can't control her emotions. A weak woman who makes awful mistakes. Over and over. But for the first time, I thought I made a mistake with the right person."

This is so wrong. Even worse is that I get it. I really do.

I wasn't enough for Mya because I wasn't good. But with Raven… She understands me in a way Mya never could. She doesn't judge me for my mistakes because she's made them before. And now she's making them *with* me.

This is wrong. I clench and unclench my fists. It's worse than wrong. It's hypocrisy. I know it is because this twisted version of love is not how our relationship began.

Raven and I used to hold each other accountable. She stopped me from using foul language, and I kept her temper in check. We made each other stronger, emotionally and spiritually. Now we've become our own weaknesses. And we're suddenly left alone in this uncontrollable flood of emotion, desperation, and lust. Neither of us can keep our head afloat. Neither of us can stop the flow. So, we drown as one, saved by the simple pleasure of sharing this misery together.

If I'm going to hell, I'd rather not go alone.

"The right person," I whisper, knowing that I'm about to stumble into chaos.

Raven nods slowly, watching me step toward her, closing the distance between us. "The right person," she repeats. "No regrets."

No regrets... It's like she's giving me permission to make this mistake. So, I do.

We make love again, right there in the same spot. And then we spend the day hand in hand, pretending to search for clues we've lost all interest in. We sleep naked, cuddled on a stained cot together. Then we stroll through the center again, nude and free and joyously blind to our sin and the consequences of our choices. That's what this has become. A choice.

The first time we had sex was a moment of weakness. But all the other times... those were decisions I made with a clear head. Walking around naked with Raven was a decision, hooking up with her multiple times was a choice, even as we searched and explored Orly Center, my mind was on our next exchange. Our next moment alone.

But who needs a *moment* when we have the rest of eternity?

"This could be us forever." Raven hums as we search a charred office. She's sitting on a scorched desk, swinging her bare legs like a kid.

"Forever?" I quirk an eyebrow, walking over to her. My next words are a murmur, whispered against her lips as I kiss them. "We only have right now. This moment."

"Then make it worth every second."

I do. I forget about the world outside, the troubles outside, the faith I had outside, and I drown in the moment. I bathe in ecstasy, I swim in lust, I drink the cup I've poured, and I savor every drop, knowing that soon I'll regret it. Soon, I'll reap the harvest of the poisonous seeds I've planted. And then I will return to reality. But for now, I'm living in a dream, and I will enjoy every second of it.

20

Caesar

I don't know how many times we make love before we grow tired, but once it's over, Raven and I sleep in that office. We're still naked and unbothered. Still so hot for each other that when we wake, we do it again, finishing with a cry and a gasp. It's only when my stomach growls that I decide we should probably do something else besides … each other.

"I need food," I say, playing with her coiled dark hair. It looks like a million springs wound into her head, bouncing around each time she moves. I yank one and watch it spring back. It's so pretty.

Raven slowly crawls off my lap, we both adjust and stretch out our legs. I don't even know where we are exactly. I think we might've stopped in a bookstore. It doesn't matter.

I stand and stretch my arms, watching Raven roll her neck. Her eyes are closed, and she looks so peaceful, like a satisfied lover basking in the warm aftermath of our passion. We're both spent. I haven't had this much sex since my freshman year in college. That was probably the wildest year of my life. While in high school, I'd been a popular kid with a relatively naïve mother who had no idea what I was really up to on weekends. But college was entirely different.

I was living in a frat house. I was on the track team. And I was finally eighteen. I couldn't legally drink, but that didn't stop any seniors from passing alcohol to me, and it certainly didn't stop me from guzzling it down. I had no shame back then. I didn't see a need to be ashamed. I was in college; this is what happens in college. I had no idea what else I was supposed to do until Mya came along and in one night she made me realize I didn't have to get blackout drunk every weekend.

I was busy with a party while she was having prayer night with her dorm. We'd come from two different worlds but hers intrigued me more than I was willing to admit. I'd wanted to be a part of that world, but I never found the strength or discipline. I thought I had at Eternus, but my butt naked booty cheeks are proof that I was wrong.

I shake away my thoughts and reach for Raven's hand as we stumble into the hall. We're on the west side of the building now, a long walk from the lobby where we left our clothes and supplies. We fill the time with idle chatter that seems to grow more and more somber with every step. It's like we both know that we aren't just walking back to the foyer, we're walking back to the beginning. Back to reality. Once we put our clothes back on, this blissful day will end, and we'll be left with nothing but consequences.

Guilt. Remorse. Regret. Condemnation. Sadness. Shame. All the typical symptoms of sin.

"What do you want to eat for lunch?" Raven asks, and she squeezes my hand when I don't answer right away.

I'm not ignoring her; I'm not even thinking about the sin stuff anymore. I didn't answer Raven because I thought I heard something. We're nearing the lobby now, just around the corner, but instead of being met with eerie silence, I think I hear movement. Voices.

"Caesar?" Raven says.

"Hold on—"

"Over here!" someone calls behind us. "Found them!"

My heart hammers as I pivot to face our enemies. I'm so scared I think I might wet myself. Raven and I are both naked. We have no weapons—we don't even have socks. This is the worst possible time to bump into looters or soldiers, but as I turn, I realize the person who found us is worse than a soldier.

It's Claudius.

He's grinning as he walks up to us, taking long, easy strides, like this is a game for him. When he's right in front of us, he leaves his rifle to dangle by its strap so he can fold his arms and laugh. "So, this is what you've been up to? You ran away to have a little privacy."

Raven uses one of her arms to cover her breasts and the other hand to cover her private, but Claudius pays our nudity no attention. He's already seen my junk before when they kidnapped me the first time, and right now his eyes are focused on me. He doesn't even glance at Raven. Which I'm thankful for. There are tears in her eyes as she moves to hide behind me. She's humiliated.

"It wasn't for privacy," I say to Claudius, but that just makes him laugh even louder.

"I don't really care why you left, kid. My job is to bring you back." He nods toward the lobby, gesturing for us to start walking. "Job's half done now."

I turn and walk in front of Raven, so she doesn't suffer the shame of having everyone on Claudius's team see her naked. Major Banks is standing by our pile of discarded clothes when we enter the lobby. Katia is beside her and Bobby is by the front door. All of them stare at us as we approach.

Now I feel embarrassed, and I reach down to cup my groin so the women can't see as I approach. That doesn't stop them from staring, but not in desire or even shock, they all look disgusted.

Major Banks slings her rifle over her shoulder as she marches toward us, glaring. "You little snot," she hisses. "I thought you might've been kidnapped. Or worse. But you're here banging your little girlfriend like no tomorrow!"

"That's not why I left," I mutter.

Claudius laughs behind me. "Could've fooled us. I heard you guys from the front doors. Thought you were screaming in *pain*."

I am horrified. How long have they been in the building? And were we really that loud? Well, there was no reason to be quiet. We thought we were alone. It never even crossed my mind that someone would hear and interpret the pounding and screaming as violence. Then again, I doubt anyone would have expected it to be desperate sex either.

I'm an idiot. I knew Eternus would send people after us. I knew they would immediately go to Orly Center because that's where we found Delilah. That's where I thought I'd find clues about the rest of my friends. But I was foolish enough to believe we had more time. To think that we were far enough ahead to gather clues and hit the road again. Maybe we *did* have the time when we arrived, but spending the day tangled up derailed us. A lot.

Now, all we can do is stand in the lobby, still butt naked, and take the verbal lashing we deserve. I knew there would be consequences to the choices we'd made, but I didn't think it would come in the form of public shame. The Bible says whatever is done in the dark will be brought into the light. I should've expected this.

"Ray..." Katia steps forward, eyes flicking between the two of us. Raven is full on crying now, her tears leaking down her cheeks in streams. She's still feebly trying to cover her body so she can't wipe them away, they drip off the tip of her chin and wet her dirty feet. "Ray," her sister says again. "Please say something. I don't know what to think of this. I don't even know..." her voice cracks, making me realize how deeply we've failed. Katia had truly believed we were in danger. She came to *rescue* her sister, not to hunt her down. But her worries have turned to shame and confusion as the truth screams at her from across the room.

Raven doesn't speak. She just opens her mouth and breaks down into tears. Her sobs are loud and grow closer to hysteria with every heaving breath. After a few moments, she drops into a squat to cover herself, and screams into her hands.

I hear movement behind me, and when I turn, I see Claudius placing his jacket over Raven's shoulders. Great. I'm happy for his sympathy, but when a guy like Claudius pities anyone, it immediately makes the other person in the room the perpetrator. Now everyone is looking at me like this is all my fault and Raven is some innocent victim.

Everything that happened was consensual. Uncontrollable, but still consensual. I didn't do anything to her that she didn't want or enjoy—or *ask* for. But that doesn't matter now. What matters is that we've been caught and now everyone wants answers or repercussions.

"Let's go," Major Banks orders, still glaring at me. "Put your clothes on."

I shuffle past her, still holding my junk, face red and hot with shame. When I get to my clothes, I don't get dressed, I turn and take Claudius's jacket off Raven's shoulders, and I hold it up to block her so she can dress with a little privacy. She takes her dear sweet time, sniffling and sobbing as she steps into her underwear, then her jeans and her shirt. Once she's done, she collapses into my arms, hugging me and crying loudly.

"Raven," I say, stroking her hair, "it'll be okay."

"I'm sorry! I'm sorry!"

I don't know why she's sorry. Like I said, it was all consensual. But I accept the apology anyway. "It's okay," I say again, still stroking her hair.

"You're sorry?" Katia storms over to us. "Were you sorry when you stole supplies and ran off? Were you sorry when you left me without saying a word? Were you sorry when you let him bend you over a desk?"

"*Katia!*" Bobby shouts, running behind her. She makes it within arm's length, but Bobby grabs her before she can do anything.

"We came all this way to find you like *this*!" her sister screams. "Have you learned nothing?"

"Katia!" Bobby grunts, tugging her away. He has to pick her up to keep her from going after her little sister, but that doesn't stop her from spewing more venom.

"You haven't changed!" she shouts, and as her strength gives out, she whispers one last thing. "Arya really taught you well."

Arya... that's the name of Raven's ex-boyfriend. The guy she was shacking up with before the Fall. She'd told me all about him before; how he'd dragged her away from her faith. How her relationship with him ruined her relationship with her mother. And how she'd watched him die after he'd gotten hurt protecting her. I guess Katia sees me as the next Arya in her sister's life. The next big mistake that dragged her away from God. But I hadn't done that. Sure, I'd made the first move, but

Raven hadn't stopped me. And she hadn't stopped herself from being with Arya either.

She'd loved Arya, warts and all. But she'd also wanted the best for him—for *them*—and she'd even prayed for him as he lay dying on her sofa. Raven's life wasn't all sin and lust. She still had light in her heart, she just needed to grasp it. So, I understand why Raven whirls away from me in a rage at the sound of her sister's words. I understand why she wants to rip her sister apart for her callousness. But I can't let her do that.

We've made enough mistakes; violence doesn't have to be one of them.

"Raven!" I shout, reaching for her, but there's only so much I can do when I'm still naked, so instead of holding her back, I quickly stoop to grab my underwear and jam my legs into my boxers. I have one leg through when I glance up to see Raven swinging at Katia. Bobby is still holding her back when she does it, so she lands a clean blow to her sister's face.

Then Bobby let's go.

Katia launches like a missile and the girls erupt into a fit of screams and blows. Bobby and I both stare in shock. Neither of us knows what to do until Major Banks yells, "Stop them!"

"They're too loud!" Claudius shouts.

I yank on my jeans as Bobby moves to intervene. He grabs Katia by the waist, but she's got fistfuls of Raven's hair, so Ray is dragged along the floor as Bobby pulls Katia away. Raven *screams*. Her voice penetrates the air in a shriek that makes me want to cover my ears, but I ignore the pain and run over to pry Katia's fingers from Raven's curly locks. They're locked in like claws, but she releases her grip when Major Banks fires a shot into the air.

We all jump, and I scramble away, protectively pulling Raven into my arms. We're right to panic. When I glance up, I see surprise on Major Banks' face, and I realize she isn't the one who fired that shot. Neither is Claudius.

"Down!" Claudius shouts, lifting his weapon. He scans the walls, staring at the windows for a sniper while Major Banks aims at the front door.

Another shot fires, and this time Bobby screams but he isn't issuing a command, he's screaming in pain. There's a red splotch blooming on his shirt, he's been shot in his side. He grabs it as he releases Katia and falls to the floor. She quickly turns to throw her body over him, screaming and crying and begging him to be okay. The only thing louder than her shrieks is the next gunshot that fires—this one silences her.

Katia's head whips to the side as blood bursts from her skull, the force nearly turns her entire body all the way around before she drops on top of Bobby's chest. Dead. He lies there in silence, staring with perfectly circular eyes. For the rest of my life, I will always remember that he never screamed. He only stared.

Raven does scream. Her sister is sprawled dead over her own boyfriend, who's also been shot. I don't have time to make sure Bobby is safe or okay, my only thought is to get Raven out of here. Like now. She's crawling over me, trying to wriggle free from my arms, but I'm not letting go. I know she wants to see her sister, wants to hold her, wants to somehow make things better. But she can't. There are shots going off all around us and I have no idea which ones are enemy fire, and which ones are from Major Banks and Claudius who have begun firing back now. All I can do is lift Raven up and run.

I'm only wearing my jeans and underwear. I don't have shoes. I don't have a shirt. I don't have a weapon. Even if I did, I couldn't wield it. I'm too busy hauling Raven away as she shrieks hysterically. Claudius is near the corner, by the hallway he found us walking naked in. He's down on one knee, providing cover for Keoni who is firing at the windows as she backs away toward us.

"Keep moving!" Claudius shouts at me. "Take the west side exit! Enrique will pull around!"

I nod as I run by, Raven thrown over one of my shoulders. She's beating my back with her fists and kicking her feet so hard I have to wrap both my arms around her ankles to keep them still. Holding her like this slows me down, but I manage to keep up a good enough pace. I can hear footsteps pounding behind me, accompanied by more gunfire. It sounds like there's a lot more people running behind me than just Major Banks and Claudius, but I don't dare turn around to check. I thunder down the hall, following the hoarse shouts of Claudius as he tells me where to run.

"Turn left!"

When I reach the corner, I pivot and grab the wall with one hand, so I don't lose much momentum.

"Take the third door!"

I kick it in and run into the torn down arcade, Raven's body bopping against my back.

"Emergency exit on your left!" Claudius shouts, then he screams, and I hear something topple over behind me.

I turn to see him scuffling with an enemy soldier. His uniform is military grade, but he doesn't have a rifle like Claudius. I guess that doesn't matter since they're fist fighting now and Claudius is too busy trying to throw him off his back to use his gun.

With a cry, Claudius falls backwards and nearly crushes the guy who screams in agony. Claudius is a big man; I wouldn't want him to fall on top of me either. He rolls to the side and lifts his gun, firing two shots without hesitation. The man dies clutching his heart. Claudius snatches the hunting knife from his hip and tosses it to me.

"Let's go! Emergency exit!"

Knife and Raven in hand, I take off running again, shoving open the emergency door to find Enrique zooming up in one of Eternus's vans. He screeches to a halt, and I toss Raven inside the doors which are already open, then I climb in and turn back, holding out my hand to catch Claudius who practically launches himself into the van like a rocket. Even Raven crawls to the side to avoid being crushed by him.

"¿Dónde está Keoni!!?" Enrique screams in Spanish.

I have no idea what that means so I don't answer, but Claudius replies in a shout, "Still inside! She's coming!"

"¡Diez segundos!" Enriques shouts. "¡Diez segundos!"

"*Twenty* seconds!" Claudius lifts his rifle at the door we just ran out of. "She's coming, Enrique, trust me!"

He starts speaking Spanish too fast for me to pick out individual words, but he's clutching the cross around his neck, so I know he's praying. Before he finishes that prayer, the emergency exit flies open, and Major Banks runs out with Bobby limping beside her. She's holding him up, leaning against her own body, so she can't raise her rifle well enough to use it. Not with great aim anyway. But Claudius is ready to take the shot when she yells, "Incoming! Get down!"

I duck, throwing my body over Raven. Claudius begins to fire as the door swings open again. Whoever is on the other side fires back. Bullets punch the van walls just above my head. Claudius falls back into the van, clutching his chest. Somehow, Major Banks makes it inside; she shoves Bobby in first and then turns to fire as more bullets rain down on us. I hear the tires screech and we take off fast, never slowing down. But the bullets don't stop. Our enemies fire as we speed through the parking lot, forcing Enrique to dodge and swerve. He screams as the van skitters to the side but manages to keep it upright by yanking on the steering wheel.

The sound of bullets hitting the van never stops. The screaming never stops. Enrique's praying never stops, not until a bullet hits one of our tires and we're all thrown sideways.

The van veers, nearly crashing into an abandoned car. We barely miss it as we careen onto the road. Enrique is spinning the steering wheel back and forth, trying to lean the van into its wobbly projection, but nothing is working. We're too off balance.

"Keoni!" Enrique screams, falling back into the driver's seat.

That's when I see the blood. He's been hit.

Enrique's holding his bloody right arm, trying to steer with his left. The van is still swerving, bullets are still spraying at us. I want to close my eyes, but I can't look away. This is a nightmare. Worse than finding Delilah's body. Worse than finding *Mya's*.

God help...

Enrique looks over his shoulder as the van goes off the road, his eyes meet mine for half a second and I see the blame in them right before a bullet shatters his window and shoots through his head. His body jerks and he falls forward, onto the steering wheel. His foot reflexively slams on the gas, and we all lurch forward, screaming. Keoni keeps her head, crawling over the seats to get to the wheel. She hesitates for just a moment before opening Enrique's door and shoving his body out, then she takes the wheel and drives us away. She keeps her head low because bullets are still punching through the van, but it's less and less now that we've made it to the road.

I feel safe enough to lift my head and peer out one of the cracked windows. I can see Enrique's body behind us, and in the distance, I can see enemy soldiers dotting the parking lot of Orly Center. They're shouting and raising their guns above their heads like they've just won some great battle.

They did win that battle.

We lost two people back there. Two more have been shot. And it's all my fault.

21

Adrian

Dinner with Mya was not awful. It wasn't even bad. I would dare to say it was *good*. My siblings love her, my mother loves her, *I* love her. When I think of it that way, there's no reason not to take my mother's advice and marry the girl, but neither of us is ready for that sort of commitment. I haven't even asked Mya to be my *girlfriend* yet, marriage seems like a massive leap in comparison. And no matter how much I love her, I'm still not one hundred percent certain that she would say yes.

Because I'm not Christian.

Yes, I've been going to services with my mother and siblings, but I haven't converted yet. I haven't officially given my life to Christ. But I've decided that I will. I made up my mind after that dinner which is exactly what I said I didn't want to do, right? I didn't want to get saved because of a woman or because of love. I wanted to do it because I saw the love of

Christ in my life, but the love I have with Mya *comes* from Christ.

I fell in love with her without making love first—yes, we went *very* far before, but for a former atheist who'd only had hookups without commitment, I'd say I'm proud of my restraint.

I'm not a saint, okay? The point is, I loved Mya with my heart before I gave her my body. And now I want to give her my heart. Stitch it to hers forever. And I want to tie our souls together, too. I can't do that if I still don't believe I have one.

I do have a soul, and I believe it was saved by Jesus. It has to be, because only God could give me the gift of joy I've received here in this bunker. I have my family. I have my siblings who get to live a happy, innocent life for the first time. Our mother is a *mother* again. She's happy and sober and cracking jokes, something she only did on holidays before she grabbed the bottle.

For the first time in my life, things are good. Peaceful. That's a gift. That's proof that God is real. He must be. And I want to serve Him because if He could do this for me while I still wore the badge of atheism, then what else is possible for me as His child?

That's the joy I carry with me to work this morning. I want to tell Mya that I've made up my mind. I'm getting saved at the next church service. I'm going to become a Christian and then I'm going to ask her to be my girlfriend. For real. Forever. I hope that doesn't scare her away.

The only sore spot in my life is my stepfather. He's still the same piece of crap he was before the Fall. Smells sour like homemade liquor every time I see him, *when* I see him. I've covered three more of his shifts in the last week because he keeps disappearing. I know he's just passed out drunk somewhere, sleeping off a hangover so he doesn't get caught and kicked out for having alcohol in the shelter.

The only reason I don't mind covering his shift is because Saloso has been giving me extra pay for it. The first time, it was an unpaid favor. The second time, she gave me an extra ration. Now I'm getting paid double for just one shift, but I'm completing double the work, so it adds up.

Normally, I get extra food or water. Sometimes Saloso lets me choose something from the wood shop to take as payment. I got a little horse figurine for Dinara a few days ago. I want to get the carved airplane she's got in there, too. Danya would love that. I'm also thinking maybe I can save up enough to trade for the rocking chair on display. It's crazy expensive; it'll only trade for 20 gallons of water plus 10 pounds of grain, but if I agree to do another week of doubles with no pay, I think Saloso might let me have it. Mom would love that chair.

What should I get Mya?

She deserves a gift just because she's beautiful and she's mine. I think of her as I strip the bark off my cut logs. I finished my pile before lunch, once I get everything stripped, I can start chopping Ryan's wood. That'll take me another few hours which means I'll be late for dinner again, but that's not a big deal. Mom's gotten used to me working doubles, so she starts dinner later now. Maybe Mya will stop by again. We've been having lunch together every day since that dinner, but she hasn't been back to the house.

It's only been a week, I remind myself, dragging the drawknife down the log. The bark strips away with a cry, and I toss it on the floor. We use the bark for a dozen different things down here. Fuel for our brick ovens, which are vented through a very complicated system, mind you. We also use it for compost in our indoor gardens, and depending on the tree, Saloso tells me to set the bark aside to be delivered to the apothecary. Apparently, the bark of certain trees has medicinal qualities. In a world without modern medical facilities, tree bark is as good as Tylenol. Literally, some bark can be used to treat pain and headaches. Who knew?

It's weird, but I like the way we live now. I like that I'm part of a community that seems to genuinely care about everyone here. I like that every day I work toward a goal that matters. Chopping wood is more than just swinging an ax. I'm making medicine. I'm making fuel for our ovens. I'm making decorations. I'm making mulch for our gardens. There is no such thing as an insignificant job at this church. Every person matters. Every person is needed. Every person serves a purpose. I like having a purpose. Now I have someone to share that purpose with.

Only a week, I tell myself again, stripping the next log. A week and I've decided I'm in love, I want to become a Christian convert, and I want to eventually get married. Crazy.

But also a week since I've had dinner with Mya. Lunch has been awesome, but I want to do something special. Something for just the two of us. Don't get me wrong, I love my family, and I definitely want to tell them about my faith too, but I want this moment with Mya to be special. She's the only one who truly knows how far I've come. She's been there through it all. Fighting with me, and then fighting *for* me through her prayers. She deserves to be the first to know. But where can I take—

Ryan stumbles into the room and burps. He blinks at me like he has no idea who I am and then a smile slithers across his face like a snake, sharp and venomous. "It's my boy!" he exclaims.

"I'm not your boy," I grunt.

He nods, scratching his chin. "I never adopted you."

"I never wanted you to."

"I know." He hiccups and then wobbles across the room to take a seat on the floor beside his uncut logs. He looks tired, even though I'm sure he just woke up. His hair is a mop of matted locks that stick to his sweaty forehead. He looks like he hasn't bathed in days, and smells like it too. I'm not sure which is stronger, his funk or the sour liquor smell. It fills the room, and I debate breathing through my mouth.

"You always hated me," Ryan says in a grumble, like he's upset about it.

If I hadn't decided to live for God, I'd turn around and slice him up with this drawknife. Instead, I take a slow breath and glide the knife along my next log.

"I hated you because you hated my mother."

218

"I loved that woman. Had two kids with her. Took care of her other kid, who hated me."

"You *never* took care of me," I hiss. "I've taken care of myself my entire life. I took care of my mother when you beat her unconscious!" My eyes grow large when I turn and see Ryan cowering in the corner, beside his log pile. He's literally holding his hands up like he's afraid of me. That makes me pause, and I exhale slowly. I hadn't realized I was shouting. Hadn't realized I'd been gripping the drawknife so tightly that my hands are shaking.

Ryan's eyes flicker between my eyes and the blade. "I-I'm sorry," he says shakily. "I'm pathetic. I know that. Why do you think I do this?" He opens his arms, as if showing himself off. He looks awful, pallid skin dewy and stained with grime. There are dark circles beneath his eyes and his facial hair is growing in patches, like he got into a fight and someone tried to rip it out. They almost succeeded.

"I'm a mess," Ryan says, then he chuckles and wipes his hand through his hair. "You always pissed me off because your mother loved you so much."

That makes me frown. For most of my life, my mother acted like she couldn't stand me. But maybe she did that on purpose. Maybe her disdain was a cover up to keep me safe from Ryan. Clearly, he was jealous of me and her love toward me pissed him off enough that we'd gotten into fights. Imagine if she had been openly affectionate toward me.

Or maybe Ryan is a drunken liar, and my mother couldn't stand me as a child because she was a crackhead prostitute dating one of the guys who bought her for a few nights. Did you know that's how she met Ryan? He paid for her, and she liked him enough to bring him home. He liked her enough to occasionally pass her cash for rent and groceries, so I guess that worked out for them.

But Mom doesn't need his money anymore and I've been buying her groceries since I got here. There's no room for Ryan in our lives. There's no room for drugs or alcohol or prostitution. We have everything we need, and we don't want anything more.

"Whatever happened in the past is done and over with," I tell Ryan.

"That include your hatred of me?" He coughs and then leans his head against the logs piled beside him. The ones he's supposed to have chopped by now. "Is your hatred done and over with?"

I want to tell him no. I will never stop hating him. But as I stare at this pathetic man on the floor beneath me, I shock myself by saying, "There's nothing left to hate."

It's the truth. Ryan is nothing to me. Not just because I've matured, but because I've replaced my hatred and my anger and even the anxiety that used to take me to my knees. I was so pissed off before, but now all I feel is joy when I think of my family. I was so hateful, but now there's so much love in my life. I'd been filled with anxiety to the point of suffering breakdowns, but now I have overwhelming peace. All of that came from God. He replaced every single bad emotion I used to harbor and filled me with the things He calls good. Peace, joy, and love. Fruits of the Spirit that dwells within me. When you're filled with God, there's no room for anything that is not of Him.

But I'm not filled with His Spirit yet. I haven't given my life to Him, which means I haven't welcomed His Spirit into my heart. But I will, as soon as I get to the next church service. Pastor Cyndi always has an altar call and performs the Sinner's Prayer at the end of service. I just need to make it there. Until that happens, I can't afford to be derailed or angered by the likes of Ryan.

I nod to myself, mulling over my thoughts, then I look him in the eye. "I don't hate you anymore, Ryan. I think one day I'll even have the strength to forgive you." I've got to if I want to call myself a Christian. That won't be easy, but I know God will help me do it. He'll help me heal from every scar Ryan burned into my childhood, and all the nightmares he forced the twins to suffer through.

Ryan blinks at me like he has no idea what to say, then he lets out a slow chuckle, shoulders bopping up and down. "You ended up becoming a better man than me."

"Yeah."

"Think you're good enough to put in a word for me with your mom?"

I stare at him, refusing to believe what I just heard. Has he lost his mind?

"My mother wants nothing to do with a drunken fool."

"You've always hated alcohol." He glowers.

I look him up and down. "For good reason."

221

"Yeah. Look what it's done to me."

"I don't know how you can live with yourself." I turn around and sit on my stool to start stripping bark again.

Ryan speaks behind me. "This is how I do it. I drink so I don't have to deal with it."

If he's looking for a pity party, he isn't going to get one from me.

"You're a grown man," I say over my shoulder. "Get it together. Your life isn't the only one that sucks now, you're just the only one who copes by smuggling booze into the shelter." I grunt, scraping the blade along my log. "Do you have any idea how much danger you're putting the church in by sneaking out and meeting with strangers to trade for beer? You're probably the reason soldiers are moving in on us."

"That ain't true."

I spin on my stool to glare at him. "How can you say that when you're sneaking out?"

"I'm not sneaking out." Ryna picks his teeth with his pinky fingernail. "I have permission to go to the surface to collect wood."

I guess that makes sense. It's not like we're growing oak trees down here.

"I haven't met with any strangers either," Ryan says. He picks something from his tooth and then eats it. "I make the booze myself. Moonshine."

I can't help but laugh. Why did I ever think he was out there meeting people in the woods to get alcohol? Of course he's making it himself. He works in a wood shop, and he understands enough about alcohol to know how to use wood to make it. Some tree bark ferments faster than barley. This is the perfect place to make moonshine when you're desperate enough, which Ryan clearly is. But that's only worked against him. He's still as insufferable as he was before the Fall, just a lot less violent.

"So, you've never met anyone outside?" I ask.

Ryan shakes his head and then groans like the motion hurt. He's probably still hungover. "I make the booze myself and keep it for myself."

I believe him wholeheartedly.

"This place is Christian to its core. I'm not stupid enough to sneak any alcohol down here."

That explains why he hasn't been caught, despite reeking of it. If there isn't any alcohol on him or in his room, then there's no proof that he's actually got any. As far as anyone knows, he just stinks, and that's not a crime.

I sigh. "Where on earth did you find the tools to make and stash moonshine above ground?"

"I've been here for months, kid. I made the time and found the tools. Wasn't easy, but I was determined."

"Clearly."

He snorts and then shoots a glob of phlegm from his mouth. "Wanna see my stash?"

"Absolutely not." I don't hate the guy anymore, but I am not about to become his drinking buddy. And also... "What you're doing out there still isn't right. I want nothing to do with it."

"How ain't it right?" he challenges. "They don't want alcohol down here, so I drink it up there."

"And stumble down here drunk, slacking off on your duties, skipping work, and stealing supplies to make more alcohol." I shake my head. "I don't want to know anything else about your stupid moonshine."

"I drink responsibly," he grumbles.

"No. You don't."

"Fine. Forget the moonshine, then. I got other places up there I like to explore."

I glance up from my log. "What do you mean?"

"Life down here is stuffy. I like to stretch my legs when I go out to collect lumber. Stumbled on this pathway that leads into the woods just outside the city."

"That's dangerous, Ryan."

"You sound concerned." He grins and I see how yellow his teeth have gotten.

"I know you might feel cramped down here after all these months, but I've lived on the surface since the Fall. Life is much better down here." I almost shiver at the memory of that cannibal father I ran into. The one I killed.

"How'd you survive up there for so long?" Ryan asks behind me.

I chuckle. "Took your gun from the safe."

"You made it back home?"

"I went there to check for Danya and Dinara. Even stayed there a while with Mya."

A sultry growl slips from his lips. "Is that where you—"

"No." I grunt, stripping more bark from my log.

"So, you haven't slept with her."

"Not entirely."

"The heck does that mean?"

"It means I'm trying to honor her Chrisitan faith." I toss my log into the finished pile and stand to grab my water while Ryan keeps talking.

"Even if y'all weren't religious, you wouldn't have gotten laid down here anyway. There's no privacy."

That's for sure. I should know since Bunny is always begging me to leave our room for at least two hours. He insists it isn't *always* sexual. Sometimes they just want a moment alone where Ae-cha's father isn't hovering, or I'm not hovering, or the rest of our friends aren't hovering. I get it. I'm currently trying to find a private place to meet with Mya just so I can tell her that I want to get saved.

Apparently, Ryan has just the place.

I groan as the thought rolls over me. I do not want to ask him for any favors, but if he's really got a great place above ground that'll give me some privacy, then I want to check it out. I need a moment alone with Mya as badly as he needs a drink.

"Tell me about this place you've got," I say in a quiet voice, like we're coconspirators.

When I look over at Ryan, I see him grinning wider than before. "It's the perfect place to take your little lady, but I ain't telling you for free."

I roll my eyes. "What do you want?"

"A good word with your mom."

I almost tell him no, but what's the harm? My mother wants nothing to do with Ryan and he's in bad shape. Nothing I say could ever get her to date him again, not when he's always drunk and smelly.

I fold my arms. "I'll put in a good word, but not for free."

He pulls a face. "Telling you about my getaway is the price, kid."

"No, that's a bonus. If I put in a word for you with my mother, I want you to get yourself cleaned up in exchange."

He drops his gaze, and I realize I won't have to fight him on this. Ryan knows he's pathetic, and he knows he'll have to get better if he truly wants to have a chance with my mom. He *doesn't* have a chance, but there's no point in me telling him that. Taking a bath and getting rid of the booze will benefit Ryan whether my mom likes him or not. And it benefits me. If I've got to feed him false hope just to make sure he gets to work on time, so be it.

"Do we have a deal?" I ask.

Ryan hesitates, but he eventually smiles and nods. "We've got a deal, kid."

22

Caesar

My life has fallen apart in every possible way.

I sit with my back against the wall, staring at the dusty floor. We're camping in a tiny shop that used to sell donuts and artisan coffee. The tables are overturned, the trendy little sofas by the floor-to-ceiling windows are slashed with knife cuts, cotton spilling onto the dirty floor. The cash register is gone, the counters are covered in dead cockroaches. At least the windows are painted over in black so no one can see inside very well.

We were forced off the road and shot at. When we found this shop, we hunkered down and didn't move. We've only been here two days, but before this, we spent two days driving. Nonstop.

When Keoni finally got the van going, she didn't slow down. Not for hours. It wasn't until sunset that she took her chances and pulled over to the side of the road. By then, we'd calmed down enough to change the flat tire; I helped Keoni do it while Raven stared at the van wall, Bobby quietly bled out, and Claudius lay unconscious on the van floor. He'd been shot in his chest, but he was wearing a bulletproof vest, so it wasn't lethal. Still, when the van spun out of control, he took a serious blow to the head. He got thrown into the wall and smashed one of the windows with his face. Spent the entire ride here unconscious.

Once the tire was changed, Keoni drove for the rest of the night and the entire following day. She only stopped for bathroom breaks once. I got a shirt, socks, and shoes from the supplies stashed in the bins beneath our seats, then I opened the packaged food and passed out rations while she drove. No one ate except me and Major Banks. No one spoke. No one did anything except cry or groan in pain.

Movement ahead catches my attention, I glance up to see Major Banks exiting the tiny employee bathroom. She's holding a bucket and has a rag tossed over her muscular shoulder. It's bloody which means she was using it on Bobby.

He's dying.

He was shot in his side at Orly Center. He was also wearing a bulletproof vest, so the bullet only grazed him because he was slightly exposed, but the wound hasn't stopped bleeding and now it's infected. There's nothing we can do except wait for him to die. He's in such bad shape we never moved him from the van, we left him lying on the floor and covered him with blankets to keep him comfortable and warm. Last night he developed uncontrollable chills; Keoni says that means there isn't much time left.

She looks over at me now, her face impassive. She hasn't spoken to me except to issue orders or updates about Bobby. It's clear that she hates me. Even now, I can feel her anger resonating around her, spilling into the shop and washing over me in shame. I can't even look her in the eye. I drop my gaze and go back to staring at the dusty floor.

"Bobby's still alive," she says in a clipped voice. "I've changed his bandages, and I checked Claudius."

"How is he?" I whisper to the floor.

"Resting in the van with Bobby. He's got a concussion, so he'll need to take it easy for the next few days, but he can handle the meeting later."

The meeting, something I have not been looking forward to. Now that we're not hysterical anymore, we need to sit down and discuss what happens next. That means addressing my massive failures.

I lick my dry lips. "Where's Raven?" She hasn't spoken to me since everything went down, but she also hasn't spoken to anyone else. It's like she's become a mute, silently drifting through the donut shop, a ghost of her former self. I can't tell if she hates me or not, but I wouldn't be surprised if she does. I ran away and convinced her to come with me. Then I used her for pleasure, knowing that I didn't share the feelings she had. And when Eternus tracked us down, I got Katia and Enrique killed. I got Bobby shot. I got Claudius knocked out. I even got us derailed from our route back home.

Keoni was afraid of those soldiers following the van back to Eternus, so she drove in the opposite direction of the camp and didn't stop for days. I don't know what we're going to do now, but if we don't get moving, we'll end up starving out here.

"Raven's holding watch out front. I'll grab her and Claudius. Shouldn't take me long."

"Right."

Keoni doesn't say anything more, she just turns on her heel and leaves. I listen to her footsteps tap against the tile floor, then I listen to the creak of the back door, and I listen to the Arizona wind blowing as she steps into the parking lot outside. Then the door shuts and I'm engulfed in silence.

I hate silence. When the world around me is quiet, I can hear my thoughts, and they are never kind. Isn't that funny? The harshest voice in my life is my own. Right now, it tells me that I'm a failure. A murderer. A liar. A criminal. That it should have been me who was shot in the head. Me whose body was left on the ground as the van sped away. Me with a concussion.

It's all true.

I bury my face in my hands and my muscles cringe as I let out a muted scream, mouth open, but no sound coming out. I don't have to stay quiet. Major Banks is outside, Bobby and Claudius are in the van, and Raven is unresponsive. I have all the privacy I need to let it all out, but I'm ashamed to do that. I don't think I deserve to let it out. This pain is my punishment. But I can't handle it. I won't survive this grief—but who can help me?

"G-God…" I whisper, but I cut off the prayer with a shake of my head. What can I even say to Him? This is all my fault. Mistake after mistake after mistake.

I bury my face in my hands again and curl into fetal position on the dirty floor. I don't know how long I stay like that but when I hear noise at the back of the shop, I peel my hands from my face and blink into the dim room. Major Banks appears by the shop counter, a tall figure beside her. It's Claudius, though he looks frail and tired. His face is sweaty, and his eyes are bloodshot, his hair has somehow gotten greyer, and when he speaks, I notice he has a busted lip.

"We're ready." Claudius's voice is hoarse. "Let's do this."

"Raven," I say, then I dumbly add, "and Bobby," as if he can actually join us.

"He isn't serious, is he?" Claudius glances down at Keoni who keeps her eyes on me as she replies, "He hasn't seen him."

"So, you don't know how bad it is." Claudius shakes his head. "You know what, let's have the meeting in the van with him."

"Claudius—"

"He needs to see what he's done."

Claudius pulls away from Major Banks and slowly walks out the back door, it takes longer than normal because of his concussion. He walks with one hand on the wall the entire time and even stops to stable himself before twisting the handle to the door. Once it shuts behind him, Keoni speaks.

"Bobby is going to die soon."

I close my eyes.

"Just be prepared." She walks past me toward the front of the donut shop. "I'm going to get Raven. I'll meet you at the van."

Left with no choice, I mosey outside and squint through the harsh sunlight. It's high noon so everything is hot and bright, that should lift my mood but as I near the van I only feel sick. The sour smell of blood and illness hits me before I even reach the vehicle, and once I do get there, I immediately understand why.

The entire floor of the van is stained red. Bobby is in the center of this great crimson stain, but the splotch on his side isn't red anymore. It's brown and oozing yellow pus. I can smell the infection festering in his wound as I stand in the doorway, staring down at him. He's shirtless and lying beneath two blankets which stick to his chest because of all the sweat. Despite this, he's visibly shivering, his lips are even blue.

"Bobby?" I whisper.

Slowly, his eyes peel back, and I stare at his dilated pupils. The unfocused gaze he gives me seems empty until his lips shrivel back to reveal his bloody teeth. It takes me a moment to register that he's smiling, and the sight breaks my heart. What is he smiling for? At *me*, of all people.

"Caesar," Bobby croaks. "Claudius said there's a meeting."

"Uh, yeah."

"I'm glad you're here." He coughs. "I'm glad you made it."

I made it. I'm alive.

"Thanks." My voice cracks. "Thanks, Bobby."

"We're here," Major Banks announces behind me.

232

I let go of the breath I'd been holding as I turn to see her and Raven. Raven doesn't speak or even acknowledge my presence; she just stares into the van at Bobby. All the color drains from her face, which is saying an awful lot considering her brown complexion. She stumbles backwards, but Keoni wraps an arm around her shoulders and holds her in place.

"It's okay," she says softly.

Bobby agrees in a weak voice. "It's okay. Don't worry about me."

"How can you say that?" the words burst from my mouth without notice, making me jump.

Claudius shakes his head. Keoni and Raven stare at me.

"I'm out of here," Bobby rasps. "No more looting. No more hunger. No more fighting." He chuckles, it sounds raw and painful. "Let's skip the meeting and just say goodbye. It's time."

What?

I step forward, leaning into the van. "You can't mean that."

He exhales slowly. "I mean every word, Caesar. I'm ready to go."

"You're ready to die?"

"I'm ready to see her again."

He's talking about Katia, the first one to die because of me. She died trying to protect Bobby when he was shot. I don't know how long they'd been dating, but it was long enough for her to decide he was worth a bullet. I wonder if she loved him before that moment, or if she'd only moved on instinct the same way I'd reflexively protected Raven. Very soon, Bobby will get to ask her.

"She just left, but I want to see her already." Bobby clears his throat. "You can understand that, right?"

I nod, but I don't get to reply because he sinks into a coughing fit so violent, Claudius has to wipe blood from his mouth when it's finally over.

"Let me have a moment alone with each of you." Bobby juts his chin at Keoni. "You first, Major Banks."

We all shuffle away to let Keoni sit on the edge of the van and say goodbye. I'm about twenty feet away, so I can hear talking but I can't make out specific words with the wind gently blowing, plus Bobby's voice is so hoarse it's like talking to a sick smoker.

After a few moments, Keoni leans over to kiss Bobby's forehead, then she straightens and walks over to us with tears in her eyes. "Claudius," is all she says, and the big man lumbers forward to hug her. They embrace for a few silent moments before he kisses her temple and peels away to limp toward the van. When he's finished, he pats Bobby on the shoulder and walks back. His voice trembles as he says, "He wants both of you together."

Raven and I exchange looks—it's the first time we've made eye contact in days, but it doesn't last long. The next moment, Raven's walking toward the van without waiting for me. I follow her at a slower pace, trying not to cry.

When I reach the van, Bobby smiles at me.

"There's a reason I asked for both of you together." He swallows and it sounds like there's glue in his throat. The sympathetic part of me wants to offer him water, but the desperate part—the part that wants to live—feels like it would be a waste. "You need each other," Bobby continues slowly. "There's a lot of pain here. But pain brings blame and blame causes division. You need each other." His voice sounds strained, he even moves his hand, using all of his energy just to reach for us.

Raven takes his hand and sits on the edge of the van. There are tears in her eyes and she sniffles as she says, "I'm sorry, Bobby. We never meant for this to happen."

"It's okay."

Those two words break both of us. I feel wetness streaking my cheeks before I know it, but once I'm aware that I'm crying, I can't stop myself. I take a deep breath and press the back of my hand to my mouth. I want to say that I'm sorry, too. I want Bobby to know this wasn't our plan, but I can't speak. All I can do is tremble as the grief wracks my body. That seems to be enough for Bobby. He watches me and Raven cry in silence, squeezing her hand, until he works his mouth to croak, "It's okay. I forgive you."

"Why?" I manage.

"Because I know you didn't mean for this to happen. You're just kids with emotions." He smiles, his lips crack when he does. "I remember what that was like. I loved Katia enough to make dumb decisions when we first got together, too. It's not your fault that this choice ended so badly." He stops to breathe for a moment. "I don't blame you. I blame the enemy. That's what Katia would want. And … it's the Christian thing to do."

I blink at him. I hadn't known he was a Believer. He doesn't wear a cross like Katia used to, and I've never heard him mention anything about his faith before. But that doesn't mean he has none. I've seen him at church services, he always sat with Katia near the front while I stayed near the back with Raven. Maybe I thought he was like me, only going because of the woman by his side. But he seems sincere now.

I reach over and place my hand on top of Raven's, shockingly, she doesn't push me away, she actually looks up at me and nods. This is her apology; this is her saying that she forgives me, too. Maybe not fully. Maybe not completely. But she forgives me enough to let me back in.

"I'm sorry," I say to her. "You know I never meant for any of this to happen, but leaving was my idea, so I'm taking responsibility. I'm going to protect you, Raven. I'm gonna get you back home. I promise."

Bobby squeezes our hands, his grip is shaky and delicate, like I could break his whole hand if squeezed back too hard.

"Thank you for this," he whispers. "Now I can tell Katia that you didn't let this tear you apart."

I feel the backs of my eyes burn again. "I'm not ready to say goodbye."

"Let me go. I'm tired, Caesar."

He looks more than tired. He looks like he's been dead for days, like he was only holding on long enough to share this moment. He told me he forgives me. He told me and Raven to trust each other again. And he said goodbye to Keoni and Claudius. The woman he loves is already gone, what reason does he have to keep suffering?

I wipe my tears with the back of my hand and nod at Bobby. "I'll bury you—"

"Don't," he cuts me off. "That'd be a waste of time. You've got to keep moving. You have to set out today, and don't look back. Don't look back, Caesar."

I stare at him, trying to figure out if there's more to his words, but before I can ask him, Major Banks and Claudius appear by my side and Bobby settles down. He slowly exhales and then releases Raven's hand. She stands beside me, closer than she needs to. I take it as a sign of her forgiveness, but I don't push my limits. She's still grieving her sister, if I take more than what's been given, I may end up pushing her away again. So instead of wrapping an arm around her shoulders, I just stand there silently, like a pillar of strength for her to lean on if she wants.

We don't watch Bobby die. He doesn't want us to. Instead, he reminds us to forgive each other and then he asks us to close the van door and not return. I wonder how we're going to pack up and leave with his body locked in there but once we get inside, Keoni immediately begins the meeting and tells us that we're out of gas which makes the van useless.

"Without the van, we'll have to travel on foot," Major Banks says, crossing her arms over her chest. Her voice is a little shaky because of what just happened, but she muscles through this meeting without breaking.

"We're screwed," Claudius grumbles. He leans against the wall at the front of the donut shop and sighs. "It'll take more than a week to walk back to Eternus. We don't have enough supplies to last us that long."

Don't look back… Bobby's words invade my mind, and I find the courage to speak up. "Is there anywhere else we can go?"

Major Banks glances up, her face looks angry, but I recognize the tension in her brow as concentration. She's thinking.

"Eternus was in the middle of establishing trade routes with other shelters," Raven says softly. "Was there communication with anyplace nearby?"

"According to our maps, we aren't far from a little city called Napam," Keoni says. "I think there's a church one town over with an underground bunker. We were able to reach them via radio communication, but our connection was patchy at best."

"And we were never able to set up a date to meet in person and begin trading," Claudius adds.

"But they know Eternus exists, right?" I ask. "If we show up, they'll at least let us in to speak. I mean, this could be a good opportunity to finally talk to them."

"We don't know their exact location." Major Banks unfolds her arms. "Secrecy is so important out here, so they never gave us a secure address."

That's understandable. Eternus goes out of its way to keep their location to themselves. Major Banks drove us away from the camp so no one could follow us there, so I understand why they never shared their locations. Especially over a patchy radio connection. Still, I don't think it'll be impossible to find them.

"If they're in a church somewhere near Napam, then we can start there," I say. "How far is that city?"

"Three days." Claudius pushes from the wall. "We've got enough supplies for four. If we don't do anything stupid, we should make it there alive." Claudius's voice is a growl, and I don't miss the hatred in his eyes as he looks at me. It's a clear reminder that Bobby and Raven have forgiven me, but no one else.

Major Banks only nods and turns to walk away. "We leave in an hour."

23

Adrian

Today I'm having a private dinner with Mya. I gave in and asked Ryan to show me his little haven, it's actually a cute patch of grass in the woods surrounded by trees and shrubbery with a brook not too far off so I can hear the sound of water gently running in the background. It's a serene piece of land in the middle of this chaos, and I absolutely love it.

The walk is about forty minutes, which isn't ideal, but we have to leave the city limits and then venture into the surrounding forestry. Arizona forests are beautiful, a stark contrast to the common red desert that takes up most of our land. I can't wait to bring Mya out here; I've been preparing all week.

I ended up taking two more doubles off of Ryan's shoulders because I needed the extra pay to trade for food. I asked my mom to make meatballs again, they're much smaller than the ones she made before because meat is rare down here, but they smell good as I leave her apartment this afternoon. Ae-cha agreed to make tea for me in exchange for an extra half gallon of water, and I'll be pulling another double off Ryan next week to pay Saloso back for the basket of apples she gave me this morning. There were six in the bundle, I gave half of them to my mom, and I'll be taking three to dinner.

I don't even know if Mya likes apples, but when's the last time either of us had fresh fruit? The apples aren't all that fresh. One of them has a big brown spot I'll have to peel off before I take them tonight, but they're better than the dried fruit we've been surviving on.

I'm so excited for the dinner, I can hardly make it through my shift. I'm not even bothered by Ryan who has a hundred questions about Mya. I answer almost each one—he seems oddly interested in the sexual part of our relationship but Ryan's a creep, so I'm not surprised by his questions. I skip over the intimate ones and tell him about our journey to get here. He seems interested in the library and listens quietly when I get to the part about the cannibal.

When I'm done, I'm surprised to see he has a gift for me; a slip of paper he thrusts into my hands as I turn to leave. "It's a map," he says. "I drew it myself, so it ain't perfect."

I unfold the paper and stare at his elementary scribbles. It's legible enough for me to make out the pathway he took me to at the beginning of the week. I haven't been back to the place since, so the map helps more than he thinks.

"Thank you," I tell him.

Ryan smiles, showing his yellow teeth, though they are admittedly slightly lighter today. And he doesn't smell as bad as he normally does. It's only been about 5 days since I told him I would put in a good word with my mom. I haven't done it yet but just the sight of him makes me think he's taking this seriously. At least for now. Only time will tell if he truly cleans himself up and stays clean, but at least he's bathing now.

"There's plenty of brush to cover you guys, but don't get too loud out there." He makes a lewd gesture I won't describe, and I cram the map into my pocket.

"Thanks."

"You can sneak by the perimeter guards right before the evening bell." Ryan nods. "That's when they swap shifts so no one's really paying much attention."

We did the same thing when we snuck out together, waited for the breakfast bell and darted past the security line. It isn't anything more than a few guards moseying around the church, but if they saw us scurrying away, we'd be in big trouble. I'm not sure how Mya will feel about sneaking out, but she's already agreed to meet me for dinner. I just have to butter her up before we make it to the border because I'm sure that'll be a point of contention for us.

But it'll be worth it.

Ryan says the guards swap shifts every eight hours, but there's a second switch for dinner after just three hours. That means we'll be able to have a few hours to ourselves and still make it back before sunset. We can eat, talk, and then I'll tell her about my decision. I'm positive we'll make out afterward, so I don't know when I should make the announcement. It seems kind of wrong to slide my hands up her shirt after telling her I plan to give my life to Christ. But, *gosh*, I need this. If I weren't planning on getting saved, I'd take her out there and strip her down before we even get to the food. But I've changed. Waiting like this is agonizing, but once I'm saved, I'm sure Mya will warm up to the idea of marriage. It seemed insane and overwhelming before but now that I realize we won't be able to touch each other until we tie the knot, I'm ready to walk down the aisle *tonight*. Maybe we can have a dual service at church, get saved and married in the same service. Wouldn't that be convenient?

Anyway, I thank Ryan before I leave, then I haul it to my apartment so I can shower. Showers are timed, seven minutes unless you're a woman who's pregnant or menstruating, then you get ten minutes. The water never gets really hot but it's better than nothing, and if you don't use all seven minutes they'll roll over for the next shower. Bunny is fast as a whip, so I have nine minutes on the timer when I step in. I listen to the clicking as I scrub my hair, it ticks as fast as my heart.

The buzzer goes off at the one-minute mark, so I have time to rinse the suds from my eyes and then I step out just as the water slows down. When I leave the bathroom, Bunny and Ae-cha are sitting on his bed reading a book together. I have a tiny little towel wrapped around my waist, so I awkwardly wave at them and then grab my clothes from my bed. The bathroom is smaller than a walk-in closet so it's tough to get dressed in there, but I manage. My hair is still wet when I leave the apartment. Bunny whistles behind me, his way of saying he hopes I get laid, Ae-cha only giggles and compliments his whistling skills.

Mom gives me a headache the moment I walk through her apartment door. The meatballs have been marinating all day, they're just now finished cooking and the whole place smells like meat and garlic. She steals a meatball for herself and a kiss from my cheek before passing me the food.

"I would give you my ring to propose but I know you are missing testicles so there is no point."

"Mom," I take a deep breath, "I have the balls to propose. I'm just waiting for the right time."

She grins. "The time is now, before you bring me an unexpected grandchild."

Good Lord, I'm not going out there to have sex! First Ryan, then Bunny, now even my mother is convinced I've planned this date for fun. No one would ever believe I just want some privacy to tell the woman I love that I'm going to join her on this spiritual journey. Now that I've seen everyone's reactions tonight, I'm glad I've kept this information to myself. They say its hard to be a Christian because then you can't have any fun, but I think it's hard because everyone around you takes the fun out of things.

I never noticed just how often people think about sex. Yes, I want to have it, too. I want it so bad, but I'd like to think that waiting on it wouldn't be so tough if everyone wasn't trying to get me to do it in the first place. Cracking jokes. Making lewd gestures. Telling me I have no balls just because I think I need more time before committing my eternity to someone. I haven't even gotten saved yet and it seems hard, but not because of God or His standards, its hard because of His children.

I shake my head as I walk to the front door, my mother meets me there and opens it for me. She slaps my butt as I walk out. "You are strong Russian man, go easy on her, yes?"

I don't even respond to that, I just march down the hall and follow the path to the back stairwell that leads to the surface. There's only one guard there but I bribe him with an apple, and he lets me by. I'll have to use one more when I go back to get Mya, but that'll still leave one for her to enjoy after dinner. I'm going to take the food out there first just so I can hold Mya's hand the entire time we walk together. That's sappy, I know, but I want every part of this night to be perfect.

I have to watch the church perimeter carefully so I can sneak by unnoticed, the shifts don't change for another hour so this part is risky, but I make it out without a problem. The meatball dish burns as I jog through the backstreets of the city; after I reach the city limits, I sit down for a break to rest my hands and check Ryan's map. According to his drawing, I'm on the right path. At least it matches the mental map I made the first time out here, so I think I'm doing pretty good—until I hear something whistle behind me.

Slowly, I turn to find two soldiers with their guns aimed directly at me. I have no idea where they came from. I have no idea why I didn't hear them, but there's no time for wondering—I take off running before they can even think to fire at me.

The soldiers shout in another language, but I don't hear any bullets go off, so I keep running. I can hear footsteps behind me and more yelling, like more soldiers have joined the chase. I can't lead them back to the church, so I push into the woods and sprint through the trees, but my foot gets caught on a root and I take a hard fall.

My hands fly out to catch myself, but my knee bangs against a rock and I cry out as I stumble back to my feet, limping forward. It's no use, I think I twisted my ankle and I'm positive my knee is bleeding, but I can't let those men catch me.

The church doesn't allow weapons, they confiscated my gun when I arrived, but I discreetly slipped one of my mother's kitchen knives up my sleeve without her noticing. I slide it into my hand now as I hear men approaching. When the steps sound close enough, I pivot and slash. The man screams as my knife cuts across his chest, it's just a flesh wound but it's enough to give me time to limp a few more steps.

I find a thick tree and set my back against it, so they all have to approach me from one direction. There are six of them, including the guy I slashed. They're wearing the same uniforms as the men in the post office, and the men I saw rape that woman months ago. But their accents are all different.

One of them strolls forward and smirks at me. I lift my knife and hold it steady, though my voice trembles when I say, "I don't want any trouble."

"English," the man replies. His accent is so heavy I barely make out the word, but I nod anyway. "English," he repeats.

"Yeah, English. That means you understand me when I say I don't want trouble."

"Where from?" He raises his eyebrows.

I glance at the five other men encircling me. They're all different skin tones, wearing different features. It's impossible to tell where they're from, but I suppose that's the least of my worries right now.

"I'm alone," I say. "I live out here."

"You come from the woods?"

I nod, but I don't even finish the motion before his arm juts out and snatches my knife away. He's so quick, I'm left holding the air before I realize it. Then he slaps me across the face, and I stumble to the side. My hands go up in defense, as I stumble. Pain shoots through my ankle and then my knee, and I fall onto my butt.

The man doesn't hit me again. He pulls up the legs of his pants and squats in front of me as the men chuckle and watch. The blade of the knife touches my nose, it doesn't hurt, but I feel a chill run down my spine. He's warning me.

"Liar," the man says. "I don't like liars."

Neither do I, but what else am I supposed to do? If I tell him I'm from an underground shelter with nearly two-thousand survivors who aren't allowed to have weapons, then I'll get everyone killed. I've seen what these soldiers are capable of; I won't let that happen to the church.

As I gaze at this man, I don't see his thick brow or his large, hooked nose, I see the younger face of the man who held that woman down in the street. I hear her screaming in my head, and the voice morphs into my mother's. The child lying dead beside her is Danya. Even worse, I hear Mya screaming, and the child is ours. That's the reality I face.

I shake my head. "I'm from the woods."

My face burns as he hits me again, an open palm to the side of my head. His hand is so big, my cheek, my temple, and my eye feels hot with pain, but I bite my tongue and ignore it. I'm not telling him anything.

He hits me again, my head whips to the side and spit flies from my mouth, but I straighten and look him right in the eye without saying a word. I won't say a word, no matter what he does to me. He must see the resolve in my eye because he says something in his native tongue and then I hear someone reply in a different language, translating the command. A moment later, two soldiers grab my arms and hold me in place. My breathing comes out in bursts, air shooting through my flared nostrils as I begin to panic. I thrash against their hold, but they're strong enough to keep me on my knees.

The man in front of me tosses the kitchen knife aside and walks over wearing a smile that tells me he's going to enjoy this. He grabs a painful fistful of my hair and holds my head in place.

"When you are ready for the truth, let me know," he says, then he punches me. Hard.

My vision blurs and my face erupts in blinding pain, but I grunt and squeeze my eyes shut. He punches me again before I can recover, and on the third punch, I see stars. The hit is so hard, he loses his grip on my hair and my head snaps to the side so hard I feel my neck crack. Blood drips down my chin, along with sweat, spit, and tears. My right eye hurts worst of all, it swims with liquid that tints my vision red. A ruptured blood vessel.

My scalp stings as the man grabs my hair again, he cranes my head back, so my throat is exposed. "Truth. Where you from?"

When I don't speak, he punches me in the throat. I scream but it's cut off by a second jab.

"Where you live?" the man shouts, but he punches me again so I can't even answer. "Tell the truth!"

Mercifully, the next punch goes to my gut, and I double over to vomit. My throat feels like I've swallowed rocks, and it burns as I spit up on the ground. The men let me sag forward as I hurl, even the guy punching me backs away because he doesn't want to get his shoes dirty. I just sit there, defeated, unable to even sit up straight. I'm on my knees, my arms held out at either side, head hanging forward. A draw of bloody spit leaks from my fat lips and dribbles all the way to the ground where it mingles with my sour vomit. I had oatmeal for breakfast with freeze dried blueberries. I count the mushy blue specks just to keep myself conscious.

"Ready for truth?" The man steps closer again, his boots squishing in the puke. He says something in his language and one of the guys holding me loosens his grip to yank my head back by my hair. "Truth?" the man says, tilting his head to the side.

I don't reply.

He punches me in the face, then again on the other side. After the third punch, he steps back to shake out his fist. His knuckles are bloody which makes me wonder how bad my face looks. I can't even feel it anymore. I just sit there and breathe when he steps back for a break. We're both tired, but he's not done.

God… I can't take much more.

He punches me in the gut now. I don't have the strength to scream, I just gag and dry heave, abs cringing in pain. My arms stretch out and my fingers spread apart as I feel my muscles lock up and seize. I'm cramping all over, my abs spasming after the next punch. The men start talking fast, afraid that I'm having a seizure, they let go of my arms and I fall face-first into the dirt. I'm engulfed in darkness but not for long. The moment all the lights go out, I see a piercing white light that illuminates everything around me.

I'm not lying in the dirt anymore; I'm standing in a white room with no injuries or pain. I even pat my chest to make sure I'm alive. I can feel my heart beating, the rhythm is smooth and calm.

"You're okay."

I turn and see a Man so beautiful, the sight of Him nearly makes me weep. He is *wearing* light, a cloak of luminescent diamonds sings as He walks to me. When He's close enough,

He reaches out and touches me. I feel warm from the inside out.

"You're okay," He repeats.

"How can you say that? They're torturing me."

"They are." He looks away, but the emotion that blankets his face is not sadness. He looks angry. "You won't suffer for much longer, sweet one."

I swallow. *They're going to kill me...*

The thought takes me to my knees, and I grab His hand, crying out, "I give my life to You!" If I'm about to die, I won't go out as a sinner. I clearly won't make it to the next church service. It's now or never.

"Jesus, You're my Lord and Savior!" I sob. I know this Man is the Christ. I can feel the truth vibrating in my bones and that vibrating turns to song as my weeping becomes laughter. I knew He was real. All along, I knew it inside. Mya would be proud... If only I could see her to tell her.

Something warm pats the top of my head and I look up to see Jesus smiling down at me. "I did not bring you all this way to let it end here."

My eyes widen. "But You said—"

"Your suffering will end soon, but not because of death. You will be saved."

My shoulders slump. I'm going to live. I deserve to live after all this.

Jesus laughs, and the sound is so beautiful it makes me blush. "You deserve to live because You are Mine."

I am His. Our course I am. I just gave my life to Him, that means I'm His responsibility. That means it's His job to take care of me. To take my worries, and my fears, and my anxiety. To guide me, lead me, and protect me. It's His job to rescue me.

Jesus kneels and lifts my chin. "I have a ram in the bush. Trust Me, Adrian."

"I don't know how much longer I can last," I whisper. "I'm passed out now because of them."

He smiles. "I am your strength. Lean on Me."

"Okay," I reply, and as soon as the word leaves my mouth, everything goes dark again.

Water splashes my face, and I gasp into consciousness. The water is warm and smells sour. When I peel my swollen eyelids back, I see a penis in my face, and I realize I'm getting pissed on.

The soldiers all chuckle as I cough and frantically scoot away. Every part of my body hurts, but in a different way than I expect. I'm not just sore, I feel dirt and rocks digging into my legs and my butt, scraping my skin.

I blink. They … they took my clothes.

I don't know how long I was passed out, but it was long enough for them to strip me naked and when I glance around, I see some of the men sitting in the grass, eating my meatballs. There's another one standing in the distance, casually holding his rifle. I guess he's keeping watch. Something smells awful, and I glance to my side to see the soldier who peed on me now has his pants down, taking a crap. I turn my head, searching for my clothes, but a shadow darkens my view, and I see the leader looming over me.

He grins and taps his foot. My clothes are folded neatly beside him but when I crawl forward, he kicks them away and squats in front of me to hold something up in my face. It's a slip of paper. Ryan's map.

My right eye is swollen shut, but I feel my left one stretch open, and it widens in shock and horror. "No," I whisper.

The man nods and tucks the paper away, then he rubs an apple on his shirt and takes a bite. I stare at his raw, bloody knuckles as he eats. "I knew you were a liar."

"P-Please…"

He shakes his head. "If you said truth before, we would be nice. But not now." He says something in his own language and two men walk over to me. I start scrambling backwards but they grab my arms and my legs and force me to lie on my belly.

The leader begins to laugh, apple juice flying from his mouth. He stands and taps my head with his boot. I've stopped fighting, too tired and scared of what's going to happen next. The leader watches me from above, his grin stretching wider as I hear footsteps coming closer. Someone is behind me, standing over me. And I suddenly hear the jingle of a belt.

No … oh God, no.

This is why they took my clothes. This is why they've held me down. This is why their leader is smirking. He wants to watch. He thinks this is funny.

I thrash like an animal, screaming and kicking my legs. Someone loses their grip, and I catch them in the jaw with my heel, but it's not enough to set me free. It just makes the soldiers angry. I get a swift kick to my ribs and then another that takes the air from my lungs in a pitiful, reedy, cry. I can't even cradle the injury because they've got my arms again, stretched me out like I'm making an angel in the grass. I'm so exposed, all I can do is cry.

I weep like a child as I hear them begin to laugh, and when I hear the sound of a zipper behind me, I close my eyes and beg God for the strength He promised me.

24

Caesar

We're on our last leg. It's been days since we set out and I feel like we're nowhere near our goal. Hopefully, I'm wrong. I'm not the one reading the map, and I have no idea what this church is supposed to look like, so as I gaze up at the tall buildings standing sentinel in the street, I can only pray that Keoni knows where she's going.

Prayer... I started doing that again, thanks to Bobby. It wasn't easy to leave him behind like that, but it was easier to let go since I knew that was what he wanted. He also wanted to forgive me, some of his last words to me were that he didn't blame me. That he didn't hate me. So, I've been trying not to hate myself, because if a dying man can leave this world without a grudge, then why can't I?

Somehow, forgiving myself is harder than forgiving others. The guilt eats away at me. The shame won't let me move on.

But every day gets a little easier. I've been saying my morning prayers each day since we left. Nothing more than five minutes, and it's usually four minutes of silence and then thirty seconds of me mumbling to God, asking Him to fix the big mess I've created, to heal the relationships I've broken, and to get us to this shelter safely.

It doesn't seem like much has changed, but only time will tell.

Major Banks stumbles on the cracked sidewalk and then hisses as she limps to the steps of a building and sits down. We all stop and sit with her, breathing heavily, wondering how much water we have left. We're on our last day of supplies. If we don't find this church soon, we're going to die. I'm positive we won't suddenly keel over, but we're doomed, nonetheless. There isn't much to loot out here. We know. We've checked. And we have no idea where to find another settlement. This is it for us. Make it or break it.

I sit on the edge of the sidewalk and gaze out at the city. It's not covered in red dust like most other places because this city sits at the edge of the woods. I can see stalks of green shooting into the sky in the distance, like oak soldiers ready to defend us from the encroaching desert beyond our view.

We don't have long before evening, that means daylight is waning so we can't afford to rest for long, but no one seems in a hurry to move. Raven is sitting beside me, still not speaking to me but not entirely shunning me either. She's panting and licking her cracked lips, thirsty as all get out. But we don't have any water to spare. We're saving our last ration for dinner and then that's it.

Claudius leans against the porch, too stubborn to sit. Major Banks sits on the stone steps like she's holding the entire building on her shoulders. This is the worst I've seen her, and that scares me. When your leader has given up, what else is there to hope for?

I clear my throat. "We should start searching buildings."

"No point." Claudius coughs and then spits. "If it ain't a church then it clearly ain't the shelter we're looking for."

"Well, we can't stay right here."

"Obviously."

I roll my eyes and stand. "I'm gonna take a look around."

"You shouldn't wander on your own." Major Banks' voice is so hoarse it sounds like it hurts to talk. She clears her throat. "Take Raven with you. We'll split up and search buildings for the next hour. Meet back here no matter what you find."

Divide and conquer. Our last desperate attempt to make it to the church. It's better than nothing.

I nod as Raven slowly rises and moves to stand beside me. "Can we have weapons?"

Enrique and Bobby both had guns, Major Banks took them but has been keeping them in her bag since we left. She doesn't trust me with one because I've already proved myself to be irresponsible, and Raven doesn't appear mentally stable enough to handle a weapon. But I'm not venturing into this city without a way to protect myself.

I hold out my hand. "You know I need a weapon, Major Banks."

She stares at my hand, but after a moment she nods and swings her bag from her shoulder. Claudius looks like he wants to protest but he doesn't have the strength to argue.

Major Banks presses a handgun into my palm. "Use it because you must. Not because you can."

I nod and tuck it into my waistband as she passes one to Raven. I wonder which gun I have right now. Enrique's or Bobby's. I suppose it doesn't matter.

Raven and I walk for twenty minutes, slowly moving to the outskirts of the city. I don't know anything about architecture but I'm hoping the church will be further out. Like, maybe they were hoping to catch travelers or new folks who've moved to the town. It might've felt welcoming to be greeted by a friendly church as soon as you arrive.

It's wishful thinking, but it sets me on a path that crosses with a stranger.

Raven is the one who notices. She stops walking suddenly and then grabs my arm and jerks me to a stop. I snap my vision down at her, but she's staring ahead so intently, I blink up the next second and immediately understand why.

There's a person ahead. A soldier. But he isn't looking at us or holding up a weapon. He's got his back to us and he's walking slowly, carrying something. When he turns to glance over his shoulder, I try to make out the item, but I don't believe what I'm seeing.

It's a casserole dish.

What the heck…

Raven is just as confused, but she acts on her curiosity by stepping forward. Following him. I don't stop her; I'm just as confused and intrigued as she is. I could raise my gun and take this guy out, get revenge for what happened at Orly Center, but he's clearly going somewhere, and we need to find that out.

If there's one thing I've learned on this journey, it's that the bad guys never travel alone. Wherever this soldier is headed, there will be more of them waiting. That thought makes me slow down and grab Raven by the wrist. I pull her off the road and whisper quietly, "Are you sure we should follow him?" We've been walking behind him for less than a minute, but it's clear he's heading straight for the woods. Unfamiliar territory. Anything could be out there, maybe even the enemy camp. I tell this to Raven, but she doesn't seem deterred.

"That's good. If there's an enemy camp, we need to find it."

"And do what?"

"Head back and report."

Okay … that's not a bad plan, but it is dangerous.

"What if we get caught?"

"Caesar, we're Runners. It's our job to be stealthy and quiet."

She's right. We had to be swift and silent during runs because we never knew if there were other looters around, or soldiers. We had to be unseen and unheard, and we had to move with purpose. That was the part that got my adrenaline pumping. The mystery. The anxiety of not knowing if I was being watched. In a strange way, it made me feel powerful, because I knew I could still get the job done even if someone had eyes on me.

This is just another mission, I tell myself. *Another day with Raven, running together again.*

"Okay," I whisper. "Stay quiet. Stay low. And don't move in unnecessarily."

We follow the soldier into the woods. It's easy to catch up to him because he's walking so slow with that casserole dish. Still, we have to fall back and take cover when he reaches a clearing, and I see more soldiers come into view.

I quickly count their heads and bite my lower lip in frustration. Six of them. That's bad news, but it could be worse.

"This doesn't look like a camp," Raven whispers.

She's right. There are no tents, no fire, and where the heck did that one guy get a casserole dish from? He sets it down in the grass and I squint to watch him eat a meatball. The sight of it makes my stomach growl so loudly I fear he'll hear it, but he keeps eating and even calls another solider over to get a taste. The scent of garlic and olive oil rides the breeze and I almost moan. I'm so hungry. Raven's hungry, too, I hear her stomach growling beside me and when I glance down, I see her lick her lips.

Two more soldiers join the two eating meatballs. One reaches into a basket and pulls out an apple.

Fresh fruit. My mouth waters.

The other soldier lifts a canteen and takes a swig of whatever's inside. I don't think he likes the drink because he frowns and caps it, then tosses the canteen into the grass. Before he leaves, he grabs an apple and strolls across the clearing. There are two soldiers in the middle. One of them walks away and takes up point about twenty yards away. He isn't facing us, so I'm not worried, but the other solider remains in the middle of the woods. The other guy passes him the apple and he rubs it on his shirt but doesn't eat it. He just stands there, staring down into the grass. I gasp when I realize it's a body.

A big, pale body is sprawled on the ground, face down, but the soldier in the middle says something I can't hear, and the other guy kneels beside him. There's some awkward movement, and then he tosses a boot into the air. Then another. After a moment, he flips the guy over and yanks down his pants.

"He's stripping him," Raven whispers.

We're crouched in the shrubbery some distance away, hidden in the evening shadows. There isn't much daylight left, and I'm sure the hour Major Banks gave us has passed by now, but I can't get myself to abandon this scene. I don't know what's happening, I don't even know if I can help, but I don't want to leave. Not yet.

Without thinking, I grip my gun and yank it from my waistband. That catches Raven's attention. She stares at the gun as she says, "We should get out of here. This looks like bad business."

Of course it does. They just stripped that guy naked, and now one of them is peeing on him. I swallow and wince at the dryness in my mouth. What am I about to witness?

The guy jerks upright with a shout, and I get a look at his bloody face. It's swollen and bruised, so I don't recognize his features, but I do recognize his voice when he yells.

It's Adrian Nikols.

How? How is this possible…

After all this time, Adrian is alive, and he's somehow found his way out to these woods. The exact woods I stumbled into. This isn't a coincidence, but could I really call it a blessing?

I left to find my friends, but not this one. The only one I hated. And I certainly didn't want to find him like this. It isn't just uncomfortable, it feels like betrayal. I hated Adrian because I saw him as my rival, one I couldn't beat. But as I look at him now, held down by two men, screaming for his life, sobbing like a child… That's not the Adrian I remember. This Adrian is weak. This Adrian has been defeated.

I hate them for that.

"If we're gonna do something, it needs to be now," Raven says, and without hesitation, I lift my gun and fire.

There's a guy standing over Adrian, between his spread legs. He's got his pants down to his knees and he's grinning. He wears that grin to his grave as a bullet splits his skull. Blood spurts from his forehead and lands on Adrian's bare butt with a splat. It's the only noise I hear until one of the soldiers whirls around and screams.

I scream too, firing more bullets before they can raise their weapons. I've got a handgun, and they have rifles, it doesn't take a genius to know we're screwed but screwed isn't the same as dead.

I fire two more shots and scurry from my hiding spot to a nearby tree. Raven calls my name and when I glance up, I see her gun spiraling toward me. I catch it and blink at her, but when I realize she's already gone, I understand her plan. She wants me to give her cover while she moves in to help Adrian. That's more noble than you think it is because Raven has no idea who Adrian is. To her, he's just a big naked albino, screaming in the woods. He isn't her teammate from track, he isn't her frat brother, he hasn't been her rival since high school. But she wants to save him anyway, and so do I. I want to save him more than she does, so I take a slow breath and give every shot my best aim.

I take down two more guys who don't see me in my hiding spot, but those shots give away my cover and the tree in front of me is shredded to pieces. I scream and roll into the clearing, stopping on my knee to fire another shot. A bullet splits my hand and sends the gun flying from my grasp, I've got another, so I pull Raven's out as I run behind another tree.

This is bad.

Having Raven's gun is one thing, but when I lift my bleeding hand, I realize I'm missing the finger to shoot it with. They *shot off* my finger.

There's no time to dwell on it, all I can do is lift Raven's gun with my other hand and fire a wobbly shot at the guy who's trying to rush me. Thankfully, he's a big guy, so even though my aim is crap, I still shoot him in the chest. But he's a soldier, so he's wearing a bulletproof vest which means my shot only slows him down. He stumbles backwards and then lifts his rifle. All I can do is gasp and close my eyes. There isn't even any time to pray, all I say is, "Please—" and then a gun fires. But I'm not hit.

I open my eyes to see a bullet lodged between the man's eyes. He walks forward and falls to his knees, then collapses. Footsteps behind me make me pivot and I almost cry in relief.

It's Major Banks! And Claudius, too, but he ignores me completely as he continues to fire into the woods. There are only two soldiers left now. One of them is aiming at us, but he goes down quickly to Claudius's sharp skills, the other turns and begins to run, but doesn't make it more than three steps before blood spurts from his head and he falls. Claudius shot him in the skull.

"You found us," I say, breathing heavily.

Major Banks nods, staring past me. "We heard the gunfire. But that means so did others, we've got to get moving. Now."

"Moving where?" I ask. "Did you find the shelter?"

She starts to shake her head, but someone calls behind me, "I can take you to a shelter."

When I look up, I see Adrian limping toward us with Raven holding him up. He's got his pants on now, but he's forsaken his shoes and shirt. I don't think he cares. The guy was *this* close to getting raped, I wouldn't blame him if he ran home naked and screaming. But he seems calm, if not relieved. He's alive. We all are, and apparently, Adrian has a place for us to stay.

I hold out my hand as he draws nearer and the smile on his face lets me know he recognizes me. "It's good to see you," he says, clasping my hand.

"Good to see you, too."

I mean it. I really do.

25

Mya

Something's wrong. Adrian invited me to dinner and then stood me up. That's what I want to believe, but I know him better than that. He would never stand me up, not after making such a big show of inviting me out. He even said it would be special. He was looking forward to seeing me. Alone. So why didn't he show up?

My eyes begin to water as I stare into my cup of tea. I'm at his mother's apartment. I didn't know where else to go when he didn't show up at our meeting spot. He said he would pick me up near the back staircase because he wanted to have a picnic on the surface. I was definitely worried about how that would go, but I trusted Adrian. I believed he had everything planned out and I had a dreamy, childish hope that he would keep me safe out there.

But now he's gone.

It's been *hours*. I waited thirty minutes before I walked to his job and asked his manager about him. I thought he might've gotten caught up since he's been working so many doubles lately, but the wood shop was empty except for Saloso. She's a tall woman who's hard to miss; her sharp features morphed into a concerned frown when I asked about Adrian.

"He got off over an hour ago!" Her voice was nearly a shout, but not in a mean way. I've been having lunch with Adrian on his work break almost every day for a week now and I've learned that Saloso only exists on two planes, shouting and laughing. She does both with equal fervor.

"Oh," I'd said. "Well, we had a date tonight, but he hasn't shown up." I had no idea why I was sharing that with her, but I was desperate and getting more worried with each passing second. "We're having a picnic. And he was excited about it because it's the first time we'll get to be alone as a couple."

Saloso had given me a very funny smile before bursting into booming laughter. Her voice was like a shock to the nerves. "Adrian loves you! He is just late, young girl. Do not worry, handsome men never pass up chance for good sex."

I smiled and left. How else was I supposed to respond to that?

I thought about going back to our meeting spot but that nagging in the pit of my stomach hadn't ceased, so I skipped that place and went straight to Adrian's apartment. Bunny answered with a huff, swinging open his door with a red face and a mean frown.

"*What?*" he'd practically yelled at me. I didn't have to wonder why he was so angry. He yanked the door open wearing nothing but his underwear with a very little friend tenting the front of it. I didn't have to ask to know Ae-cha was in there somewhere. The shelter was really strict about coed visits, there was probably twenty minutes before guards would come through and start knocking on doors. I could understand Bunny's frustration at being interrupted, but I'm sure Ae-cha's father would thank me later. He's a member of the church, attends every service he can, and has more than a few reasons to pray that his daughter joins him soon, but that moment had no time for judgment.

"I can't find Adrian," I'd said, tossing away all thoughts of Bunny and his girlfriend. Why did I care if they sinned, I clearly had bigger things to worry about. "He was supposed to meet me for our date."

Bunny paused but only for a moment. "He's probably at his mom's apartment. Did you check there?"

I hadn't yet. His mother's place was a last resort because I didn't want to worry her, but I didn't get to explain this to Bunny because he said quickly, "Check there and don't come back unless he's dead!" Then he slammed the door in my face, and I turned to leave with the sound of Ae-cha giggling behind me.

Before I went to his mother's place, I stopped by our meeting spot one last time. By then, it'd been a full hour past the time he said he'd be there. Adrian is a punctual person. He would never leave me hanging like this. Not without a good reason. Not unless something was wrong.

Just to be sure I wasn't overreacting, I forced myself to wait at our meeting spot for thirty more minutes before nearly sprinting to his mother's place. When I got there, I pounded my fist on the door, tears springing to my eyes, but they dried up when a strange man answered instead of his mother.

"H-Hello?" I'd taken a step back, wondering if I'd knocked on the wrong door. "I'm looking for—"

"Let her in, Ryan." I recognized the voice of Adri's mother and felt myself sigh in relief when she appeared beside the man named Ryan. Her eyes were red. I still had no idea what was going on, but it was clear she already knew something was wrong.

"Um…" I stepped into the apartment, staring at them both. Ryan was looking everywhere but at me, fumbling with the hem of his dirty t-shirt. It was a long-sleeved shirt with holes punched into the sleeves so he could poke his thumbs through like a teenager. His nails were all jagged and misshapen, and his hands were stained with dirt, caked under his nails, and seemingly rubbed into his skin like lotion. There was a layer of grime on his face, but I hardly noticed as I blinked at him and said, "I can't find Adrian."

"Yes, I know," his mother replied. "This is Ryan, he's the father of the twins."

I must have made a face because Ryan took a step back like he was suddenly ashamed. Even Adri's mom paused, like she was ashamed, too. It's a wonder how someone as filthy and smelly as Ryan managed to land Adrian's mother, but I didn't have time for that. I was more shocked that he was here than with how he looked.

"What's going on?" I said.

"Ryan works at the wood shop with Adrian."

Huh. Adrian never told me.

"I went back to the shop to grab something I left," Ryan explained, "my manager told me a pretty young lady came in asking about Adrian." He bobbed his head, still fiddling with his shirt. "When I heard that, I came here because I have information."

"What information?" I licked my lips. My mouth was dry, but I swallowed anyway, hoping to work moisture into it. All the moisture was in my eyes, tears misting each one, pooling at the rims and spilling down my cheeks. I still had no idea what'd happened, or if anything had happened at all. But I was crying, nonetheless. Like my heart already knew what Ryan was about to tell me.

"I know Adrian was planning a date," he said. "I know where he was planning it. So, if no one has seen him, then something is wrong. Really wrong."

At that moment, someone knocked on the door and I heard laughter in the hall. Adrian's mother said something in Russian before she ran to open it. The twins dashed inside, hugging their mother around the waist, but they froze in place when they caught sight of Ryan. He froze too, staring at them like they were alien creatures.

His eyes turned red and brimmed with tears. That's when it hit me. *He hasn't seen them.* Maybe they arrived at the shelter together, but the stunned look on Ryan's face was clear. *He almost doesn't recognize his own kids, and they don't recognize him.* I wondered if he looked this bad the last time they were together.

"Hello, Mister." Danya waved.

"To your rooms," their mother ordered, and when they protested, she yelled, "TO YOUR ROOMS!" Then she slammed the front door and marched back to the middle of the living room.

No one spoke until we heard the bedroom shut down the hall.

"Adrian wanted to take you beyond the perimeter," Ryan said.

Adri's mother started speaking Russian, but I didn't need to translate to know that she was upset. I was upset, too. How could he be so reckless…

"Beyond the perimeter?" I'd squeaked out. Anything could happen out there. Anyone could be out there. And no one would ever know.

After that, my memory is foggy. I remember turning to leave—to go find Adrian—but then the room started spinning and I missed a step and was suddenly on the floor. I don't remember getting back up. I don't remember moving to the sofa, but that's where I woke up a few moments ago.

Danya sits beside me now, holding my hand. He's a sweet boy; his nearness comforts me in a way that makes my chest hurt. He looks just like his older brother but smaller. White-blonde hair and clear eyes that seem to take in everything around him. They're big and round, a complete contrast to the sharpness of his features. His chin is always tucked down, like he prefers to stare at the floor instead of the people around him. I bet he prefers quiet places and hates crowds, just like Adrian. I wonder if his wrinkled brow is permanent, if he realizes he's always scowling. And the pinch of his full lips is just like his brother, like he's always on the verge of an outburst.

As angry as he looks, Danya is a happy boy, even now, he smiles at me as he looks over. Though the smile is clearly forced and draws all of his strength. His hand trembles in my grasp. "Adri will be okay." He swallows and then nods at the tea he'd brought me. "You should drink it while its warm."

"Of course," I whisper, lifting the cup to my lips. It's hot and sweet and makes me wonder where Adrian's mother got sugar from. It makes me feel guilty that she shared it with me. "Where is your mother?" I ask Danya.

He lets my hand go so he can point down the hall, toward her bedroom. "She went to lie down after you fainted. Dad put you on the sofa before he left."

I notice he called Ryan 'Dad' I guess some things were explained while I was out. I'm tempted to ask how long I was unconscious, but I don't care. I just want to know what's going on with Adrian.

"Any updates?" I ask.

Danya shakes his head. "After Dad left, your friends came by and said a team was dispatched to find Adrian."

"That's good." I think of Hayden and how his team rescued me and Adrian. They were frightening at the time, but ultimately good at their job. They had weapons. They had maps. They were formidable. "They'll bring him back," I say, more to myself than to Danya, but he nods anyway and reaches for my hand again. I let him take it, squeezing gently.

"Dinara won't come out of our room," Danya whispers. His voice cracks on the last word, and I see tears rolling down his pink cheeks. "I've gotta be strong for her."

"You are strong," I tell him. "The strongest here right now. As strong as Adrian."

"Is he really coming back?" He looks at me through his tears and I know my answer will live with him for the rest of his life. I can't get this wrong, but I don't have all the facts. I can't look into the future. This is out of my hands. But I know it isn't out of God's.

I nod. "God will bring him back."

That makes Danya pause, his little white eyebrows scrunching in a frown. I expect him to say something negative, like Adrian probably would, but he doesn't. Instead, he asks, "Can we pray?"

For the first time, I feel a spark of hope come alive inside. "Of course, we can."

My tea sloshes around the cup when I set it down on the little table beside the sofa. I wipe my sweaty hand on my pants before reaching for Danya. He closes his eyes and begins to hum, it's the sweetest, most peaceful thing I've ever seen. The faith of a child... I feel a tear burning down my face as I stare at him, wishing I had his bold faith. Wishing I could blindly believe that Adrian was fine and everything would be alright.

That's what I have to believe, I tell myself. So instead of praying for Adrian, I pray for all of us.

"God, please give us Your strength. Give us Your faith, like You did for the disciples." I sigh, squeezing Dayna's hands. "The truth is that I'm scared, Abba. I don't believe that Adrian's okay... but I want him to be. And I know if anyone in all of creation can keep him safe and bring him back, it's You. Only You. So, Danya and I come to you, in faith and hope, and we place our worries at Your feet. We ask You to keep Adrian safe. To heal our hearts of these dark fears. And to reunite this family. In Jesus' Name we pray, amen."

Danya says amen and then sniffles as he releases my hands. "Thank you," he whispers.

I pull him close for a hug. "It'll be okay."

We sit like that for a little while, holding each other, listening to the hum of the communal generators whirring in the walls. I think there's one in each unit, hidden in the back of the living room closet. I've never looked. But the sound of it working in the background is almost comforting now. The generators are unseen, yet they keep the entire shelter running. They're small but powerful. They are the heartbeat of this entire operation. Kind of like faith.

God, please... I squeeze Danya a little harder, and he squeezes me back until the sound of someone knocking on the front door yanks us apart. We stare at the door, shocked and unsure if we heard knocking.

Down the hall, I hear a bedroom door squeak open and Adrian's mother drifts into the living room. Her face is puffy and swollen, she's definitely been crying, but she dries her tears on the sleeve of her shirt before she swings the door open and says, "Yes?"

"Ms. Nikols!"

I recognize Bunny's voice immediately, the sound of it drags me to my feet and before I know it, I'm at the door behind Ms. Nikols. Bunny looks at me, his face apologetic. I don't know what to make of his expression, but he speaks before I can dwell on it.

"They found him."

My heart stops and restarts. I hear Danya gasp behind me and then his little footsteps dart down the hall. "Dinara! Dinara!" His voice disappears inside a room.

"Where?" Ms. Nikols whispers. I see her shoulders shaking, but she holds her head high, gripping the door handle like it's the only thing holding her up. "Where is my son?"

"The infirmary. He doesn't look good—"

"I'm going." Ms. Nikols turns away, leaving me at the door to face Bunny. He's wearing that apologetic face again, and it makes me want to scream.

"What else is there?" I ask.

"I ... I'm sorry. You came to me earlier, but I didn't believe anything was wrong. I sent you away." He coughs to cover the way his voice breaks. "And then other people—camp officials—showed up at my door, asking if I had seen him."

"Bunny, you didn't know. It's okay. They found him, that's all that matters."

He shakes his head. "There's more."

I brace myself.

"He was found with other people, Mya."

"His captors?"

"No." He takes a shaky breath as tears fill his eyes. "Th- They found him with Caesar."

For a second, I can't breathe. They found Adrian. He's alive, in bad shape, but still alive. And they found him with Caesar. Julius Caesar. It's almost overwhelming.

Now I'm gripping the door handle. "How do you know? Are you sure it's him?"

Bunny nods. "The camp officials asked me to verify his identity when he arrived. Jupiter too."

"Oh my gosh." I cover my mouth with my hand, but I don't let myself cry again. I don't know how to feel about Caesar's arrival. What does it mean? How am I supposed to handle it?

Ms. Nikols returns to the door with the twins beside her, each one holding her hand. "We are leaving now," she says, walking right by me.

Bunny steps aside, but he calls to me as I close the front door. "Caesar isn't at the infirmary."

I stop. "What?"

"His hand was badly injured, but they treated it pretty fast. He's being kept in the holding center." Bunny points over his shoulder. "This way."

Now I get it. Caesar and Adrian are in opposite directions. Two different locations. I can't see them both at once, so I've got to choose. I haven't seen Julie in months. I've prayed for him every day since he was taken from me. I've cried for him. Ached for him. Missed him with every part of my heart. But I gave my heart to Adrian. He must come first.

"I'll see him soon," I say to Bunny, then I turn away and run to catch up to Ms. Nikols. She smiles as she sees me from the corner of her eye, turning to nod at me. The gesture is small but holds the weight of my future on it. She knows I just made an important choice. She's seen for herself that my feelings for her son are genuine. True. And she's thankful for it.

So am I.

26

Adrian

I'm alive. I can't believe it. Even more shocking than the fact that I haven't died is how I managed to live. God saved me. He sent His own soldier in to rescue me in the form of Julius Caesar. I've never been so happy to see the guy in my life. I thought I'd hated him. I thought he was the worst guy I ever met. I thought he'd ruined my chances with Mya forever, therefore ruining my life. But in the end, he saved me. Without thought or hesitation.

My eyes peel open to take in the hospital room around me. A thin mattress beneath me, a somewhat comfy looking chair in the corner, beige walls, that nauseating smell of bleach and sickness. My body aches from head to toe. My face throbs with every movement and expression, I can't even raise my eyebrows without feeling like my skull is being pried open. My abs hurt, ribs are even worse. The nurse told me I bruised six of them, cracked another. I had a concussion. My nose was broken. Lip busted. A vessel in my eye had ruptured, things are still tinted pink in my vision. Two days later.

I drag my blanket from my body and swing my legs over the edge of my bed. It happens slowly, as if I'm moving against time. My body feels larger, and I can't seem to get a grasp on just how much room I take up. I'm so clumsy now, bumping and tripping into everything. The doctor says it happens with trauma. Considering I got my head bashed in, yeah, I'm not surprised I feel a little dizzy. I just don't like it.

I grip the wall as I walk slowly toward the on-suite bathroom, hissing through my teeth. The cold tile floor might as well be covered in needles. Sharp pain shoots up each one of my toes, through my foot, into my sore ankle. I'd twisted it running away from those guys, busted my knee, too. I've got a nice boot and a knee brace. The infirmary doesn't have many of these, and it was tough finding one in my size, so I won't get to hold on to it for long. Thankfully, I don't plan to be here long. I need to get better so I can be released. I need to be with my family again. They've visited me every day since my miraculous return. Mya too. She's the one I want to see the most.

I'll never forget the feeling I had when I first woke up in the hospital and saw her crying. She was by my side. Even though Julius was here. Even though she'd loved him first. And hadn't seen him in months. And had spent every day praying for his return. She chose me.

My heart had melted as she clung to me, wetting my bandaged face with her tears. If I'd had the strength, I would've cried too. But all I could do was close my eyes and whisper a prayer.

"Thank You, Jesus."

He'd kept His Word. He brought me back alive. I didn't have to hold on for much longer, just like He'd said. Help had arrived at the perfect moment. Seriously.

I told Mya everything. About me encountering Christ. About how I dropped to my knees and gave my life to Him. I told her how He'd promised I would be saved. And that all I'd wanted was to get back and see her again.

I told her other things, too. That I was in love with her, and I didn't want our time together to ever end. I told her I wanted to take my mother's advice and hold on to her while I could. For as long as I could. For eternity.

I guess that was as close as I'd get to getting down on one knee, but Mya accepted it, nodding and crying and telling me she loved me, too. Our reunion was sweet, probably sweeter than that dinner would have been. In a strange way, I'm thankful for it.

There were other things I told Mya. Details I didn't want to think about. She knows more than my mom does. More than my siblings. Certainly more than Ryan, who's apologized profusely for telling me to go out there in the first place. I'm not mad at him. It wasn't his fault there were soldiers out there, and if I hadn't gone, I never would've bumped into Julius. So, it's all good.

I think of Ryan as I wash my hands and grab the toothpaste from the side of the sink. He visited me once in the hospital; Mom and the twins were there so I think he feels awkward coming by. The time I saw him, he looked a little better. To a stranger, he's probably still a smelly mess, but having worked with him for the last few weeks, I can tell he's taken at least one bath in the recent days. That's progress for him, trust me.

Someone knocks on my door when I leave the bathroom, and I have to quickly hobble over to get it. I peek outside to see Mya smiling up at me. I want to lift her from the ground and spin in a circle, but I don't have the strength. Instead, I settle for a ginger hug as she wraps her small arms around my middle. She feels so warm.

"How are you?"

"Good." My voice sounds hoarse, but I'm doing better than I sound. I try to prove this by walking to the comfy chair across the room all on my own. I sway a little but manage to stay on my feet.

Mya claps for me. "You really are doing better."

On the chair is a pile of clean clothes, a pair of grey sweatpants and a dark t-shirt. The pants are two sizes too big so the legs can fit over my knee brace and ankle boot. I have to tie the drawstrings in a tight knot to keep them from falling back down. Mya offers to help, but I'm just not ready to have anyone's hands near my personal areas. Not right now. Not yet. Not soon. I don't know when.

I swallow and let go of a shaky breath.

"It's okay," Mya says. She's gotten good at catching my facial expressions. Knowing what I'm thinking. Understanding how I feel.

When the Fall first happened, I saved her from some thugs who'd tried to rape her. She was a mess for a few days, but things were so chaotic, there was no time for her to dwell on it. All I've got is time now, and the freedom leaves me with nightmares. Little gifts left for those who survive their trauma.

Still, Mya understands what I've been through. She's felt the same fear. Felt the same darkness overcome her, fear invading her mind. Madness swallowing her sanity. I saw the look on her face when I'd stopped those guys from attacking her. I wonder if mine looked the same to Julius when he saw me.

"You're okay." Mya is beside me now, taking my hand. I feel her fingers intertwine with my own and I give them a squeeze.

"Thanks."

"That's what I'm here for."

"I thought I'd never see you again," I whisper.

"God brought you back."

"He did."

The look on Mya's face makes me smile hard, she's so happy about me giving my life to God. I think she wanted that more than she wanted to marry me. I barely proposed, so her enthusiasm about it shouldn't be counted against her, but still. I told her I wanted her forever and she said she wanted the same. That's like a proposal, isn't it?

Mya fidgets beside me, catching my attention. The look on her face doesn't make me grin anymore. She looks worried about something, chewing her lip and avoiding my eyes.

"What is it?"

"Julius… He wants to see us."

I nod slowly. We haven't really talked about him. I know he's here and I know Mya chose to come to my room instead of his when we first arrived, but that was the extent of our conversation about wonder boy. Now that I'm getting better, I suppose we need to address what happens next.

"I understand," I say honestly. "I want to see him."

"Are you sure?"

"Mya, he's your best friend. I want to get along with him, and I think I can do that now, considering he saved my life."

She lets out a sigh.

"Have you seen him?" I ask casually.

"No. I wanted us to go together."

"I see." I don't say more because I'm afraid my voice will crack. I don't want to start crying, but I am emotional. Mya really chose me. Truly chose me.

I exhale slowly. "What about Bunny and Jupiter? They've seen him, right?"

She nods. "Uh, Bunny moved him into his apartment."

"What?"

That place was already cramped. How on earth are *three* of us supposed to fit in there with only two beds? I'm not sharing.

Mya laughs and sits on my bed, swinging her legs. "You're moving in with your mother. I hope you don't mind."

I honestly don't mind at all. I'll have to sleep on the couch, but I've lived in cramped quarters with them before. I know I can survive it.

"That works perfectly," I say.

She nods, covering her smile with her hand. "They say *we* could get an apartment. If we… Well…"

My eyes widen. "If we what?"

Mya giggles again but a knock at the door cuts her off and we both jump in surprise. I sigh as she moves to open it, then I sigh again when Bunny walks inside. All the times he's yelled at me for interrupting moments with Ae-cha, I could strangle him for interrupting this with Mya. Marriage is so much more important than his quick hookups. Yes, they really are quick, one time they were together and finished before I got out of the shower. Seven-minute timer, remember?

"Adrian." Bunny says my name like he can't believe it's me. Apparently, he didn't want to help Mya when she came to him, so he's been going above and beyond to help me out now. Yesterday, he brought me some of Ae-cha's dumplings and tea. It was a welcome gift since I'd only been eating soup before that.

"Hey, Benson." I nod.

"Is something wrong?" Mya asks.

"No. Not really. I just thought I'd come help Adrian get to the meeting room."

Mya steps aside to let him help, I don't mind because he's a bit stronger than her, so it won't be so awkward to lean on him. We walk slowly down the hall, but I gather more strength with each step. By the time we stop outside the conference room, I'm standing on my own, though I'm slightly panting. My ribs burn and it takes all my focus not to curl up in fetal position and cry. Mya will never let me out of the infirmary again if she realizes how much pain I'm in, but all that pain vanishes the instant Julius opens the door.

He stares at me, then his eyes quickly drop to Mya, and they blink at each other in the growing silence. It isn't until I shift my weight from one foot to the other that he finally looks away. He doesn't even bother acknowledging Bunny.

"Come in," he says, stepping aside.

The room is small and plain; just a table and a few chairs with drinks and what looks like mini sandwiches set out in the middle. Jupiter, Ae-cha, and another girl are already at the table when we approach. Bunny sits beside his girlfriend while Mya hugs Jupe. Julius takes his place beside that other girl, and I suddenly recognize her from the day they saved me. She was the one who ran out and got me, placing almost all my weight on her shoulders and dragging me away from the bullets. She even had the concentration to snatch up my clothes, so I didn't have to walk back to camp naked.

I never got her name, so when Julius introduces her as Raven, I smile and wave at her. Mya glances between us but says nothing. I'm not sure what to make of that so I choose not to acknowledge it at all.

"It's been a while," Julius says. He fiddles with his fingers, and I notice one of them is wrapped in gauze. I'd heard he injured his hand, but now I realize that was an understatement.

285

One of his pointer fingers is missing from the knuckle down. Did that happen when he rescued me? Did he seriously sacrifice one of his appendages for me?

I stare at his hand as he talks, but I'm not listening. I'm trying to understand why. Why would he do that for me? Why would he think I'm worth one of his *fingers?*

"Julius—"

My voice is lost to the group laughter. Apparently, Julius said something funny, and the atmosphere has suddenly shifted like we're all friends again, sitting in the basement of Mya's house, huddled around the latest slop they served up.

I sit back in my chair and watch everyone smiling, talking, catching up. The scene brings a sad smile to my face. The truth is that we were never close friends like this. At Mya's house, we did nothing but fight, and when we weren't fighting, we were all hooking up, when we weren't hooking up, we were getting shot at, kidnapped, and starving to death.

The truth is that this is the closest we've ever come to being real friends. It's crazy what it took to get us to this point.

"Adrian."

I look up to see Julius's eyes focused on me. He looks handsome, always has. I can admit when someone's a good-looking guy, I've no shame in that. I've never had trouble understanding why Julius was so popular in school. He was enigmatic and charming and full of life. He had the face of his namesake, a true leader if I've ever seen one. Nothing about him has changed except his finger. His hair is longer, his body looks a little thinner. But he's still Julius Caesar, and he's just called my name.

The sound leaves his lips like a song, silencing the room. I stare at him until I realize he's waiting for a response. "It's nice to see you," I say. The words seem to calm everyone, Bunny's shoulders visibly relax. Even Mya seems to exhale held breath. Sheesh, it's like they were all waiting for me to start screaming or something. Julius and I didn't like each other much, but it wasn't impossible for us to be around each other. We'd lived in the frat house together for years before the Fall. And I'd kept my mouth shut while he cozied up with Mya for a while. Now it's his turn to keep his trap shut.

Slowly, I relax in my chair and rest my arm on the back of Mya's. Julius watches but doesn't comment. So does the girl beside him. I don't know what their relationship is like, but she seems oddly close to him. Almost protective.

"You saved me," I say to Julius. "Thank you. Seriously."

"You're welcome."

"We're so happy you're here!" Jupiter's mouth is full of food and she's smiling hard enough to show it. I don't think she's ever been a fan of Julius, but after everything we've been through, it's easy to set our college drama aside. Jupe's exclamation sparks a series of conversations and introductions. Bunny shows off Ae-cha and tells everyone the story of how they met. Then Jupiter tells us how she and Bunny ended up here in the first place. Once she's finished, Mya takes the spotlight and shares our story. It's a very filtered version, she doesn't even include the cannibal, or the fact that we're together now, but she doesn't shift away from me when I scoot my chair a little closer. I guess that's all the detail we need.

Julius speaks last, he reintroduces Raven and tells us what happened to him after he was kidnapped form Orly Center. It turns out, he wasn't kidnapped at all. Those people who took him were good to him and he's been staying at their settlement all this time. With Mya's father.

She screams at the news and turns to cry into my shoulder. I whisper to her that it's okay, that I'm happy for her, all while Julius (and Raven) watches closely. When she's settled down, Julius tells everyone how he found me—not that I was naked or anything, just how he ended up there in the first place. It's a terrible story that silences the room and leaves Raven in tears once its over. Her sister was killed when Orly Center was suddenly raided. And so were other people on Julius's team.

"We had no choice but to run," he says now, staring down at the half-eaten sandwich in his hand. "I thank God we made it here. It's only because of Him that I'm alive. And it's because of Him that I found Adrian. He brought me to you." Julius looks right at me, and I look back, but my expression isn't angry. I'm honestly surprised. He was as religious as me back in the day, not exactly an atheist but certainly no church boy. That was the reason his relationship with Mya ultimately fell apart.

I glance sideways at my girlfriend now. She's wearing an equally shocked expression, and it makes me wonder what she's thinking. If she's sorry that she moved on. If she wishes she would've waited a little longer.

288

Julius didn't just come back; he came back as a Christian. He's everything she's always wanted, but it's too late now. She's mine.

I take her hand underneath the table to remind her of this, and she interlocks her fingers with mine, squeezing it hard. This is difficult for her. I don't know how I feel about that.

"Anyway," Julius clears his throat, "I wanted to meet with everyone altogether because there are some things you need to know."

We all shift uncomfortably.

"Delilah is dead."

Mya gasps. Jupiter covers her mouth. Bunny drops his head into his hands while Ae-cha rubs his back.

"How do you know?" I ask.

"I found her body in Orly Center. My team buried her and then returned to camp, but I went back a few weeks later to search for clues." He sighs. "I was hoping to find something that could lead me back to you guys."

"Ultimately, you did." Mya sniffles and bobs her head. "You found your way back to us."

"Yeah. I did." Julius fidgets, his hands twitching on the table, but he clasps them together and swallows. He wants to reach for her. It would be so easy to extend his long arm across the table and take Mya's small hand. To intertwine their fingers, like ours are now. But he controls himself. And Mya makes no move to initiate contact either. We all just sit here in this tense silence, a hundred different emotions bouncing around the room.

"How did she die?" Jupiter asks.

"I think she starved to death," Julius replies. "We found her alone. No obvious marks or injuries on her body. She was clutching a radio in her hands."

My heart stops. That radio was the reason I sent Delilah away, and she died holding it. Clinging to it for life. Her death is my fault...

Mya squeezes my hand beneath the table, bringing me back from my thoughts. I take a deep breath, my eyes wide open and blinking madly around the room. The moment is already heavy with emotion, so no one seems to pay me any attention. They don't know how badly I'm freaking out. They don't know I'm *this* close to having another panic attack, but as Mya squeezes my hand, the warmth of her palm reminds me of the radiant warmth I felt when I was face to face with Christ Jesus.

Peace immediately blankets my shoulders. I feel it roll over me from head to toe, washing away the fear and the guilt and replacing it with a somber understanding that, yes, Delilah is dead, but no, it isn't my fault. Sending her away didn't kill her. Starvation did. She could have starved anywhere. She could've found help instead of sitting at Orly Center. I won't blame myself, but I will apologize for the role I played.

"I sent her away," I confess. "She took that radio from one of the soldiers who captured you, Julius."

He stares at me.

"When I found out she had it, I panicked. I thought the guys who took you were bad people. I thought they could trace our location with that radio, but she didn't want to let it go..."

I pause, letting go of Mya's hand so I can clench my own into fists. I stare at them on the table, the knuckles turning red then white, my nails digging into my palms. I'm already sore, but it's the sting of this regret that hurts the most.

"I'm sorry," I whisper. "She wouldn't have been out there if I hadn't told her to leave."

The room falls quiet for a long time. I can feel Julius's eyes on me. Feel the questions he has storming between us, waiting to be channeled into judgment or forgiveness.

"I was there," Mya speaks up, shocking me.

I turn to look at her and she offers a small smile. It isn't a happy one, it's one of companionship. She's on my side; she's going to defend me.

"We were all there," Mya says, forcing Bunny and Jupiter to take accountability. They both stare at the table now, too ashamed to meet anyone's gaze. "We all saw the radio, and we all agreed with Adrian's decision. No one tried to stop her from leaving."

"We gave her supplies before she left," Jupiter says, like she's trying to explain herself.

Bunny nods agreement.

"Okay." Julius's voice is quiet, but he clears his throat and then says in a more confident tone, "I'm sure you did what you thought was best."

"There's more news," Raven says. "We were attacked by soldiers at Orly Center. But you were also attacked." She looks at me.

"We faced soldiers at the post-office, too," Mya adds. "That's how we ended up here."

"I think this camp might be in danger." The look on Julius's face is serious, there's no more grief or concern for Delilah anymore.

"I thought you guys took out all the soldiers in the woods?" Bunny stares back and forth.

"We did. But there's no way to tell if they were truly alone or not. If there are other soldiers out there looking for them, it's only a matter of time before they end up here."

I sigh deeply. "They also found my map."

"You had a map?" Mya asks.

"Ryan, my stepfather, drew one for me before I left. The soldiers took it from me, that's why they were beating me."

"But they're dead now. So, it doesn't matter if they found that map." Jupiter's voice trembles. "Right?"

"Maybe," I say. "I passed out during the torture. They could have radioed their location to other soldiers and even mentioned the map, maybe they tried to follow the map and relayed that on their radios." I shrug. "There's just no real way to tell."

"I've spoken to Major Banks about this, and I wanted to present the idea to you guys privately." Julius glances at Raven who nods, encouraging him to continue. "I want you guys to come back with us. To Eternus."

"Hold on," Bunny says, "you want us all to leave?"

"It's safer there. And there's plenty of room—"

292

"Ae-cha's family is here," Bunny says, reaching for her hand. "We can't just abandon this place. I want to protect it. I want to fight for it."

"What if we can't fight?" Julius challenges. "What if our best option is to simply leave?"

"And give up this place?" Bunny shakes his head. "I went through too much to get here."

"We all did," Jupiter whispers.

"I'm ready to go."

I snap my head down to stare at Mya. "You are?"

"My father is at Eternus, Adrian. I have to go."

I don't reply. I knew Mya would probably want to go; we had conversations about it before Julius ever showed up. There have been more and more sightings of enemy soldiers lately. Leaving really is a good option. But... we've been doing so good here. This place has become my home. I don't want to go back out there again.

"Obviously, this is a lot to think about." Julius stands and Raven does, too, this creates a domino effect where we all rise one by one. It's clearly time to go. The reunion is over. "Think on everything we've said," Julius tells us. I notice he said 'we' as if he and Raven are in complete agreement. Like they're a pair. "We don't have to decide anything right now," Julius continues, "but we've got to do it soon. Every day is a risk."

"We understand," I say, reaching for Mya's hand. She takes it and stands beside me, but she keeps her gaze leveled on the table.

"We'll get back to you," she mutters.

27

Caesar

Bunny is angry at me, but I don't care. We haven't spoken much since that great big reunion two days ago. He's been giving me the silent treatment because he wants to stay and fight and I think he should pack up and go. I understand his desire to protect this place, I just don't understand why he's treating me like I'm the one threatening it.

Maybe because I'm the reason things have been rushed along. I heard there were talks of leaving the church shelter before I arrived, but when my group showed up and shared our story of what happened at Orly Center, the church leaders moved everything forward and gave the folks here two options; leave with us or stay and fight.

Staying is a suicide mission. Bunny knows this, *everyone* knows this, but there are still a few dozen volunteers who have chosen to remain here anyway. I get it, I really do. There is a certain pride in being here. A place hidden and protected by God. All the blood, sweat, tears, and prayers that have built this community brick by brick. And then to see it fall to the sort of thugs who rape, kill, and burn everything they see. It hurts. It makes me angry. But it doesn't make me stupid.

We don't have the fire power to fight these guys. They are ruthless. They will overrun this camp or seal the exits and burn it down just to destroy it. If they can't have it, then neither can we.

This church has no idea what's going on out there. We are living in World War III. I still remember when Major Banks explained it all to me, how the United Nations imploded and treaties fell apart, allies who'd stuck together for centuries became enemies. And the world spiraled into war.

The US was attacked from all sides, all at once. First, they took out our power, then they moved in for the kill. Thanks to places like Eternus, we've been resilient and have managed to survive the worst of it. They were able to establish early connections with Canada, Mexico, and parts of South America to form the United Americas—an entirely new country. I still proudly wear their patch on the sleeve of my shirt, even though I haven't represented them well. Still, my mistakes don't negate what's going on out there. The men we are fighting come from every part of the world, driven by every sort of dark passion and grab for power. They will tear this place apart in their ruthless search for world domination.

This is the ugly side of war. The enemy needs shelter and supplies just like us, but they don't have the connections established or the knowledge of the area like we do. So they have to take what we've built. That's the way the world works. It isn't right. It isn't fair. But it is what it is. We can cry about it or find a way to get through it, to overcome it.

Leaving is the safest option. No one will get hurt and we'll be able to travel at a pace that won't deplete our supplies or draw too much attention. That's the upside of moving in such a large caravan. We've got too many people to conquer. I just wish they all had weapons. Maybe then we could stand a chance, but as it is, the church is very rigid about their nonviolent approach to things. The owners are die-hard pacifists who deny entry to anyone carrying a weapon. They took our guns when we first arrived, which almost sparked a vicious fight with Claudius, but Major Banks made him stand down. We needed to get into the camp more than he needed to keep his rifle. And to be fair, they gave it back later. Once it became clear that we would need it.

I stuff clothes into my backpack and then swing it over my shoulder.

"Moving out?" Bunny asks. He's lying on his bed, staring at me from beneath his long bangs.

"No. Just staying ready."

"The caravan is supposed to leave in three days."

"Yeah."

We let the silence linger while I grab another bag to pack.

Over my shoulder, Bunny asks, "Are you really leaving? Again?"

I hate the way he adds 'again' to that, as if I had a choice in leaving the first time.

"I want to return to Eternus," I reply. "It's a good place."

"What about your foster mom?"

That makes me pause right in the middle of folding a t-shirt. I've always wanted to find my mother. That hasn't changed. I've already checked with church officials; her name isn't on the roster and there's no information on when my neighborhood was evacuated. It was turned over to the National Guard pretty early on, but no one knows what happened after that. So many shelters have been lost and overrun by enemy forces or even lost to mutiny. There are survivors out there just as violent as the soldiers. I still have hope to find my foster mom, but that won't happen if I stay here and get killed.

"I will never stop searching for my mom," I tell Bunny.

He hums and I hear his blankets rustling. "I believe you. Since you never stopped looking for us."

That's true. I'm only here now because I snuck out of Eternus to find everyone. I never told my friends about the day I spent alone with Raven and how that got us caught and shot at, but still. I left for them.

"Is this gonna be goodbye?" Bunny asks.

I turn around and sit on the edge of my bed. Bunny is sitting on his bed, his hands in his lap like a kid. He's always looked so young, so it was easy to treat him like my little brother back in college. I remember his first day at the first house, moving in with his large suitcase and unblinking eyes.

He was deathly afraid of Adrian and Memphis, but when I cracked a joke about beating them up for him, he laughed so hard that he snorted and we've been friends ever since. We trained together, had a few classes together, partied together, and on nights when we were too tired to go out, we sat together like this.

So much has changed since those simple, boring nights.

"It doesn't have to be goodbye," I say.

He nods slowly. "Ae-cha—"

"Would you regret leaving her?"

"I would."

"Then stay."

"Caesar—"

I stand. "Love is hard to come by in this world. You should hold on to it if you're one of the few who finds it."

He doesn't say anything, but I feel him staring at my back. I know he's thinking of Mya, wondering if I traveled all these miles, braved such dangers, just to see her again. And find her with Adrian.

Yes, I was lovesick enough to do all of that. And I don't regret it. I regret not doing it earlier. I lost her. I lost the one who mattered.

"To Adrian, of all people," I grumble without realizing.

Bunny shifts behind me. "I should go," he says.

I turn to tell him it's alright, but he's already at the door and when he swings it open, Mya is standing there with her hand poised to knock. She seems as stunned as we are to have her presence suddenly revealed.

"Oh! Sorry," she says quickly. "I was just going to knock."

"Oh boy," Bunny mutters.

"Excuse me?"

He glances back at me and then smiles. "Nothing, Mya. You're right on time." Bunny steps aside and dramatically sweeps his arms out to allow Mya to pass. "I was just leaving."

"Perfect timing," I say.

He winks before he shuts the door, leaving Mya and me in the muted silence that follows. She stands awkwardly in the middle of the room. It's oddly reminiscent of a college dorm; two small beds crammed against either wall with a dresser between them.

"Wanna sit?" I wave at Bunny's bed as I sit on mine. This bed used to belong to Adrian. I wonder if he sat here with Mya before I showed up. I wonder if they cuddled together. If they made love on these blankets. There's so much I don't know. So much I *can't* know. So much I don't want to know now.

I sigh. "What did you come here for?"

Mya looks stunned and hurt by the question, but she recovers quickly and offers a vacant smile. "I wanted to see you. Alone."

"You wouldn't be here to confess your undying love, would you?"

The joke is bad and earns a stern look from Mya, but I shrug it off.

"Didn't think so."

"I came to tell you that I've missed you. I didn't get to tell you that earlier."

"Is that all?"

"Don't be a jerk." She crosses her arms. "Of all the times to act like Julius Caesar—"

"What's that supposed to mean?"

She disarms me with a goofy laugh. "There he is. My Julie."

Gosh... I exhale a chuckle and wipe my hand through my hair. The tension seems to ease a bit, and I feel like I can breathe again. Nothing unites old friends like a quick fight.

"I've missed you, too," I say softly. "I've missed you a lot."

Mya moves fast, I don't see her cross the little space between us, but I feel her suddenly there. Her arms wrap around my neck, her cheek presses against mine. I hug her hard, feeling wetness crawl down my face.

"I can't believe you're here," she whispers.

"Neither can I."

We stay like that for a long time, longer than we need to. I don't want to let her go, because once we untangle ourselves, she'll go back to being Adrian's girlfriend. And I'll be alone again.

"I'm sorry I came too late," I say into her hair.

She squeezes me tighter. "No, Julie. You're right on time."

I let go of her to blink in shock but the look on her face tells me I'm not about to hear that confession of love any time soon.

"What do you mean?" I ask in a sigh.

"God brought you back into my life when I was ready to have you here in a way that pleases Him."

I grunt because I know she's telling the truth. I knew it when I made that awful mistake with Raven. I knew it when I saw her with Adrian. I knew it when I held her in my arms and didn't feel that heart-stopping passion we used to have before.

I still love Mya. Madly. Deeply. But the love between us has changed. I love her as my best friend. As my sister. The way God always intended. She was never meant to be anything more than what she is to me now. My support. My strength. My gentle reminder of the love of Christ. Now that I've discovered that love for myself, I don't need to cling to her so hard. I can let her go. Move on. Learn to love another.

I just ... I don't know if I want to. I don't know if I'm ready.

Mya touches my cheek. "I'm so sorry."

"What are you sorry for?" I lean into her hand. "I don't regret a second of my life with you, Mya. I'd look for you all over again if I could. And I'd find you."

She leans down and kisses my forehead. I close my eyes and exhale slowly.

"Do you love him?" I whisper, and I feel her nod against my head.

"We want to get married."

Those words should break me, but they don't. They just make it clear that Mya isn't the one God has for me. That sucks. It really does, but I know He'll give me strength to get over it.

"I want your blessing," she says softly.

Gosh. It's not enough to break my heart, she's got to ask permission first?

I don't really know what to say, so I stare at Mya, searching her eyes for the truth. Trying to see if this is truly what she wants. I see the girl I grew up with, smiling and laughing beside me. I see the girl I ignored in high school and set aside for later use. I see the girl who took my breath away in college, and then I see the girl I fell for. The one I kissed and snuck away with, the one I promised I'd try so hard for. The one I let slip away. I let her go to chase after sex, and I've been running behind her ever since. Hoping to make things better. But it was God's plan to make *me* a better person all along. I don't like it. I really don't. But what else can I do except accept it?

It's pointless to fight God, besides, surrendering to His will here only means there's something greater in my future. If I have the patience to wait.

"Is this what you really want?" I whisper.

Mya nods. "More than anything. But it isn't just about Adrian. It's about you, Julie."

"How can you say that?"

"I want your blessing because I need to know that you're okay with this. That *we're* okay."

I see. This is as hard for her as it is for me. Not because she still has feelings for me but because she cares. I don't know what God saw in Adrian that He didn't see in me, but Mya really wants this, and she has permission from God to do this. So … as long as she's happy, then so am I.

I take a breath and nod, but not for Mya's sake. I do it for myself. I've got to move on and find happiness, too.

"You have my blessing, Mya. I'm happy for you."

Her eyes brim with tears but they don't fall, she blinks them away like she's ashamed to cry in front of me.

"Thank you," she whispers.

I take her hand. "You've got my blessing but please don't let Adrian ask me to be his best man."

That makes her laugh. "I don't know when we'll get married. But we want to. First, we have to decide where we'll be in the next few months and plan from there."

"You haven't made a decision yet?" That catches me off guard, considering her father is at Eternus. I thought there was no discussion necessary. Of course she's leaving with the caravan.

Right?

"Mya, you're coming to Eternus, right?"

She hesitates—and before she can answer, the lights shut off and a piercing sound screams through the bunker halls. The emergency low lights flicker on, they're set into the floor, so the room is aglow like a nightclub. Mya is silhouetted by the light; I can just make out her panicked features as she covers her ears and yells over the alarm.

"What's going on!?"

Shouldn't I be asking that? I'm the new guy here, but it doesn't take a genius to figure out something's wrong. Very wrong. There can only be one answer to her question.

"Intruders!" I shout back.

I'm on my feet the next second, tugging on my backpack and reaching for Mya's hand. She takes it without missing a beat and we fly into the hall to find it filled with people. The sound of shrieks can be heard over the wail of the alarm, but it's clear the voices aren't screaming in pain. They're calling names, searching for each other. There are too many people in the hall and not enough light. It's impossible to get my bearings, especially since I don't exactly know where I'm going. What's the protocol here?

Mya grips my hand and takes the lead, tugging me in the opposite direction of where I thought the stairwell was. She shouts over her shoulder, "We can find him this way!"

Him?

I tug Mya into an alcove, shielding her from the crowd with my body. We're face-to-face with her back against the wall, but she doesn't seem to mind the proximity. "Where are we going?" I ask loudly.

"To the infirmary! I need to find Adrian!"

My nostrils flare in frustration. I'm not angry that she wants to see her boyfriend, I'm annoyed that we aren't on the same page right now. Adrian isn't my priority here. I already saved him once. Right now, I need to find Major Banks and the rest of my squad so we can form a plan.

"I've got to find my team!" I tell Mya.

She stares at me. "Julie—"

"Get to the exit gates!" I shout. "I'm sure evacuations are underway. You need to get out of here, Mya. You and Adrian."

"We need to leave together!"

"I'll see you again," I say quickly, then I hug her. Squeeze her. "I'll see you at Eternus."

28

Mya

I watch Julie run in the opposite direction, his shoulders bouncing with each stride, his strong body moving nimbly through the crowd. He is the image of a hero running into battle. Brave and fierce and handsome. And then he's gone, swallowed by the panicking campers. The hall is flooded with noise. The alarm never stops blaring and people never stop panicking, shouting, pressing against each other as they search for family and friends and a safe way out.

Something whistles in my ears, louder than the bell ringing, louder than the voices ever rising. It is fear. Grating and constant. It echoes through the chambers of the shelter, trapped in these concrete walls. When it finds no exit, it blackens with anger and darkens the hall. I see it settle on the crowd as pushing turns to shoving and shouting turns to screaming. We are no longer pressing toward the exit but rushing the doors, our minds brimming with fear. Fear that makes us angry. Fear that makes us irrational. Fear that ruins us from the inside out.

I'm shoved against the wall by a man twice my size. The force rips a scream from my lungs, but it gets caught in my throat as I trip and stumble headfirst toward the floor. I grab the wall and just barely manage to stay upright. I can hardly breathe from the pressure of the crowd. That man who shoved me is still right beside me, his body flush against mine. The crowd seems to move as one, like we've become a single unit, a fat snake winding through the hall.

I scream and try to push away from the wall, inching further down the corridor. Someone steps on my foot, then I get kicked in the shins. Hard. I grunt and dig my nails into the wooden doors I pass, shuffling sideways, heaving and shoving my way forward. I cannot stop moving. If I stay still, I will be crushed. If I am crushed, I will never see Adrian again. I'll never see Julius again. And I'll never be reunited with my father.

God didn't bring me this far to die here. Like this.

I take a breath and exhale a scream, pushing back against the bodies that crush me. There's a woman pressed against me now, she has a bag strapped to her back; I grab it and yank hard, using the leverage to pull myself forward. Her head tips back and she cries out, but I don't care. I'm getting dragged away by the people behind me, and it only gets worse when gunshots fire down the hall.

Chaos strikes like lightning, a wicked bolt of fear and raw panic shoots through the crowd and sets the mass ablaze. People begin to climb over each other, shoving and clawing their way toward the stairs. More shots go off behind us and the crowd moves like a current. I'm swept away in the rolling waves of bodies, my feet moving against my will. I crane my neck to get a sense of where I'm going, to try to map out the dim hallway, but I can hardly see around the frightened faces that surround me.

Suddenly, there's a break in the crowd, pressure is released as people move away from me. They've found the staircase. I can hear howls of relief showering down from the top of the stairwell and I cry tears of joy. The door has been opened; we can leave. We can escape the gunfire that sounds so close now.

I move on shaky legs, following the crowd as it empties into the next corridor. At the top of the stairs are members of the church's strike team, dressed in cargo pants and holding meager weapons. Some of them have guns but most are armed with knives and even metal poles. It won't be enough to fight the soldiers who are moving through the crowd, but we won't have to fight if we can get away and shut the door behind us.

When I reach the top of the stairs, I feel tears burn my eyes. I nearly died in that crowd, so I'm almost overwhelmed when I grasp the helpful hand of a Strike Team member. "Thank you," I blubber, and the kind man inclines his head.

"Mya?" he says, and I blink away my tears to realize it's not a man at all. It's a small woman. The one who was with Julius.

"Raven," I whisper.

She pulls me into a hug. It's awkward and shocks me so badly that I take a step back and my knees buckle. She's stronger than she looks, pulling me away from the crowd so we aren't blocking the staircase.

"How'd you get down there?" she asks.

"I was visiting Julius."

She stiffens at his name, pressing her lips together before she speaks. "He left to guard the northern exit. I've been assigned here."

"You're helping the church?"

"Of course. We need to stick together if we want to survive."

I'm still used to living outside where it's every man for himself.

"Is Julius safe?" I ask.

Raven nods. "He went with Major Banks. I'm here with Claudius."

I have no idea who those people are, but I nod anyway.

"Mya, if you can walk, you need to follow the crowd to the surface. There's an evacuation route you can follow. Do you remember it?"

I shake my head. I do remember the evacuation route; the shelter had a meeting in the church yesterday where we went over emergency protocols again. They even passed out maps with all the exits highlighted. I remember where I'm supposed to go from here, but I don't want to leave. I'm not ready yet.

"I won't go without Adrian."

The declaration makes Mya pause. She has a pretty face with gentle features, her brows naturally arched, her forehead smooth and creamy brown. All of her features seem to harden as she tries to make sense of what I've just said.

"Mya, the shelter is in chaos. You need to evacuate while you can."

"Not without Adrian."

"You heard the gunfire—"

"Would you leave without Julius?" I snap.

I know it's a low blow for me to use her emotions against her like this, but I need Raven to understand what Adrian means to me. I'm not a fool, I can see how much she cares for my best friend. I can see how much she loves him. It's written all over her face and it's in her eyes each time she looks at him. The only thing I'm unsure about is whether *she* knows how much she loves him. And if he loves her back.

Raven slowly closes her eyes. "Going back in there is a death wish."

"I'd rather be dead than leave without him." I find the strength to walk back toward the staircase. There are still people escaping, madly sprinting up the steps with their eyes blinking around the hall, their mouths open in wordless screams. I push past them, ignoring the shouts of the Strike Team behind me. They're all telling me that I'm going the wrong way, but I don't respond, and I don't look back, not until I feel something grab me roughly by the arm.

I'm yanked to the side and shoved against the wall. My mouth opens in a snarl, but I stop when I recognize Raven. She's shoving a hunting knife into my hands.

"Take this!"

I grip the handle and then stare at her in confusion.

"I'm not your bodyguard," she says, lifting her handgun. "If we're gonna move together, you're holding your own weight."

Move together?

"You're helping me," I say softly.

"He wouldn't forgive me if I didn't." Raven turns away before I can ask who '*he*' is, but in my heart, I already know.

To my surprise, Raven lets me take the lead, though I shouldn't be surprised at all considering I know this place much better than her. I haven't been here for long, but I'm positive I can find the infirmary before she does. She's positive about this, too, because she walks quietly beside me the whole time, waiting for me to pick a direction, turn down a hall, cut through a room.

We move slowly, taking a shortcut through a room that connects with the fire exit to avoid the soldiers down the hall. I can't see them clearly because most of the lights are out, but I hear their voices, like shadows talking in the distance. Their presence is haunting, figures shaped like men marching through the church halls. Halls I'd considered safe not even an hour ago.

"What do they want?" I mutter, leading Raven down a short hallway. She has her handgun raised, ready to fire at a moment's notice.

"What do you think they want?" she replies. "To kill us all."

"What did we ever do to them?"

"Exist in a place they wanted."

I guess that's all the reason they need to invade our home and try to take over, but if the gunfire I hear is any indication, I'd say they aren't taking anything without a fight.

All I've got is a hunting knife, but it feels like the sword of a mighty knight as I grip it in my sweaty palm. I walk so close to Raven, I can hear her breathing. The sound of it is comforting. I match my own breathing to hers and realize how calm she is. My heart rate slows with how deeply I'm breathing now, I fear it will make me sluggish, but when a soldier rounds the corner ahead of me, I scream and lunge without even thinking.

My knife flashes out in a twinkle of silver, slicing through the darkness shading the hall. The soldier is surprised enough that he steps back, but he raises his weapon at the same time.

He never gets to fire.

Raven sets off two shots and he slumps against the wall—but there's another soldier right behind him. This one pulls the trigger faster, but the hall is dark, and his aim is off. Bullets spatter the wall just over my head, I duck and scream, but I don't let go of my knife. In fact, it's clutched in my hand when I crouch and move forward. I swing at his midsection, too close for him to step away, and Raven fires again. It isn't until he stumbles sideways that I realize we got him. Both of us.

Raven clicks her tongue as she checks her weapon. "My gun is jammed."

I can't help her with that, so I kneel to check the bodies of the soldiers and pass her one of their fancy automatic rifles. "This is better anyway." I grunt as I lift it. It's heavier than it looks.

"There's another one." Raven nods at the body of the first soldier but I shake my head. "It's okay for Christians to defend themselves," she tells me, and I almost laugh.

I'm not afraid to shoot someone who's invaded my home, I'm afraid I'll end up jamming the gun or hurting someone innocent.

"I don't have great aim," I confess. I got Adrian's gun jammed when he was fighting that cannibal. It's a miracle I didn't accidentally shoot him in the process.

Raven's mouth pinches in the corner. I think she's smiling. For some reason, that melts away all the anxiety I felt earlier. It takes a certain sense of confidence and faith to smile about anything right now. Yet, Raven thinks it's funny that I can't shoot. She's choosing to smile instead of rolling her eyes or complaining.

In this odd, bloody moment, I realize I like this girl. There doesn't have to be any animosity between us. We don't have to hate each other just because we both love Julius.

I reach for the other soldier's rifle and sling the strap over my head. "My aim isn't great, so I won't fire unless I have to."

Raven nods. "Even if you don't use it, its better for us to have it than them."

She's right. Plus, I can give it to Adrian when we find him. Which we are most certainly going to do.

"Let's go," I tell Raven. "We're almost there."

29

Adrian

The alarm snatches me from my sleep with an anger so violent, I wake up screaming. There's a frightened nurse huddling in the corner of my room, but I can't tell if she's afraid of me or the blaring noise. Or what that noise means.

Enemy soldiers—not nearby—*inside* the shelter. That's the only reason they would kill the lights and sound the alarm. I know because we had a meeting with the entire camp yesterday, lasted three hours with everyone crammed into the church, the only place large enough to hold everyone. I didn't sit through the entire meeting because I had to leave to take medicine and then my mother insisted I lay down to rest. I wish I'd stayed. I wish I knew what the heck is going on because right now all I can do is hobble to the door and stare outside like a frightened old man.

The nurse starts crying behind me and even screams and runs out the room when someone bursts through the door. Honestly, I scream too, falling back and snapping my teeth shut when I put too much pressure on my ankle. However, there's no fear in my scream because I recognize the person who walked in.

It's my mother.

"Adri!" she shouts, then she runs over to help me up.

"How'd you make it through the crowds out there?" The halls are filled with people madly trying to get to the exits as the bell screams behind us. Somewhere in the distance, I hear the punching sound of bullets, and I take a shaky breath. "Are the twins—"

"Safe." Mom nods, helping me sit on the edge of my bed. "They are with their father. I was already coming to visit you when the alarm went off. I wasn't very far."

"Where's Mya?" I ask. "Was she with you?"

Mom shakes her head. "I came here from the library. Haven't seen your pretty girlfriend."

I push off the bed with a grunt, cradling my sore ribs. "I've got to find her."

Mother doesn't speak which draws my attention. She always has something to say. But when I turn around, I find her standing by the door with her arms folded and her face darkened with worry.

"Adri, you need to find the exit. There are soldiers—"

"I'm not leaving without her."

She doesn't budge as I approach the door.

"Mom, there's no time to fight about this."

"Then don't fight me. Come with me. Let's leave together."

"Without Mya? The woman you said I should marry?"

She pauses, even has the shame to glance away. Thank God, at least she knows what she's saying is crazy. Whether she admits it aloud or not is another thing, but I don't care if she owns up to it, I just need her to step aside so I can leave. I'm willing to move her myself if she doesn't. Mercifully, she gives in.

With a string of Russian words dancing over her lips, Mom turns and grabs the doorknob. "I'll come with you."

"You will?"

She looks back over her shoulder, giving me an exaggerated glance at my ankle boot and knee brace. I look awful. Not to mention the fact that my face is still bruised and slightly swollen.

"You need all the help you can get," Mom says.

That's one thing we can agree on.

Mom quickly helps me change into a pair of baggy pants and a sweatshirt, then I slip on one shoe, and we slowly walk to the door together. I'm leaning on her, but she's strong enough to hold me up without any problem. I wish I weren't so big, I feel like I'm crushing her, but Mom doesn't complain. We don't really have time for it anyway.

She opens the door and takes a breath. "Don't let go of me," she says, "no matter what."

"I won't."

I didn't come this far to lose my family again. I didn't survive a vicious attack, and attempted rape, just to die underground in a dark shelter with people screaming around me. I didn't travel around the state, protecting the woman I love, just to perish without marrying her. And I didn't give my life to Christ to lose everything immediately after.

God, I pray inside, *I have no idea how this new relationship with You is supposed to work, but I want it to work. I want to have Someone in my life who will never leave me. Mya says that person is You and I believe her. So, please keep me safe. And my family. And Mya, too. Protect all of us, just like You have been. In Jesus's Name I pray, amen.*

My mother shifts her weight with a grunt, and I try to stable myself. I lost focus during that prayer, but now I slide one hand along the wall and try to stand upright as much as I can. The boot is awkward to walk in, not to mention the knee brace, but it's also difficult to see through the dark and people are still crowding the hall. We get bumped and jostled, someone even shoves Mom aside once, but she recovers and takes my arm again without a word.

"Not much farther," Mom tells me.

"We can take a break," I say.

She shakes her head. "Soldiers are inside, Adri. If we stop, we die."

She's right. But I don't know where to go from here. What happens if we make it to Mya's room and it's empty? Should we just leave without her? Should we search other places? We're already putting ourselves at risk by staying down here for as long as we have.

At the end of the hallway, I see someone waving people along, telling them which path to follow to get to the emergency exits. He sees me walking with my mother and frantically motions for us to hurry. We try to pick up the pace, but I can only walk so fast, it isn't until bullets tear that man to pieces that I realize my sluggish pace is a blessing.

The screaming intensifies as bullets shred the hallway. I scream and grab my mother, shielding her from the crowd with my own body. She hugs me, wrapping her arms around me like squeezing me will somehow make me bullet proof.

The hall is dark but sparks of light slice through the darkness with gunfire, like tiny explosions. It's haunting to see flickers of violence flashing in and out of my vision. I want to squeeze my eyes shut, but I also don't want to look away. I need to see what's happening.

I feel terror climbing up my back, digging its claws into the back of my head, stabbing my skull. Piercing my mind. I can't let it in. I can't panic now.

God—

Gunfire interrupts the prayer. I scream and grab my mother's hand; together, we shove through the escaping survivors and make a beeline for the exit. My mother trips and I go down with her. We're a tangle of limbs, trying to regain our footing, trying to scramble to the door. I hear the voices of soldiers behind us. To the side of us. Ahead of us, too. We're surrounded. We're going to die.

God!

Bullets pop around us. We duck and cover our heads, but something grabs my arm, and I lunge forward, swinging hard. The voice that screams catches me by surprise, my chest actually aches like I'm having a heart attack.

It's Mya. Her eyes are huge, and her mouth is open. She's speaking to me, yelling for me to get up as her hands grasp my bicep. I feel her fingernails dig into my skin, the pain snaps me out of my frightened trance, and I get to my feet with a gasp.

"It's you!" I yank Mya into my chest, crushing her in a hug. She hugs me back, but it's awkward because of the rifle she's holding. I feel it press against my abs, and I pull back when my ribs begin to ache. "Where'd you get a gun?"

"No time to explain." Mya swings the strap over her head and passes me the weapon, but my mother steps forward and snatches it away before I can even touch it.

"You can barely stand," she says. "I do not trust you to shoot well."

Beside her, Raven laughs, making me notice her for the first time. She's holding point with her own rifle, only giving us half of her attention. The rest of her concern is on the hallway, eyes darting through the dwindling crowd for soldiers and enemies.

"We gotta go," she says loudly.

Mya grabs my hand. "Stay close."

I don't like being led around by Mya, my mother, and Raven. I feel weak as I limp and pant for breath. I feel pathetic—as useless as Bunny, but even he had plans to join the church's Strike Team while all I could do was lie in my hospital bed and sleep. I bet he's out there saving people. Julius too. Meanwhile, I'm the one being saved, and by a bunch of women no less.

Don't get me wrong, I know Raven is tough as nails. She's saved me once already. But I want to be there for Mya. I want to be there for my mother. This feels so wrong to have them looking out for me. Then again, isn't that what love does? It fills in the gaps, it makes up for my own weaknesses.

With a sigh, I accept things as they are and let Mya take the lead, pulling me along with one hand while she grips her hunting knife with the other. We stop and check corners, cut through rooms as shortcuts, and do everything we can to avoid soldiers. When confrontation is inevitable, Raven takes point and fires her weapon, shooting down enemies before they even spot us. My mother ends up spraying down two soldiers, she does it screaming and with her eyes closed which scares the crap out of me, but her bravery saves our lives, so I don't complain.

Mya keeps her knife close the entire time, never releasing my hand. I interlock my fingers with hers as we finally climb the church staircase and make it to the upper levels. We're in the sanctuary now, with people screaming and trying to establish order.

It's clear that we're some of the last evacuees. There are only half a dozen church officials in the room, guarding the doors and watching for more people to stumble up the stairs. When we emerge from the darkness below, two men grab us and quickly shuffle us toward the back corner of the church.

One of them is yelling orders, giving us instructions on what's going to happen next, but I'm hardly listening. I can't hear much over the gunfire outside, and even if I could, my beating heart screams in my ears and drowns out everything else.

Vaguely, I recognize the shouting man as Hayden. He found me and Mya at the post office and took us to the church. He hadn't wanted to let us join, but his group outnumbered him and his callous choice to leave us out there was overruled. Now, I wonder if he regrets that vote. I wonder if he blames me for the destruction of the shelter.

I got caught in the woods, and my map was stolen. A few days later, hordes of enemy soldiers showed up and invaded the shelter. The connection is clear. But I won't let myself spiral into such despair. The church shelter had already gotten reports of nearby soldiers before I ever arrived. Maybe it's not entirely my fault, but the role I played leaves me feeling guilty as Hayden takes us to the backdoors and gives us the cue to make a run for it.

I squeeze Mya's hand, and we push into the fray together. Raven is still in front with her rifle, my mother is behind us. I glance back to make sure she's alright, but I'm really looking at the church. We're on the backstreet behind the large building now. It looks different from this angle, like a massive theater instead of a cathedral. I've only seen the church from the outside once, that was when I left and almost got myself killed. The first time I arrived, Hayden had me and Mya bound, and our faces covered.

I wish I had paid attention to the church when I had the chance. When I was sneaking off through the woods, I wasn't thinking that the next time I saw the church I'd be escaping from it. If I had known this would happen, I would've appreciated the place more. I would've enjoyed the simple design of the building and how it hid the massive catacombs of bunkers below. I would've been impressed with the ancient-looking stained-glass windows and the bricks stacked high to form the pillars of the church. But right now, all I see is a building crumbling into ruin. I see men and women with guns pouring from the doors, escorting survivors into the woods. And I see soldiers hiding in the shadows, crouched behind abandoned cars, and set up in the windows of other buildings. Before they can even take aim, the church's strike team opens fire.

The neighborhood erupts into war. Raven screams as she pulls the trigger, mowing down a soldier who'd charged at us. I hear my mother shooting behind us, and I crouch low, squeezing Mya's hand just to make sure she's still with me. She squeezes back, tugging me along.

I never would have guessed that this would be the start of our relationship. That I would nearly die, give my life to God, and be saved by the guy I'd hated for so long. I never thought that Mya would rescue me through her prayers and in person.

As we move together, I steal glances at her, taking in her sweaty forehead, her wrinkled brow, the way her jaw seems to tighten each time we duck for cover. We travel to the outskirts of the city, never slowing our pace, never stopping to fight or even to defend. By the time we reach the highway, we're full-on sprinting, my boot crashing into the pavement.

I double over to breath when Raven finally stops outside a large building. It looks like a warehouse which makes every hair on my body rise. This place can't be safe. Would the church really make arrangements for survivors to evacuate and meet here?

Raven knocks three times, pounding her fist on the garage door. After a moment, someone knocks from the other side, and she whistles back. Finally, the door lifts to reveal members of the Strike Team holding one gun and three rakes as protection. It's a pitiful sight, but when I glance behind them and see hundreds of survivors sitting on the floor, huddled in groups, hugging family members and friends, I realize they have all the protection they need.

"You're safe now," a woman says, reaching for my hand. "We're glad you made it."

"Do you know how many others are left out there?" a man with a rake asks.

I mutely shake my head while Raven stops to relay information. I feel numb as I'm ushered forward, still holding Mya's hand.

Is this it? Are we really safe?

"What happens next?" I whisper.

Mya looks up at me. "We keep moving."

"The twins," Mom says, glancing left and right. "I have to find Danya and Dinara." She's still holding that rifle, clutching it now with a shaky grip. I think her adrenaline is wearing off which means she's coming down from a very strong high. I can see reality settling in as her survival instincts slowly recede. Now she's faced with the worries of a mother, and I get a firsthand look at the nightmare weaseling into her mind.

"Mom." I touch her shoulder and give her a firm shake. "We'll find them."

"There are two other warehouses," Raven walks over, holding up two fingers. She's still carrying her rifle and begins to reload it as she explains. "The Strike Team has radios to keep in touch. If we can't find your family here, we'll let them know."

That news seems to bring everyone a bit of relief. Mom wants to find the twins. Mya and I have each other, but I'm still worried about Bunny and Jupiter, even Ae-cha and Julius, too. I wonder if Ryan made it. I wonder if Saloso got out. I even wonder if the rest of Raven's group is doing okay.

I'm sure she's wondering the same thing as her head swivels to take in the room. The survivors have grouped up on their own. Pockets of families, friends, even coworkers seem to have found their way to each other. Everything happened all at once, leaving little time to plan or respond. There are no welcome tables set up, no church leaders to greet everyone and take names down to help sort and recover survivors. Right now, the best way to find our loved ones is to simply walk around and look.

So we start doing that. Mom walks away first, bravely pushing into the crowd to ask a complete stranger about her children. "Have you seen a twin brother and sister?" she asks, pointing to her own face. "They look like me. Russian. Blonde. Beautiful."

The man studies her but shakes his head and she quickly moves on. In my peripheral, I see Raven approaching a group but she's too far away for me to hear who she's asking about.

Mya tugs on my hand. "Let's start over there." She points in the opposite direction of my mother and Raven, and I nod.

"Good idea."

"We'll find them. Don't worry, Adrian."

"I'm not worried." Surprisingly, I'm telling the truth, not just putting up a brave face. I know we'll find my siblings. We found them once, against all odds. God united me with everyone I loved and cared about. People I never thought I'd see again. And He gave me a wonderful home that I felt safe in. That home is burning somewhere in the distance, but I don't feel worried about it. I don't even feel afraid anymore.

"Everything's going to be fine," I tell Mya.

She manages to smile. "You're mighty confident."

"Don't you see why?"

"Not exactly. We just got to that shelter, and now it's being overrun. Everyone is separated again—"

"Not for long," I say quickly. "Have faith, Mya."

Now her smile widens. "You really have changed."

"Who wouldn't change after everything that's happened?"

"Some people let their storms crush them. They give in to the despair and the sorrow. They grow bitter in their trial."

"I grew up bitter." I chuckle. "I got tired of that."

"So, what are you now?"

"Hopeful? Faithful? Trusting?"

"Trusting in what?"

"You know what."

She sighs, walking quietly beside me. "I want to hear you say it."

"I trust God."

It feels so weird to say that, but it's the truth. I have no worries as I drift through the warehouse. I don't see my siblings or Ryan, but I don't let that bother me. In the middle of the chaos we've survived, I feel at peace. I've seen death up close, I've witnessed what this broken world has to offer, and I've learned that it's better to take what God offers. It isn't always comfortable. It isn't always what I want. But it is better. It's safer. It's easier. It's peaceful.

Without God, I'd be screaming and running through this place, desperately searching for my family. I'd be blaming God for the destruction of the church. I'd be so angry that everything is falling apart yet again. But I've learned on this journey that some things may fall in your life, but if you dare to stick with God, He'll fix it. And you'll come out better than you were before.

So, yes, it does pain me to see all this destruction playing out. To see the country being torn apart by war. To see the repercussions of that war with my own eyes. But I know God has a plan for His children. He has a safe place for us. Now that we've finally emerged from underground, we can go to the shelter He's built for us. And let Him keep us safe.

It will be a long journey to Eternus, but if God brought us this far, He'll keep us again.

I squeeze Mya's hand. "Let's keep looking."

"Okay," she says. "I'm with you."

Forever.

30

Caesar

When I reach the top level, I see members of the church's Strike Team gearing up for battle. I march over and, to my joy, some of them recognize me. I entered the camp under insane circumstances, and then I spent a day or two in meetings with Major Banks and church officials, telling them all about Eternus. So, a lot of people already know my name here, which is a good thing because it makes things flow more swiftly when I offer help.

"I can shoot, if you've got an extra gun," I tell the Strike Team leader, a woman named Jade who glances down at my hand before she answers.

"Hard to shoot without a trigger finger."

"I'm ambidextrous."

It's true, I can write with my right and left hand and pull the trigger with both pointer fingers, if I had two. The pointer finger on my right hand was shot off when I helped rescue Adrian. I don't regret helping him, I haven't even felt much different missing the top half of my finger now. But it is a hindrance, at least in Jade's eyes.

She raises an eyebrow and tucks the gun into her waistband. "Afraid I have to hold on to this one myself."

"Come on," I plead, but a large figure appears beside Jade and cuts me off.

It's Claudius. He hasn't spoken to me since we got here, and I understand why. He's still not over what happened at Orly Center. But things are too dire for him to ignore me now. He passes me a gun from the holster at his side and jerks his head. "Follow me."

I nod at Jade and briskly walk behind him, craning my neck to hear him speaking over all the noise. There's gunfire and screaming and people crying in the background. I've gotten so used to these stressful situations, it isn't difficult for me to blot out the noise and focus on Claudius.

"The church has multiple Strike Teams setting up a perimeter to gather intel on enemy forces, form a blockade to defend evacuations, and escort those evacuees to the safety points they've marked on these maps." He holds up a dirty slip of paper.

"Blockade of defense," I repeat. "We aren't going to counterattack?"

"We don't have the manpower or the weapons. Our focus is to get out alive, Caesar. Can you help them do that without screwing everything up?" He stops walking to face me and I almost bump into his back.

The look in his eye is filled with hate. I don't blame him, really, I don't. But I have to look past that hate if I want things to work out here. I can't fail twice. I wouldn't be able to live with that shame.

"I can do this," I tell him.

He shoves an ammo magazine into my chest and then turns to grab more supplies from the cart in front of him. I watch in silence as he grabs a pocketknife, another map, and a flare gun. His breathing is heavy, and his forehead is slick with sweat. Claudius is an older man with salt and pepper hair but a body of a guy my age. He's big with thick muscles and wideset shoulders. More than intimidating. But right now, he looks tired. I wonder how long he's been up here; I left as soon as I heard the alarm, and I was assigned to a team with Major Banks. After her evacuation began, she sent me back here. Has he been fighting all along?

Claudius passes me the supplies and grunts out his words like he's trying not to cuss at me. "I'm stationed here to help with the main evacuation site. Major Banks is on the west wing, that's where you're headed."

"I just left the west wing," I say.

"Well, you're going back."

"Why?"

He glares, unblinking.

Something isn't right.

"Where is Raven?" I ask.

Claudius glances to the side, and his voice comes out in a shockingly gentle tone. "She was here with me. But she ran back inside."

I turn away, but Claudius yanks me back by my elbow.

"You're not going to look for her!" he snarls, twisting my arm. "You have a job *here*. I'm not letting you screw it up!"

"I have to find Raven!" I try to tug away, but it's no use. The man has the grip of a bear.

"Raven can handle herself. We need you here, Caesar. *I* need you here."

I pause long enough to look up at his face. His eyes aren't filled with hate anymore, they're filled with worry.

"What's going on?"

"Major Banks is at the west wing, but our comms are down. We haven't had communication with that Strike Team in nearly an hour."

Now I get it. Claudius wants me to go help. The hatred I saw in his eyes earlier wasn't just for me. It was for him, too.

Claudius's breathing isn't just heavy, it's labored. And his forehead isn't just sweaty from nerves, he's sweating because of strain. He's hurt. I can recognize the smell of blood quite easily. I was covered in blood at Orly Center when Katia was shot right in front of me. I smelled the sickness of infection and the tinny smell of blood on Bobby as he lay dying. And I smelled my own blood when the end of my finger was shot off in the woods.

I smell blood on Claudius now, but I don't see any obvious wounds. My gaze drops to his legs, and he shifts

332

uncomfortably. That's when I notice the tear in his jeans, right above his knee. Was he stabbed? Or shot? Maybe even hit by debris? Whatever the case, Claudius is too injured to make the trip to the west wing himself. He needs me, just like he said. And he hates that. He hates that he can't go to Major Banks himself. He hates that he's weak right now. And he hates that he's got to depend on me to save someone he cares about.

But if I go after Major Banks then I won't be able to go back for Raven.

Claudius sees the indecision on my face and gives my arm a firm shake. "Caesar, Raven can handle herself."

"So can Major Banks."

"She trusted you," he says. "Even after everything you did and everything you caused. Major Banks still trusted you. When we heard gunfire in the woods, I knew you'd gotten into trouble again." He swallows. "I wanted to leave you out there. But Major Banks went after you. She knew you hadn't done something reckless. She trusted that you were out there fighting for a good reason. And you were."

Major Banks helped me rescue Adrian. At the time, I didn't question her assistance, I was just happy to have it. But I had no idea Claudius hadn't wanted to help. He'd told Major Banks to leave us in the woods that day. If she hadn't disagreed with him, all three of us would've died out there. We were outnumbered and outgunned. I was already missing a finger when they arrived.

Claudius steps closer. "Major Banks trusted you that day. Prove that she wasn't wrong to do that."

Sheesh, he's trying to guilt-trip me into saving his unofficial girlfriend.

"She's in the west wing?" I ask.

He nods. "About half a mile from here."

"If I go after her, you have to promise me you'll keep an eye out for Raven."

"Of course I will."

I turn to leave. "I'm not doing this because you asked me to. Or even because Major Banks trusts me. I'm doing it because I'm the only one who can."

I take off before Claudius can respond, proving exactly what I just said. Claudius is old and injured. I'm not in my best shape, but I'm better off than him. And I'm doing exactly what God created me to do. Run.

Dr. Brown's words drift into my head as I tear through the surrounding streets, moving toward the west wing at break-neck speed. *God gave your speed a purpose.*

He told me that after I busted my leg trying to escape from Eternus. All my life, I thought I was fast because I was meant to be a sports superstar. That was my dream in life, to run and win and see myself on the cover of magazines. I didn't view my goals as vain, I saw them as practical. What other hope was there for a kid who had no talent except charisma and speed?

Now, I realize there was much hope. Hope for survival. Hope that I can make a difference when it matters most. God used me to run supplies for Eternus. Then He used me to save Adrian, even in the midst of my own failures. And now He can use me once again to save more lives. To make up for the ones I so recklessly caused to be taken.

God, let me make it in time, I pray, leaping over rubble. I cut through an alley to avoid a cluster of enemy soldiers and then I run through the backlot of a small plaza to emerge behind a dilapidated building. As a Runner, it was our job to stay hidden while we waited for shipments to arrive, so I know where to look to find people, but as I walk through the parking lot, someone calls my name before I've taken five steps.

"Caesar!"

I spin to find none other than Major Banks waving from behind an abandoned truck. When I run over, she hugs me and then slaps my shoulder. "You made it."

"Claudius sent me." I think it's important for her to know that he's alive and thinking of her. The spark of hope in her eye tells me I made the right decision. She closes her eyes for a moment and then takes a deep breath, returning to the soldier I know she is inside.

"Thanks for coming."

"Of course." I nod.

When Keoni whistles, figures rush from the shadows and my jaw drops open. There are dozens of people here. Families. Groups of survivors who made it out alive. People who want to live. Bunny and Jupiter are two of them; they run over and swarm me with questions, but Major Banks makes them hush. She has more important things to discuss and not a lot of time.

"I was supposed to escort this group to the safehouse nearby, but we got turned around by enemy soldiers. We've been hiding for a while now."

That's why comms went down. Major Banks and her group had to drop everything and move off track to hide. I want to look over at Bunny now, but I keep my eyes focused on Major Banks. He wanted to join the Strike Team, but it looks like he ended up evacuating with everyone else. Did he get turned away by the Strike Team or just chicken out?

I brush away those thoughts and pull out my little map. "How much further to the safehouse?"

"About a mile," Major Banks answers.

Easy for me to run, but that could take us an hour in a group this size. There are even children here—

My eyes widen as I catch a glimpse of two angelic figures. Pale skin with rosy cheeks and whiteish blonde hair. Like tiny copies of Adrian. I instantly recognize the children as his twin siblings, and I make my decision right there. We are getting these people back safely, no matter what it takes.

Is this another chance? I ask God. *Another chance to save lives instead of foolishly getting them taken.*

"How many can run?" I ask Major Banks.

"All of them. But we'll have to move slowly."

"I can lead the way."

"I'll help too," Bunny volunteers. He specialized in marathons, running long distances in large groups, so he's perfect for this.

Major Banks nods at him but her words are for me. "Keep moving west. Look for a large warehouse." She lifts her rifle. "I'll be your overwatch."

My heart skips in excitement. Claudius was right, Major Banks does trust me. She has no hesitation when she lays out orders and she lets me run at the front of the group without argument. Maybe she's just making the smart move, I am a Runner, so it makes sense to let me lead. But she doesn't waste time giving me a lecture about my failures, so that's a plus.

I stretch out my legs as Keoni rounds up the group. Adrian's siblings stare at me but a tall man grabs both their hands and pulls them into the crowd. I'm guessing they know him since they don't fight him—I heard Adrian's stepfather lived in the church, too. Maybe that's him.

Major Banks appears beside me. "Caesar, thank you for coming. I couldn't lead these guys on my own and I had no idea if help was on the way or not."

"We can do this."

"No." She slaps my shoulder again, gripping it firmly. "You don't understand—"

"Claudius told me you still believe in me."

She looks stunned for a moment.

"He told me he wanted to leave me in the woods the day we rescued Adrian. But you insisted on helping." I pause. "Thank you, Major Banks. I know I messed up—"

"You made a mistake, but no one could have predicted what ended up happening. I'm done blaming you, Caesar. I miss my friends, but I have to move on."

"I guess this is my way of making it up to you."

She smiles. "Consider this the greatest apology I've ever received."

I cost three good people their lives. I could save the world, and I don't think it would be enough, but it would be worth it. It's worth it to at least try to do better. I'm grateful Keoni sees that, and it seems like maybe Claudius sees it, too. Raven forgave me in her own way, still quietly keeping her distance but staying close enough for me to know that she doesn't hate me. Slowly, we're all healing. Things will never go back to what they used to be, but this is a step in the right direction.

"Everyone!" Major Banks says loudly. "Keep your eyes on Caesar and follow him. We must move quickly and quietly. Do not stop moving, no matter what." She lifts her weapon again. "I'll be watching our backs, so don't worry. We're going to make it out of here safely. I promise."

It's dangerous to make promises like that, but I can see the desperation on everyone's faces. They need those promises. They cling to them like a lifeline and use each word as fuel to keep them going. I take advantage of that, pushing them hard, arms pumping, legs snatching up the earth, stealing speed with each swift step. I'm running so hard my eyes burn and my vision blurs. I can hear voices behind me, the sound makes me panic.

What if I'm moving too fast? What if I've lost them?

I slow my steps and the shift in speed snaps me back into focus for a moment, long enough to realize the crowd is not screaming for me to slow down. They're cheering for me. Telling me to keep going.

So I do.

To the sound of excited voices, I sprint through the backstreets and down alleyways. Tear down the sidewalk and cut through parking lots with a trail of dozens of people crying out in victory. We could attract attention with all the noise we're making but I think it's having the opposite effect. We don't sound like the frightened, unarmed people I found hiding in the shadows. Right now, we are soldiers marching into battle. Fearlessly running toward our enemy.

We have nothing to fear because the worst is behind us. They invaded our home, opened fire in our halls, and chased us out of our own sanctuary. What more could happen?

There is no room for fear in our hearts. Not anymore.

During the last leg of the run, I raise my fist and fire a shot from the flare gun Claudius gave me. Red smoke billows into the air like fluffy fire stretching toward the sky. The crowd cheers at this, too, and I smile at their excitement. At this point, I've slowed down enough that Bunny catches up, panting and waving.

"What was the flare for?"

"Stragglers can follow it."

"Enemies too."

I shake my head as I slap his shoulder. I'm running up a hill now, the inner city behind me and the outskirts of town right before me. There's a highway winding over my head, taller than the trees that dot the surrounding forestry. As I crest the hill, I let out a howl and the following crowd erupts into cheers again. There are hoots below me as well, excited voices shouting up to celebrate. Bunny looks confused by the noise, but I give him a wink.

"Doesn't matter if enemies find us out here, Bun." I point to the bottom of the hill, at the warehouse waiting below. "We made it. We can defend ourselves from here."

The Strike Team members guarding the warehouse raise their guns and makeshift weapons above their heads as more survivors stand beside me at the top of the hill. It's the greatest moment of my life, finally celebrating victory instead of failure after failure after failure.

I listen to their cheers, and I can't stop myself from smiling, even though my chest is heaving, and my lungs scream for air. I am smiling in pure joy.

The warehouse doors open and more church survivors pour into the parking lot to stare up at the hilltop. My grin stretches, I even hear Bunny laughing beside me.

"The gang's all here!" He throws his hands into the air and hoots. I almost hoot with him. Just below us, I can make out the distinct pale figure that is Adrian Nikols. He's big enough and pale enough to point out even at our distance, so I know for a fact that the small brown woman beside him is Mya. There are more figures moving through the crowd to join them, a woman standing beside Adrian, and another brown-skinned figure that makes me suck in a gasp. It's Raven.

Claudius told me she ran back into the church, but he didn't say why. Now, it's obvious. She went to save Mya. Her selflessness melts my heart. I don't know if she did it because of her feelings for me or because of my feelings for Mya, but I hope she knows what it makes me feel for her. The emotions aren't entirely romantic, but they are there. I care about Raven, and I will spend my life trying to make up for the sacrifices she's made for me.

I see Katia's face in my mind's eye, and I wonder if she would be proud of me. I left Eternus to find my friends, but I got so many people hurt and killed along the way. In the end, however, I think I've started to make amends. I think I've begun to earn back some of the respect I lost amongst my peers. The dozens of survivors beside me are proof of that. I helped save lives today. I wasn't responsible for the ones that were lost. I wasn't the cause of all the chaos for once. I was finally part of the solution.

"Are you proud of yourself?" Bunny asks, leaning against a tree.

I shrug, trying to play it cool. "All I did was run."

"That's all you had to do." He slaps my shoulder and starts down the hill, waving his hands and cheering with the others. I watch him run toward Mya and Adrian, they embrace him and undoubtedly drown him in endless questions.

"Good job, kid." Major Banks steps beside me, her eyes scanning the crowd below. "You did well."

"Finally."

"There's more work to be done."

"Isn't there always?"

She nods and turns to look at me dead on. "There's always more work, but for the first time I feel like you're actually ready for it."

Her words nearly bring tears to my eyes. "Really?"

"You've been through a lot. Made a lot of mistakes."

I glance away.

"But you've learned from them. I can tell you have."

"What makes you say that?"

Major Banks nods toward the warehouse. "You left Eternus to see that girl down there, yet you haven't moved from this spot."

"Maybe I'm just too tired from running."

"Or maybe you're content."

I tilt my head to the side, mulling over her words. Am I content? Am I finally okay with the position God has placed me in? I didn't end up with the girl of my dreams. I didn't even get to stick around with my friends for very long. But I'm okay with that. Even when we were reunited, all I wanted was to report to Major Banks and make plans. Find a way back to Eternus. My home. But now I get to share that home with the people I've been chasing after for so long. Maybe it's because I stopped chasing them—for just a moment—and finally started chasing God.

It took complete ruin and death for me to get it through my head that I couldn't achieve this without Him. But I've learned my lesson. And I won't make that mistake again.

I take a deep breath and slowly nod. "Maybe I am content. Right here."

"On the sidelines?" Keoni smirks.

"In the background. Taking care of the tough jobs. Protecting them."

"You'll have a lot of that now. There's a long journey ahead of us."

"Are we taking them to Eternus?"

She smiles. "Of course we are. And you're going to lead the way."

My heart double thumps. "You're serious?"

"After that performance you just put on, I wouldn't have it any other way." She claps my shoulder. "Isn't that what Runners do, anyway?"

It is. And for a very long time, I was only ever running away. Trying to leave Eternus. But now I'm running toward it. I'm leading people to it. I'm taking my friends to our eternity.

Epilogue

1 Year Later

Caesar

I resist the urge to straighten my tie as the bride finally kisses her groom. I feel like this part of the wedding is sacred, any sudden movement might mess it up. Maybe I'm being dramatic. The bride is totally in love with the groom, her eyes sparkle as he lifts her veil. She looks like a teenager in love, and he looks just as excited. They're a good-looking couple, her white-blonde hair and his shaggy brown locks, stained grey at the scalp. In their late 40s now, this is their second chance at love. They look like they're ready to do it right this time.

"Not bad for the second time around." Adrian nudges me as he claps.

I chuckle. He would know. That's his mother and stepfather getting remarried up there. Regardless of my familiarity with them, anyone can tell they're happy and their joy with each other makes all of us happy, too. Even Adrian.

It's hard to believe he hated Ryan before this, he's clapping the hardest right now, cheeks bunched in a grin that leaves his pale face flushed red. I guess I shouldn't be so surprised, Adrian once hated me, too. Look at us now. Standing side by side at his mother's wedding.

The twins were the perfect flower girl and ring bearer. They walk side by side now, trailing their parents as the couple walks down the aisle. Adrian joins the procession next; he was the best man; he reaches for Mya's hand as she meets him at the front of the aisle. She was the matron of honor. What a perfect couple.

The two of them got hitched a year ago, on the way to Eternus. After everything we survived, they didn't want to waste anymore time. They got married on the side of the road while the caravan set up camp for the night. When evening fell, we celebrated with a song and gave them the best portion of our rations. The entire camp was excited, even though at least a thousand of them didn't even know who Mya and Adrian were. Weddings will do that to you. In this dark world, it's so easy to get caught up in the negativity. In the stress of survival and the frustration of failure. Weddings are like little sparks of joy and encouragement. A reminder that there is life out here, happiness too. If you're willing to search for it.

I'm glad Mya found that with Adrian. I haven't exactly found it myself, but I'm closer than I was before.

As the procession moves, I step forward, I'm also one of the handsomely dressed groomsmen—ahem—and reach for Raven's hand. We've been dating for the last couple of months. It's a complicated story, but to put it shortly: I like her. I didn't want to admit that to her for a while because I wanted to make sure my feelings for her were real. I didn't want to like her because she was the next best thing or because she was my replacement for Mya. I wanted our relationship to be genuine.

It has been. We're both still Runners, and we train together every day. It feels like therapy for us; pushing each other, striving to get better. To get over the things we did and the mistakes we made. It wasn't an easy journey at all. First, we had to forgive ourselves and each other. Then we had to learn to live again. To trust ourselves and to trust God. A year later, I think we're back to what we used to be. Now, it can only get better from here.

Bunny and Ae-cha walk behind me, followed by Jupiter who takes the hand of Dr. Brown. They are not dating. Jupiter is still a single pringle, and Dr. Brown is old enough to be her father. Jupe needed a date since she agreed to be a bridesmaid, so she was paired with Dr. Brown, the only groomsman who didn't have a partner.

They look like father and daughter as they grin and walk together. I'm glad she got to be his partner. Jupiter's grandfather passed in the church invasion, so attending this wedding with her best friend's father is like filling the hole that's been left in her heart. Dr. Brown fills that same hole for me. I never found my foster mom, and I never had a dad at all.

I needed that parental figure in my life, and he's been happy to give it.

Even better than Dr. Brown, I've discovered my Father in Heaven. I thought my relationship with God had been broken for good. Thought I'd caused too much trouble. Made too many mistakes. Big mistakes. I even tried to earn back God's love by putting myself in danger at the church shelter. I thought saving all those people made up for the lives I'd cost. I thought giving up Mya and staying away from Raven made up for my years of promiscuity. It wasn't until I laid it all down and simply said, *I'm sorry God*, that I realized I'd already been forgiven.

It might be difficult for people to understand that. Major Banks and Claudius took a long time to accept me as their friend again. Even Raven needed time to grieve her sister and heal. But I'm not here to earn the forgiveness of man. I am sorry for what I did. I wish that I could bring back the people who were lost because of me. I don't take their deaths lightly at all. I never have. But God wanted me to know that I had His forgiveness, and that this was all I needed. Once that settled in my heart, it was easier to forgive myself, and it got easier to pray for those who hadn't yet forgiven me. We're not all buddies again, but things are better.

Major Banks wanted me to stay on the Search-and-Rescue Team, but I turned her down. Searching for my foster mom is at the forefront of my mind. But I've seen what happens when I take missions too personally. I'm going to focus on running and being useful to Eternus in the best way possible. I trust

347

that God will bring my foster mom home one day; He can do that through Major Banks, or maybe someone else. Who knows?

Adrian joined the Search-and-Rescue Team, so maybe he'll end up bringing her back to me. Meanwhile, Bunny joined the Eternus Strike Team. He'd always wanted to fight and defend his land, now he's finally got the chance. Most of the team is made up of members of the church shelter, like Hayden and Lori. They're good people and we've never had anyone get past our gates, so I guess they're doing things right.

I follow the procession outside, still holding Raven's hand. She squeezes my fingers and gives me a big smile. I give her one just as grand. It comes easily, cheeks lifting, lips pulling back. I couldn't hide my smile from her if I tried. But I'm not just smiling because of her, I'm smiling because of the moment.

"They're perfect," I say, nodding ahead at the bride and groom.

She nods. "The most beautiful couple ever."

"Love looks better the second time around."

"It does."

I leave the conversation at that. There isn't really much else to say with everyone moving into the open area for food and drinks and music. The bride and groom take their place at the special little table set up for them, but the rest of us scurry off to find a bit of privacy.

I see Adrian and Mya making their way through the crowd, followed by Jupiter and Bunny who holds Ae-cha's hand as he moves. We meet some distance away, close enough to still hear the music from the celebration, but far enough that no one can hear us.

I stop and lean against the wooden beam of a log cabin. Raven stands beside me, waiting quietly for one of the others to speak. We're all blinking at each other, unsure how this is supposed to go.

"I'll start." Jupiter steps forward. She's holding a cup of water and pours a few drops onto the ground. I stare at the wet spots as she speaks. "Today, we are celebrating a beautiful union, but we also want to acknowledge those who don't have the chance to join us. Delilah," she whispers, "Connor. Both of you are dearly missed. You have not been forgotten."

Major Banks and her team buried Delilah's body back at Orly Center, where we also buried Connor months ago. We held a similar 'funeral' back then and it was just as awkward as this one. But beneath the awkward air is something somber and familiar. We're all together again, and we finally have the chance to put this behind us.

We hold a moment of silence before Adrian clears his throat and says, "Connor, you ran with me when I had no one else. Thanks, buddy."

I nod. Guess it's my turn now. "Connor was a frat brother and a track teammate. He was one of us. I won't forget him. And I won't forget Delilah either. I'm sorry," I say softly. I can't produce anything else, or I might burst into tears, so I just cram my hand into my pocket and step back.

"Both of them were part of our team," Mya says. "We'll always remember them."

Bunny nods, he's too choked up to say anything, so he just closes his eyes, and we all take a moment of silence. Eventually, it's broken by Raven who says, "My sister wasn't part of your group. Neither was her boyfriend, Bobby or our driver, Enrique. But I miss them, and I'll never forget them."

"Neither will I." I take her hand, and she lets me pull her close enough to drape my arm over her shoulders. We stay like that for a long time, all of us with our heads angled downwards, our eyes staring at the ground, our mouths shut. We don't speak because the moment seems too fragile for words. So, we just stand there until, one by one, we slowly return to the wedding.

I don't even notice when it's just me and Raven left. She lays her head on my shoulder. "That wasn't as bad as I thought it would be."

"Does it hurt to talk about her?"

"Not as much as it used to."

"You know I'm sorry, right?"

I feel her nod against me. "You know I don't blame you, right?"

"I know. I just—"

"It's behind us now," she whispers. "That's why we did this. To let it all go and say our final goodbye. It's finally time to move forward."

"You're right." In my heart, I know she is. Sometimes it's just hard to think of everything we went through and realize that it's truly over. This is it.

Is it though?

We travelled across the state, we overcame the odds and not only survived, but we made it back to each other. We tore down the walls between us. We learned to heal. We learned to forgive. We learned to put God first. Now, we're not just saying goodbye to friends we lost, we're shutting the door on the past altogether. This is our new beginning. The first day of eternity.

I hug Raven. "I'm glad I get to start over with you. I'm glad I get to do things right."

"Me too, Caesar. Me too."

Adrian

I stayed up late after the wedding. I had to put the twins to bed and then I spent the night with Mya. The mood was quiet and heavy after our little memorial. I'm glad we did it, but I was shocked by how it left everyone. I needed to be alone. Mya walked around in a daze. The others spent the rest of the night wiping their eyes. I felt bad because I was celebrating my mother's wedding, it should have been a happy event. It was, but we sort of soured our own moods. Still, I'm glad we did it. I'm glad we got that off our chests and put it behind us.

After a while, the wedding reception got better. I smiled for my mother, danced with her, and even grinned as Ryan danced with Mya. He loves her, and so do the twins. She's really joined the family. I mean, we are married, so it's no surprise. She's part of the family whether they like it or not, but I am glad they like it.

Our wedding wasn't nearly as great as this one. There was no white gown or music playing, no decorated church or flowers to throw. We were tired, unbathed, and marching across the state with the hope that we didn't get ambushed along the way. That's why we got married. We were honestly afraid that we might not make it to Eternus. But we did. God kept us, just like He always has.

The wedding night wasn't so fancy either. I was still wearing a boot and a knee brace. My face was bruised. My ribs were still busted. And Mya was tired from walking all day in the caravan. We made it work. But things got so much better when we finally made it to Eternus.

Our lives haven't been the same since. I spent so much time worrying over Julius and then worrying over our survival, it was strange to finally be safe. To simply be alive. We didn't have to worry about food or water or the rest of our families. Mya's father is here. My family is here—my mother just got remarried. Everything is finally doing better. It took me a year to embrace the peace. To accept the love Mya had for me. But I think we've gotten the hang of things. A year later. Better late than never.

Mya stirs beside me in bed, I glance over and then lean down to kiss her temple which makes her hum. "Morning, beautiful," I whisper.

"Morning." Her eyes slowly open and she smiles warmly. "Sunrise?"

"Just about."

"You're up early."

"I want to go for a run."

She nods. "Do you have a mission today?"

"Not yet. In a few days."

I've been training for a big job coming up. We've heard rumors about another shelter not far from here, maybe a week or two of travel. Major Banks wants to check it out, but I have my own reasons for going. If the information I've heard is correct, then there's a chance Julius's foster mom might be at this shelter. I don't want to say anything and get anyone too excited, but I've been digging for clues and hints since I joined the Search-and-Rescue Team a year ago.

Julius saved my life, and then he helped save Eternus. He accepted my relationship with Mya and over the last year, he's worked things out with Raven. He's changed. And so have I. I want to help him find his foster mom. I won't question his reasons for rejoining the Runners, but I will do whatever I can to return all the help he's given me. We're not enemies anymore, and I've learned over the year that he isn't a bad friend. I've learned that maybe we could have been friends all along, but I'm grateful we've established something now. Mya is too. She's finally gotten what she always wanted, to have both of us in her life without tearing each other apart or forcing her to choose one of us. Peace is better, especially when it comes from God.

"I'll be back before breakfast," I tell my wife. She hums again, closing her eyes as I kiss her once more. "Sleep tight. I love you."

She doesn't speak until I'm almost out the door. "I love you too."

Sweetest words I ever heard.

Mya

"Is it ready?" I ask.

My father grins as he turns around, adjusting his circular glasses on the tip of his nose. "It's ready."

I've been helping my father collect and assemble parts for months now. Finally, our project is done. He holds up our creation—or reparation is more like it—and my eyes widen in amazement. It's beautiful. Absolutely beautiful.

The pocket watch sways back and forth as my father holds it by the silver chain. It looks just like the one I had in college before the Fall. The campus used it to help tell time, along with the old grandfather clock in the Kappa Pi dorm. I don't remember when I lost the watch, but I'm glad to get my hands on a good replica now.

It took months for us to put it together, that was mostly because parts were tough to come by. I'd tell Julius what to look for whenever he went out on a run, he had no idea what I was trying to build, but he brought back whatever he could find. Things also took forever because I was relatively unskilled and ignorant of mechanics and engineering. My father has taken me under his wing, so I've been learning well, but my shaky hands and lack of knowledge made the whole process tedious.

My father was patient. Guiding me. Instructing me. Now, our hard work has finally paid off. We've rebuilt the pocket watch I used to wear, but it's not for me. I'm giving it to Julius as a gift to congratulate him on his engagement. He made the announcement the other day at dinner, smiling and holding hands with Raven. I hadn't said much beyond the obligatory well wishes, but now I want to show him how much I really care.

Only Julie would understand the significance of such a gift. Only he could truly appreciate it. That's why I want him to have it.

"Thanks, Dad," I whisper, watching the watch swing as if on a pendulum.

My father sounds proud. "You did good, kid."

"Do you think he'll like it?"

"Of course, he will!"

I laugh, embarrassed about my nerves. Of course, Julius will like it. I wouldn't have gone through all this work if I didn't think he would. Though, I'll admit that this gift hadn't started as an engagement gift, but I'm happy to present it, nonetheless.

When I first approached my father about the project, the idea was just to give Julie something to remind him of the good old days. Something to say, *I'm still your best friend, despite all that's happened.* Now, the gift is different, but it holds the same meaning. I'm happy for Julius. I really am.

"You've grown up so much, darling." My father takes the pocket watch and presses it into my hands, holding them in his large ones. They feel like warm mittens.

"Thanks, Dad."

"I mean it. You left my house as a little girl and came back a woman." He snorts. "A married woman!"

My father was shocked to see I'd settled down when I showed up at Eternus, but he was even more surprised to learn that it was Adrian who'd stolen my heart, and that Adrian had given his heart to Christ.

"So much good news!" he'd cried, holding us both in his large arms. He'd meant every word. Despite missing the impromptu wedding, my father was happy for me, and he was happy for the love I'd found. I wish he'd found love, too. I wish we could celebrate his second marriage just like we did with Adrian's mother, but my father is content with being single. He says my mother is the only woman for him, and he's counting the days until he can see her again.

I pull my hands away from my father and then hug him. The action takes him by such surprise that he stumbles back and says, "Oh!" I feel his arms wrap around me, and I sigh into

. his shirt. He's wearing a work smock, stained with sweat and grease, the smell I remember most on him. If I close my eyes, it's like nothing has changed. We're back in my home and he's just come up from the basement, tinkering with a project I had little interest in. We'll chat about our day and then share a pizza together and laugh about silly, unimportant things. Then we'll go to bed and repeat it all again the next day.

That was life for us, and in some small way, we've gained that back. Maybe we don't get so much pizza anymore. Maybe the things we discuss aren't so mundane and silly. But we have each other. We have the love we thought we lost. And now, it's not going anywhere.

"Thanks, Dad," I whisper. "I love you."

"You're welcome, darling." He hugs me tighter. "I love you, too."

I leave my father and dash through the camp to find Julius before he leaves for a run. I'm out of breath when I catch him walking out of his tent. He looks confused to see me.

"Mya?"

"Hey," I wave because I'm panting too hard to say much more.

"Is something wrong?"

I shake my head. "I brought you a gift."

Now his eyebrows rise, and I see his eyes skirt over me, searching for his gift. Julius is still such a kid.

"Walk with me," I say, breathless and slightly dizzy. I feel like I'm about to tip over, but as I walk beside my childhood friend, I feel the headiness slip away and I can focus again. "I've been working on this gift for a while now."

Julius glances down at me, his head tilts to the side so his bangs fall into his face. He gives me a boyish grin that used to make my heart flutter, now I just snort and swat his arm. "It was a gift to remind you how much you mean to me." I hold up the pocket watch. "But now I want it to be a gift for your engagement."

He stops walking and stares at the watch, his eyes following its pattern as it swings back and forth. It looks like I'm hypnotizing him. I wonder what thoughts are flowing through his head right now.

"Do you like it?"

He finally nods, reaching up to gently take it from my grasp. "I love it, Mya."

"I'm glad. I wasn't sure how you would react to it."

"What do you mean?" He stares at me.

"I mean… I don't know." I look away, genuinely unsure why I was worried. Julius and I have been friends for so long, it should be natural to give him a present. But as he holds the pocket watch in his hands, all I can think of is everything that we used to be, and this gift suddenly feels like goodbye.

He steps closer. "Mya, I'll always love you. Just because the love we have for each other is different now, doesn't mean it isn't love."

"Thank you," I whisper. "I needed to hear that."

He sighs as he hugs me. "You know, a watch is the perfect gift. Not just because it's like the one you used to wear. It means something different now."

"What does it mean?"

"It means time doesn't affect us. We'll always find each other, no matter how far apart we are. No matter how long it's been. No matter who we loved in between." He pulls away and holds up the pocket watch, staring at it. "In one way or another, we belong together, Mya."

I smile because he's right. God blessed us to find each other and love each other the way He wanted, and it's so much better than the love we tried to force between us without Him. This love is raw, pure, and everlasting. How fitting that we would find it here, in Camp Eternus.

Did Julius ever tell you what *Eternus* means? That it's the Latin word for *eternity*? I'm sure he did, but I wanted to remind you again.

I laugh. "This is our eternity."

Julius Caesar grins. "I wouldn't have it any other way."

He winks before he turns and starts a slow jog through the camp. Running. Always running.

ACKNOWLEDGEMENTS

A big thank you to Jesus Christ for getting me through this! It was tough but we made it! Thank you all for finishing this trilogy with me. This was honestly one of the more difficult series for me to write and I wasn't very confident as I finished the story. I thank God for all of you who stuck with me through this, for the silent supporters who have been reading each page with a smile on your face, and for the very vocal readers who have hunted me down on social media just to share your wonderful thoughts. All of you have been gifts to me from God, I hope you saw this story as a nice present too. I have more to give. Will I see you in the next one?

Follow me on **TikTok, Lemon8, Amazon** and **Instagram** [@ValicityElaine] to get updates on new releases, pre-orders, and reduced prices on my books.

More books by Valicity Elaine & TRC Publishing!

Christian Fantasy
The Scribe

Cross Academy

Christian Post-Apocalyptic Fiction
The Barren Fields

The End of the World series

MAGOG saga

Christian Science Fiction
I AM MAN series

Christian Romance
The Living Water

Withered Rose Trilogy

Beautiful Lies

The Gap

Decipis Trilogy

Fractured Diamond

The Woof Pack Trilogy

Singlehood

Christian Children's Fiction
Too Young

The Rebel Christian Publishing

We are an independent Christian publishing company focused on fantasy, science fiction, and romantic reads. Visit therebelchristian.com to check out our books or click the titles below!

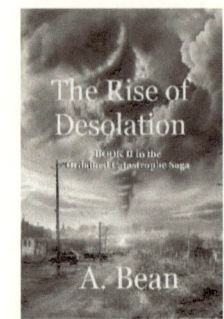

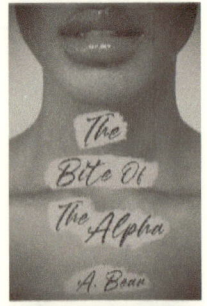

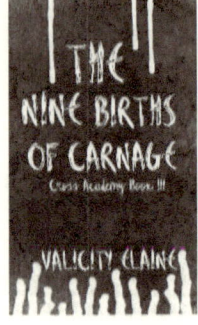

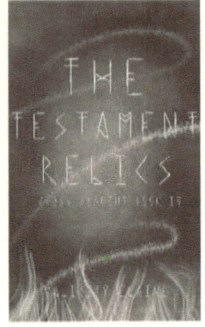

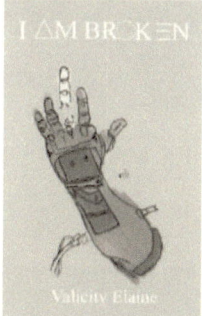

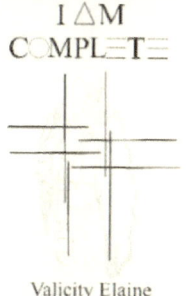